ONLY FOOL RIDING

SACRED HEARTS PNW CHAPTER - BOOK VII

A.J. DOWNEY

COPYRIGHT

Editing & book design by Maggie Kern @ Ms.K Edits
Cover art by Dar Albert at Wicked Smart Designs

DEDICATION

To Clint for inspiring Blackjack and for all your help. Thanks for being my East Coast Bestie and for making life across the country easier in so many ways.

PROLOGUE

*B*lackjack...

    It was late. So late, it was probably getting on toward early, but I'd stayed behind at Mav's request. It'd taken a long while for him to deal with whatever needed dealing with when it came to Tic.

None of the rest of the fellas had really been feeling it after church, and most of them had fucked off to do whatever. Any of the guys with women had probably gone off to fuck them.

Suckers.

I didn't play that. The whole having an ol' lady was overrated. Hell, Dahlia was enough fuckin' drama for the lot of us as a free fuckin' agent.

Anyway, Mav had asked me to hang back and talk with him, and hang back, I did. I had a feeling he wanted to talk to me about my position within the club thanks to us losing our road captain for the foreseeable future.

Sure enough, that's what he'd wanted. As soon as Tic was out the back door, he was calling for me up the hallway at the bar to step into his office. Sure enough, he was asking me to step in as a temporary de facto road captain and was asking if he thought I could pull double duty or if I thought someone else would make a good tail gunner or what.

"I can do both," I said with a nod. "That's no problem. But Tic, he's coming back, right?"

He heaved a big damn sigh and told me, "That's up to Tic, but yeah, I think he'll pull through and he'll make it. He just needs to sort his shit out."

"Am I overstepping if I ask about Dahlia?" I asked.

"Yep."

"Consider my mouth shut."

We stared at each other over his desk for a long while and it was like the clubhouse itself held its collective breath before Mav finally let his out in a harsh rush and asked, "You mind keeping my confidence with this one?"

I'd said, "I always got your back, man. You know that."

It'd been a long fuckin' talk after that, and a bit of an eye-opening one. I think I understood a hell of a lot better Dahlia's stack of issues. Shit, she had 'em taller than the Space Needle, but fuck me... didn't we all?

I wasn't so lost in thought that I was the only fool riding out here, even though in all actuality, *I was the only fool riding* out here. It was cold, it was clear, but there wasn't but a cage or two out here with me. Still, I was alert, my mental faculties right where they needed to be, and yet still, it had to be some kind of divine intervention that I even fuckin' saw them.

Way up ahead, on one of the overpasses, a high one over I-5, someone was climbing over the railing.

I let off the throttle, whipping my head over my right shoulder and giving the handlebars a twist to skate across several lanes as the figure clad in light jeans and what looked like a gray hoodie with some kind of blue logo on the front straightened up and stood, looking down on the unforgiving pavement below.

I pulled onto the shoulder and glided up to a stop below and in front of them. I shut off my bike and got off.

"Hey! Hey, yo!" I cupped my hands around my mouth and fuckin' did everything I could to *project*. The figure slipped, their arms going back up and over the railing, barely hanging on.

I heard sobbing, faintly, on the wind.

"Go back, man!" I yelled and waved him back. "Go back! I'll come up there and talk to you!"

The person sort of let their arms hold them and halfway crouched down. They shook and I could tell they wept, they cried, and they were dead-ass fuckin' serious right now.

"Go back! It's not worth it, man! Alright? Okay?"

"What do you care?" the person shrieked, and the voice was so shrill with upset that I couldn't tell you what I was looking at – a he, a she, or one of those neither persons that I couldn't think of the name for them, but it didn't matter all that much to me in this very moment.

Nonbinary.

It popped into my head unbidden, and I batted it away with my hands in an effort to frantically get the person above me to stop, to wait a minute, and to *think*.

"I do care!" I yelled. "I-I'll take you for a ride on my motorcycle!" I shouted, thinking it was fucking ridiculous, but if it *worked*... "Just go back over the railing! I'll come up there, and we'll go for a ride. It'll make you feel better!"

"What?" they shouted down, standing up but turning slightly. I felt a surge of triumph. I think I was getting close.

"Just go back over the railing! I'll come up there and I'll take you for a ride on my motorcycle. We'll go somewhere and talk, man! Okay?"

I mean, shit, a ride always made *me* feel better.

What the fuck are you doing, man? Are you serious right now? I thought savagely to myself, and the answer was simple. I'd been there before, sitting alone, a half a bottle or more of Jack in my system, ready to suck-start my fuckin' .45...

I'd been there more times than I cared to admit, and you know what? Someone had been there for me. Had picked me up, sobered me up, talked me through, and helped me get my shit together. Had been my guide off the battlefield and into the club.

3

I owed that motherfucker everything.

"Just go back, come on! Please! Don't do this! Don't make me watch you do this!"

Yeah, it was dirty, but if it worked…

"You'll come get me?" they called down.

I yelled back, "Yes! I promise, just go back over, and I'll come get you! We'll go for a ride!"

"Okay!"

"Okay?" I almost couldn't believe it.

"Okay, come get me!" they shouted.

"Go back over!" I shouted.

"I'll go back over when you come and get me!"

I was about sixty-five percent certain what I was dealing with was female at this point, but it didn't matter. Not one iota. What mattered was keeping them *alive*.

I got back on my bike and fucking put the hammer down, fucking *flying* to the next exit and figuring out just what fucking overpass they were on. There were like forty-fucking-six and two over downtown, but this was one of the last ones before the Montlake cut.

I got myself fucking oriented and kept the corner building that had been behind them as a reference point in my field of vision, looking up, and looking up, and *there! There! They were climbing back over!*

Yeah!

Yeah!

Fuck yeah!

They heard the bike, they knew I wasn't lying, and they climbed the fuck back over. Thank fucking God!

I pulled up just as they rolled their ass over the big fucking metal tubular railing and fell on their ass onto the sidewalk. I pulled over and jumped off the bike as they broke into fresh heaving, just *racking* sobs that shook their slim shoulders under the oversized gray hoodie. I dropped to my knees and grabbed them, not caring at the wild scream of fear that barreled out of their chest as I bear hugged them into me and refused to let go.

"I got yah, buddy. It's okay, it's okay. I got you."

They wailed, all worked up and stopped pushing against me. They just fucking sobbed into my cut, the bike chugging next to us, the warmth radiating off of the engine and the pipes probably doing them a little good. I mean, it was cold out. Cold as fuck. And all they had on was a pair of jeans and a goddamn hoodie. No telling if they had anything layered on under either of each.

I pulled back, looked down, and pulled the hood off of glossy black hair pulled into a loose ponytail. They, no *she*, looked up at me stricken, mascara running down her cheeks in awful black muddy tracks. Her false eyelashes all but cried off, and her brilliant blue-green eyes catching the streetlight overhead made all the more vibrant with their red rims from her crying.

She may be ugly crying, but it had a weird and fucked-up effect of making her beautiful.

Like damn beautiful.

"It's okay," I said. "I don't know what it is, but there's no sense in a permanent solution to a temporary problem. I've got you now, girl... and it's all going to be okay."

"Nothing is okay," she said, and her voice broke. I nodded.

"Come take a ride with me," I said. "I'll take you wherever you want to go, and we'll talk. I'll help you figure it out."

"Why?" she asked brokenly.

I gave her a crooked self-deprecating smile and said, "Because more people 'n I can count did it for me."

"I'm a nobody to you," she tried to argue.

Without thinking, I said, "Not tonight, you're not. Tonight, you're my everything."

We sat there on the cold, hard ground, glittering with ground and broken glass like so many of the sidewalks around these overpasses did for whatever reason and she asked me, "Who *are* you?"

"You can call me Blackjack. All my friends do. What's your name?"

She searched my face and sniffed, tensing, and I realized she was young. I couldn't tell you *how* young or old for sure, but she didn't look like she was much over the age of fuckin' consent, which made the hair rise on the back of my neck.

"Angel," she said. "My name is Angel."

"Is that a nickname or like your name, name?" I asked her.

"What do you think?" she asked, and I smirked.

"Fair," I said. "Totally fair."

"What do we do now, Blackjack?" she asked, and I took a deep breath and looked this way and that up and down Denny and shook my head.

"How about we go for that ride?" I asked.

She nodded, and I helped us both get to our feet.

"How old are you, Angel?" I asked her and she sighed.

"I know you won't believe me, but I'm twenty-nine."

"I'll believe you until you give me a reason not to, fair?"

She nodded.

"Fair."

"Same goes," I told her. "You can trust me, only I promise I'll never give you a reason not to. That's not how I roll."

She didn't say anything, just searched my face as I whipped my rag outta my back pocket, wiping at her muddy tear tracks.

"We'll go for a ride, find some twenty-four-hour place where you can clean yourself up in the bathroom and we can get something to eat and talk," I said judiciously. I wanted to hear this story – whatever it was.

"Sounds good," she agreed, shivering, whether from emotion or cold, I couldn't tell, and nodded her head.

"Come on, let's go."

I led her to the bike, got on, and helped her to get on. She huddled against my back and put her arms around me. I stuffed her hands into my coat pockets to cut the wind and try to keep them warm.

"Hold on to me. Here we go!" I pulled out onto Denny and down. There was a place I knew that was twenty-four hours – high-end as fuck, but they kept it dark, and it would be a hell of a lot quieter than any of the diner places around here on a weekend night. That, and it was close, just down the road.

I didn't want to take her far, but I promised her a ride, so we wouldn't go *straight* there, just when she felt calmer and like she was ready to talk.

I had no idea what I was doing here. I was just winging it. What I did know was either Angel had a guardian angel looking out for her hide, or mine had some shit to say about her situation. Either way, this whole thing smacked of the divine in some way.

Raven's mystical witchy woo-woo ass is gonna have a field day with this story if I ever tell it, I thought.

It was gonna be an even longer night.

1

Angel...

    I wanted to die, but let's face it... I was too chickenshit to do it myself. With absolutely nothing to lose, getting onto the back of this motorcycle with a strange man was honestly the last thing I had to worry about. I mean, if I was lucky, he would do me a favor and would get the job done where I couldn't.

Could he rape me first? Sure. Probably. *Would it hurt?* Hard to tell. Perversely, I wondered; *would I like it?*

I didn't know... I didn't know anything anymore. Just that I couldn't keep doing this push and pull, this back and forth, with Devin anymore.

I didn't want to... and *shit*. If this guy *did* rape me and somehow let me live and I wound up back on Devin's doorstep, he would probably accuse me of liking it and that it counted toward cheating on him – which I never did. Which I never would, despite how much and how often he accused me of it. Only to find out *he was...*

I didn't understand why love had to hurt so much.

"Hey." I startled and the man tapped my knee twice and I realized – we'd stopped. I shivered, and he tapped my knee twice a third time and said, "That means you need to get down for me, sweetheart – but be careful! The pipes are real hot and I don't want you to burn yourself."

I carefully, and stiffly, got to my feet and stepped back. He got off his motorcycle, leaning it to its side slightly, onto whatever stand held it up, giving the handlebars a twist as he stood up.

I didn't even know what he looked like. His helmet was one of those full facemask ones, and though the thick plastic visor wasn't tinted, you still couldn't really get a measure of what a man looked like with a helmet like that on his head. Especially in the dark, in the middle of the night, like it was. All I had was his voice, and that was nice enough.

He pulled off his helmet, and I got a look at something more than just his intense dark brown eyes and I had to say, I was pleasantly surprised.

He had to be in his thirties, and he was incredibly handsome. Like, *incredibly handsome* – long brown hair falling around his face in wisps that were coming loose from his ponytail, a trim brown beard surrounding full, lush lips.

I hadn't honestly known what to expect, but... but this wasn't it. This wasn't it by a longshot.

"Come on, let's get you warmed up and something to eat," he said. He came around his motorcycle and captured my elbow with a firm hand.

I guess my hoped-for murder wasn't going to be a thing... although at this point, I was honestly only half disappointed. My curiosity had firmly been engaged now, despite how tired, how hollow, how raw and just... *empty* I was feeling.

I wouldn't wish this kind of hurt on anyone, I thought as he led me to the glass double doors of the tan cinderblock building.

It didn't look like much. A windowless building, the paint fresh-ish but covering unsightly blotches where the previous paint layers had chipped and flaked, falling away.

Inside was dim, barely better than the dimly lit street outside... dare I say, even darker. The light a muted orange-yellow from above the tables.

Someone came out from behind the bar off to our left and said, "Welcome to Thirteen Coins, just the two of you?"

"Yeah." My unlikely savior gave a nod, and I kept looking at the décor in here. It was very posh nineteen-fifties with the light fixtures and waiting area couches.

A light tug on my arm had me following the biker into the restaurant and to one of the booths across from the bar. He sat me, back to the door, and slid in across from me where he could get a look at me.

I was afraid I wasn't much to look at.

My hair was probably a mess from hanging loose, the hood of my sweatshirt having been blown back. Mousy and a brown darker than his, but otherwise unremarkable. I had some interesting eyes – blue in some light and against some colors I wore, but greener in others and with others... but right now, I bet they were red-rimmed and bloodshot, and I looked as crazy as I felt.

I don't know how to describe the feeling, honestly, but I could try. It was like... it was like feeling blasted apart, but at a certain point a freeze frame went into effect, so that I felt like I was trapped. Like everything had just stopped mid-explosion, but though the world and the blast had been stilled, the fire of it? The flames still ravaged the ragged hole left in the center of my chest where my broken heart was still feebly trying to pulse, the shattered bits and edges grinding into each other painfully.

I flashed back to the night before to the fight with Devin, to me on my knees, begging him to be honest with me, to him screaming at me about how I was crazy, how I was paranoid, how what I thought was happening and what *was* happening were two different things and how I was living in my own fucked-up reality independent of everyone else and how I needed to stop being a paranoid bitch... but I knew what I'd found and I knew they weren't mine.

"Hey."

I ripped my eyes from the coins that were trapped under the lacquer or resin of the tabletop we'd been sat at and met deep set dark brown eyes that were shadowed by his furrowed brow. I put my hands flat on the table and dug fingertips in slightly, leaning back in my seat; flinching away from that angry look which almost immediately softened.

"You're okay, Angel," he murmured.

"What's your name?" I asked.

"I told you, my friends call me Blackjack."

"No, I mean your real name," I said, eyes darting over his face.

He sniffed, leaned back in his seat, and regarded me for a moment before giving in and saying, "Clint."

"Clint what?" I asked. I couldn't tell you why it was important. I mean, it wasn't really... nothing was important, but...

"Clinton Nathan Shumway, okay? US Marine Corps veteran. You're safe," he said, and his voice had quieted.

I slid my hands forward over the table, my palms making a squeaking noise as they rubbed over the high polish on it and he glanced down, his eye movement freezing and his brow furrowing again.

"Sorry, I'll stop," I said and lifted my hands to pull them back into my lap, but his hand whipped out lightning fast. I flinched, but his rough fingers gripped mine from the second joint down with just the lightest touch. I froze and my gaze flickered from where he grasped my fingers to his eyes, which were intently searching my face.

"Who did this?" he asked and with an equally light and gentle touch, he slid the stretched-out sleeve of my oversized hoodie up my too-thin wrist, revealing a leopard spotting of bruising in a ring around it that climbed up my forearm.

I stared mutely into this man's gaze and blinked once, slowly.

"It was an accident." The lie slid between my lips with practiced ease and he cocked his head slightly, his mouth turning down at the corners.

"Oh, no, no, no, baby... it's too late to put that genie back into the bottle," he said with a sardonic little half-grin. "I just pulled you off of an overpass about to jump and I may not look it now – but I've been there. I know I may have been a little rough reeling you in up there, but these aren't that fresh." His tone dropped an octave and he glanced around our table to make sure we weren't being overheard.

"Tell me the truth, I can take it… and I promise I'm on your side."

I stared at him numbly across the table in disbelief and that was all I could do… simply stare for long moments. A waitperson came to the table and Clint, I mean Blackjack, held up his hand and waved them off, his thumb swiping back and forth gently over the backs of my fingers as he waited me out.

"My boyfriend and I get into these horrible fights," I finally said, voice cracking. "He says I'm crazy, that I'm paranoid and being a bitch and all that I want, all that I'm asking for – *begging for* - is for him to pay *attention* to me… you know, like he used to."

I looked away, staring at the wall, eyes brimming with fresh tears. His grip on my fingers tightened and then his hand slipped away, back across the table and I don't know… it made me feel all alone, bereft all over again.

"Stupid, right?" I asked and finally got the courage to look in his direction again, half expecting to see him absently scrolling through his phone or not listening, but he was staring fixedly at me; gaze shuttered and face unreadable.

"How'd you get the bruises?" he asked.

I pursed my lips, unsure how much I should tell, how much I should share, but… but he was *listening*. I just so badly wanted to be heard that it outweighed my hesitation.

I spilled my guts, everything just pouring out of me in a torrent, and he only stopped me but once to put in a food and drink order when the waiter came back to our table. He looked me over and asked me what I liked. I said I wasn't hungry because I wasn't. He told me too bad and ordered something for me anyway.

I didn't argue. I didn't *want* to argue… I couldn't honestly remember if I had eaten that day, or even when the last time I'd ate even was.

When the waiter had gone and I'd been silent too long, he'd prompted me with a gentle, "Keep talkin', darlin'. I want to hear this."

"It's… it's distressing, you know?" I asked, and he nodded.

"I know, but it sounds like you really need to get some shit off your chest, and I'm here for it, so keep on with it. Tell me what else…"

I told him everything. He would slow me down and tell me to breathe when I started to get too worked up and eventually that was all... there was nothing left to tell. Our plates had been brought, and they sat empty before us both. I thought the steak with a side of spaghetti was a little weird, but by the time it'd been set in front of us, I'd been ravenous and had devoured everything in sight.

He leaned back at the end of my long tale and harrumphed, "Hmph, seems to me your boyfriend is an abusive prick, and you ought to run."

I blinked a long slow blink and kind of turned my head, trying to absorb what he'd said.

"No..." I disagreed, but a sinking feeling was taking root in my chest. "I'm too much," I said finally.

"You're not," he said with a sniff. "Your boyfriend's just a punk ass bitch that doesn't know how to handle you. You want I should handle *him?*"

I recoiled, my shoulders thumping against the high-backed booth.

"No!" I cried. "I mean, I'm calm now," I said and swallowed hard. "Devin is probably worried by now. I left my phone, and I should probably just go home..."

"Tch!" Blackjack made a disgusted noise and shook his head. He looked up and to my left, like he was silently asking for patience or something, which, yeah, I sort of had that effect on people, Devin especially.

I sighed and deflated. I didn't honestly know what to do, what else there was. I mean, Devin had all of my stuff, like my important documents and things, hidden away in our apartment.

"I don't have anywhere else to go and he has all my things... like my important papers and shit," I confessed, and the biker raised an eyebrow.

"So, you do want to leave," he said and cocked his head. I bit my lips together and felt my eyes well all over again. Finally, I let out a defeated sigh.

"I'll be okay," I lied, and I knew it was a lie. "I'll get my things somehow and I'll get out."

"Angel," he said, and I cringed a bit.

"That's what he calls me," I said quickly, and he stopped.

"You haven't given me another name to call you, darlin'." His tone was gentle, soothing, like I was a scared cat in a corner and I couldn't deny that it fit.

"Ember," I blurted. "Ember Richards."

He searched my face and nodded slowly. "Nice to meet you, Ember."

"Um, nice to meet you, too, Clint. I wish it were under better circumstances."

He made that scoffing noise of distaste again. "Tch! Blackjack, please," he said.

"Sorry," I murmured, and he shook his head.

"You're fine," he said gently.

"What should I do?" I asked softly, and I don't know what I wanted him to say. Probably anything to spare me the decision. My heart plead for him to say '*well you should probably...*' with an inserted option of *anything* but going back to Devin or to make the decision on my own, but of course it was the lesser of those two evils that he chose.

"I can't tell you that, darlin'. You have to make that decision all on your own. *You* tell *me* what to do and I'll do it."

I nodded solemnly and asked, "Why didn't you call the cops on me?"

Again, with that noise!

"Tch! Cops don't do shit. They would have called you an ambo and shipped you off to the headshrinkers and social workers. The hospital would have put you on a grippy sock vacay and piled you up with a bunch of mind-control substances, turning you into a fuckin' zombie."

"You sound like you speak from personal experience," I said, a bit taken aback by the vehemence in his tone.

"Yeah," he said with a blasé little shrug. "We all have our demons. Some people let themselves be consumed by them and others learn to play nice with them."

"I take it you're the latter kind of person?" I asked.

Again, he shrugged and simply looked at me, wordlessly. I realized with a jolt after the silence stretched that it wasn't that he just wasn't going to confirm or deny anything either way – it was that he was waiting for me to make some kind of decision.

"I guess right now I just want to go home," I said, defeated, shoulders slumping.

He nodded slowly and said, "I'll take you wherever you want to go."

I nodded and sniffed. "Thank you," I whispered.

"For?" he asked, arching an eyebrow.

"Pulling me down off that overpass," I said. "For listening to me?"

He grunted. "Mm, for all the good any of it did," he said and *ouch…*

"I'll get out," I promised. "I just—"

"Have to try one more time?" he asked.

More like I had to get my things – my ID, my birth certificate, my social security card – all the things Devin had hidden in a safe place and that I needed to locate – also, I needed to find someplace else to go.

Leaving wasn't as easy as just not going back. I knew this wasn't good, that this wasn't healthy, but neither was a permanent solution to what should be a temporary problem.

I knew that now. Now that I had calmed down. Just talking about everything made me feel better. Loads better.

"Come on," he said, looking at the check and peeling off a couple bills out of his wallet and laying them down.

I nodded, warmed up and just ready to go home and start working on an exit strategy.

"Where am I taking you?" he asked out at his motorcycle, the horizon starting to get light with the first hint of dawn.

"Summit Ave on Cap Hill," I said.

He nodded and got onto his bike, fishing in one of his pockets.

"Look, you change your mind, or you ever need to get the fuck outta there for a few before shit gets too real or whatever, you call me. My cell number is on that," he said, handing me a business card.

I looked at it and all it read was *Blackjack,* with his phone number and the Sacred Hearts MC logo in the corner.

"Thank you," I said.

"Can't get you to change your mind? Let me beat the shit out of him?" he asked, and I shook my head.

"I think that would just make things worse, don't you think?"

He barked a laugh. "Not for me – certainly for him, though."

"I meant me," I said softly with a softer, sadder smile, and he looked me over and nodded.

"Suppose you're right," he mumbled.

"I'm grateful," I said, and he nodded and hefted his helmet over his head, putting it down over it and clapping the visor shut. He stood the bike up and fired it up and waved me onto the back. I got on behind him, his card safely stowed in the back pocket of my jeans.

I pointed, he turned, and we roared up Denny onto Capitol Hill. I pointed, and he made elegant sweeping turns down roads and up streets, winding our way sideways across the hill face above I-5 until I tapped him on the back of the shoulder and pointed out my old brick building. It was a small block of apartments called Summit Inn and they were far overpriced for what they were... but it was home. Sort of...

He killed the motor, let me off, and called out through his helmet, "Sure I can't get you to change your mind?" I shook my head sadly.

"Can I call you?" I asked before he went to start the bike.

"That's what the card's for," he said, and I took a step back onto the sidewalk and halfway to the steps leading up into the old building.

He fired up the bike and I sighed, watching him ride away... my unlikely savior.

2

*B*lackjack...

I thought a lot about Ember and while I'd told the guys about her in passing, I kept it well out of earshot of the club's women. I didn't want them descending on the incident like a bunch of gossip mongering... well... women. I don't honestly know why it was even important to me.

It was colder than a fuckin' witches' tit out there as the seasons changed from fall to winter, and the winter was only getting deeper when I got the call from an unknown number. Usually, I just ignored that shit. They were usually just fuckin' robo calls – but something in my gut told me to answer this one, and so I did.

"Hello?"

There was a long enough pause that I thought sure I'd duped myself and this *was* just another robo call when her voice came over the line.

"Blackjack?"

"Yeah? Who's this?" I asked, needing to be sure.

"I-it's Ember," she breathed. She was silly enough to ask me, "Do you remember me?"

"I remember," I said quietly, and I couldn't really keep the disappointment out of my voice when I said, "I didn't think I would ever hear from you again. It's been a couple of months."

"Yeah, well, it um took me that long to get away," she murmured and she sounded... wounded, somehow.

"Where are you?" I asked. "Someplace safe?"

"Um, yeah, now... I'm at Harborview. I'm supposed to go to a domestic violence shelter, but they said I shouldn't call anybody once I got there and... and I'm scared."

"Scared of what?" I asked, clenching the phone and knowing that the bastard was on law enforcement's radar and outta my reach – at least for now. There would come a day when he wasn't, and I'd carpe fucking diem when that shit happened. For now, I was zeroed in on what Ember was saying.

"...they believe me now, but I don't... I don't know. I don't feel like I should be taking up resources that someone who really needs it but I don't have any place else to go or anyone to talk to that isn't really one of Devin's friends and..." she took a breath, and I could tell by the soft warble in her voice she was getting worked up again.

I made a few calculations in my head before finally sniffing and asking her, "Do you want me to come get you?"

She couldn't get the phone away from her mouth fast enough for me to miss the sob that got out of her, and I felt a hot, fierce well of anger. I leaned back in my seat at my desk at home and said, "Take your time, darlin'. You just say the word and I'm on my way."

"Yes, please," she finally said. "Yes, please come get me. I don't want to go to that place."

"Okay, I'm on my way. You got a social worker or anyone else sitting near you that I need to talk to?"

She took the phone away from her face and I heard soft conversation, her lilting question to someone unknown in the background. The phone was passed and the unknown person got on the line. "Hello, Mr. Shumway?"

"Yeah," I said, gritting my teeth against my given name.

She introduced herself as a social worker with the city of Seattle and University of Washington Medicine and ran through a bunch of shit that basically boiled down to Ember being good to go as long as she was released to someone who she felt safe with who was willing to provide a safe place for her to stay and an address or what the fuck ever.

I bobbed my head, remaining polite when what I really wanted to do was snap at the bitch to get to the point.

When she put Ember back on the phone, I told her, "Hang tight. I'm on my way to come get you. When I do, we'll get you all taken care of."

"Okay," she murmured, and I got off the damn phone and shot a text to Mav, dictating it into my phone for expediency's sake while I divested of my cut and hung it off the hook on the inside of the door of my hall closet. I hated that, but I didn't want any suspicious looks from any hospital staff or whatever.

I wanted to ride, but I took my work truck instead, figuring if she was in the hospital about to be released to a domestic violence shelter, then she might be hurt enough that riding wouldn't be in the cards for her.

It wasn't too late, but it was dark as fuck outside as was customary, being this far north in the dead of winter. We were past the Solstice, but not by much. The only reason I knew about it was because Mace's pagan ol' lady wouldn't shut the fuck up about it and its significance the other night when she got herself lit up like a Christmas – I mean, Yule tree.

It was raining, the drive from where I lived over in Kenmore kind of fuckin' miserable and I was glad I'd made the right call with my work truck, dingy and beat up as it was – it afforded protection from the cold-ass rain. Plus, I didn't know how much she had with her or if we would need to go pick anything up or what.

My headlights, dim as they were, swept the inside of the Harborview Medical Center garage as I went to the top to find some-place to park the bigger than a compact truck. I found a spot, threw it into 'park' and sat for a minute and listened to the rain patter on the rusting metal roof of the old pickup.

I stared sightlessly at the glowing windows of the hospital across from me, the view of the harbor and Puget Sound at my back, and how the hospital had gotten its name. I worried vaguely about this woman I didn't even fuckin' know.

I didn't know how bad it was, and I was tearing myself up on the inside that I hadn't left a better impression. I mean, if I had, she would have called me before now.

She hadn't left my thoughts hardly at all over the last couple of months. I wondered about her through the holidays. Through Thanksgiving and Christmas, her red-rimmed blue-green eyes haunting me as the fireworks went off on New Year's Eve as I pickled myself in alcohol to numb the painful memories the booms brought with them.

Just one more casualty of war you couldn't protect, I thought bitterly to myself.

I sighed, a frustrated sound more than anything, and got out of my truck. A beastly 1990 Chevy 3500 crew cab that looked like a fuckin' rusting tank – dented, fucked up, but still serviceable – just like me.

It was a steady plod through the rain to the nearest stairwell, then another dash across a couple of lanes of traffic to the doors leading into the main lobby of the hospital.

Harborview was *massive*. The biggest la-de-da trauma center in the region, and when I said region, I meant it. They flew motherfuckers over here to Harborview from as far as Montana, the other side of fuckin' Idaho, and down from Alaska, depending on whatever shit happened to 'em.

I followed the directional signs to where I needed to go and found Ember's bay in the emergency department fairly easily – after I stopped and got my authorization sticker that I was allowed to be there.

She was lying on the gurney, eyes closed. One was ringed in red, her cheekbone swollen, and she was sure to have a fuckin' shiner in the morning. One of her wrists was splinted and resting on a pillow across her lap.

I let my eyes rove her from head to toe and back again and tried to decide how I was going to put a hurt on the motherfuckin' boyfriend… not even questioning why I was going to do it when I probably should have.

I mean, *why?*

What was it about her that was so fuckin' special?

I sighed and her brilliant blue-green eyes flickered open, the muscles around them and in her jaw tightening ever so slightly.

"Don't," she said softly.

I raised my eyebrows and asked, "Don't what, darlin'?"

"Don't judge me," she said.

"About what?" I asked, genuinely confused.

"Let me tell you what happened first," she said, and I gave a sort of little half-smile.

"You don't owe me any explanation," I said. She raised her eyebrows then.

"Don't I?"

"Nope, not a fuckin' one," I said with a shrug, my hands buried in my rugged construction jacket.

"It took me a while to get all my things," she said. "When I finally had them all and tried to leave, he went ballistic," she said, and she'd been right. I *had* been judging, I guess, the question of *'why didn't you leave sooner?'* echoing in my mind.

"What happened exactly?" I asked, coming closer and dropping into the chair at her bedside.

She told me, said she'd gotten all her shit gathered in a backpack and a couple of totes. That she'd finally cracked where he'd been hiding her documents, that she had them in hand, and was ready to fucking skate a full two hours before his dumbass was slated to return from work. That it was just her bad fucking luck the son of a bitch had gotten his ass fired and he walked in just as she'd been shouldering shit to leave.

That he'd given her the sob story of getting axed at his job – which was totally his own damn fault, by the way – and she guessed she'd not been sympathetic enough and had stated her intentions of still leaving and he'd fuckin' lost it. Punched her in the face, the front door of their place still standing open. He'd grabbed her by the wrist to haul her up from where she'd fallen against the couch, intending to wallop her again when one of the neighbors dragged him off her and basically sat on him until the cops arrived.

Seattle PD had him in custody. So at least there was that – the fuckin' pigs weren't usually that helpful when it came to these types of things. Too much fuckin' paperwork.

"My stuff is still back at the apartment," she said. "I have keys. At least the cops were nice enough to give me a ride here, so I didn't have to pay for an ambulance."

"Shit," I said with a scoff. "Useful twice in the same fuckin' day? That's a miracle."

The curtain whisked aside, and I jumped to my feet, resisting the urge to draw down on the nurse standing there, a woman with a clipboard behind her.

"Mr. Shumway?" the clipboard carrier asked.

"Yeah, that's me."

"Okay," she said with a nod.

We talked, signed paperwork and discharge papers, and they let Ember walk outta the ER on her own. Used to be you couldn't leave the hospital any other way than in a wheelchair. I guess they didn't do that anymore. Probably cost extra and Ember sure didn't have any money. One of the pieces of paperwork she'd done with the social worker was to declare financial indigence, so she didn't have to pay the full bill walking outta here.

I'd had her put down my home address to receive any further paperwork. I'd take care of the rest when it came in, probably in a few months. That seemed to be how long it took for this shit to get through billing. Goddamned ridiculous if you asked me.

When we got to the top of the garage, I opened the passenger door of my truck for her and helped her up onto the bench seat.

"We'll go by your place and get your shit," I told her.

"Thank you," she said and when I went to pull back my hand, hers tightened around it. I stopped and looked up at her. She was staring down at me with a grim pallor to her face and something in her eyes –

a sincerity that said that she was saying thank you for a lot more than just helping her up into my truck.

I pulled my hand free of hers and grunted, "Don't mention it," and shut the door on whatever she was going to try and say next.

I honestly didn't want to hear it. I wasn't and didn't do anything all that special.

I got into the driver's seat and fired up the truck, glad it was still warm-ish from the drive down here. I didn't expect it, to be honest. It was fuckin' cold out there and the shit with the social worker and discharge or whatever took longer than I'd liked, even though I guess in retrospect, it probably could have taken a lot fucking longer.

We were both silent as I drove her back over to what was soon going to be her old place. Yeah, I remembered where it was. I'd be lying if I said I hadn't dipped off the fuckin' freeway a fair few times and ridden by just hoping I'd see her and know she was doing okay. I hadn't though, seen her that is. I'd also be lying if I said I hadn't felt disappointed every time. I guess some people, some experiences, they just left an indelible mark on your soul after having them. A sort of spiritual tattoo.

I went upstairs with her. The likelihood of him being out of jail already was pretty much slim and none but when it came to perps walking, they seemed to let the scum of the fuckin' earth, meaning assholes like this guy, out within what felt like fuckin' minutes.

She was having a hard time unlocking her front door with her dominant hand all splinted up and shit, so I took her keys from her and got the job done.

"Sorry," she murmured, and I shook my head with a down-turned mouth and gave a shrug. No-big-deal like, because it wasn't.

Inside the apartment was a bit of a mess. Her bags toppled, papers strewn, and more papers and the like sloshing out of another.

She went to her knees a little stiffly and gathered things up. I took up her bags as she finished them and hated that it wouldn't be a fast draw on my gun if we needed it, but I couldn't and wouldn't expect her to carry anything.

Now that we were out of the hospital, the adrenaline had

completely worn off, and she was almost out the door for the final time. The girl just looked *exhausted.*

"You doin' okay?" I asked, measuring her response when she raised her eyebrows, staring a little sightlessly while giving me a nod.

"We got time, darlin'. Anything else you want to take outta here?"

She shook herself as if waking from an unpleasant dream and turned her head in my direction slowly, her eyes taking a moment to track as they seemed fixed on that indeterminable point in space.

"Do we have time?" she asked.

"We have all the time in the world," I told her. Although there didn't look like there was going to be much else we needed to haul outta here. There wasn't much to begin with.

She looked thoughtful and said, "I almost left my jewelry. Some of it was family—"

"Go get it," I ordered firmly, but not unkindly. I wasn't trying to be short with her and regardless, she seemed sensitive, jolting slightly and apologizing before dashing off to get her jewelry box.

When she came back, she had this look on her face that could only mean one thing.

"Everything okay?" I asked anyway.

"Some of it's missing," she murmured, and her face screwed up like she was going to cry.

"We'll get it back," I assured her, and she just sort of looked at me.

"He probably gave it to the girl he was with," she said and shook her head.

"Probably," I said. "And we'll get it back."

"I don't see how," she said.

"We'll deal with that later," I told her.

We both managed to carry all of her shit down to my truck in one trip between the both of us, me carrying the bulk of it. She'd added a couple of paintings that she'd put in a trash bag to go with us, and I didn't argue or complain. I mean, her belongings fit in like four reusable grocery totes, a small carryon suitcase, and the trash bag. That was it. That was all she was taking, even though I asked her what else. She just shook her head and wouldn't look at me and said, "Let's just go."

Getting her out of the depressing little apartment suddenly became my pleasure – not that my dusty old house was a million times better or anything. I was a bachelor living alone, prone to bouts of paranoia and depression. My place was what it was, and I guess it would have to do, but it certainly wasn't any place I was proud to really bring a girl into.

Most of the time if I did, it was just to fuck her and kick her out. I didn't honestly know what I was going to do with Ember when we got to my place.

Did I have rooms? Plenty. Did I have any with the furniture actually assembled or in a usable state? I had to think about that one, honestly… probably not?

Hell, what was I getting myself into?

3

*E*mber...

The ride to wherever we were going was silent. I huddled with my temple against the cool glass of the passenger door and stared out sightlessly at the cityscape rushing past the window. I wasn't scared. I mean, I knew I *should* be scared – I didn't know this man from Adam... but I wasn't scared. I didn't know if that had to do with the medication that they'd given me at the hospital to calm me down or if it had more to do with the fact that I was just... I don't know... hollowed out and empty after all that'd happened that day.

We were on the freeway for a surprising amount of time before he dipped off on the Lake City Way exit. We rolled to a stoplight, not many cars out here at this time of night on a Tuesday, and I felt his eyes on me.

I resituated myself into the semblance of something a little more comfortable as the light turned green, half expecting him to say something, but he didn't.

We were on Lake City Way for a long time, passing car lots and marijuana shops all closed up in the dark, their neon signs glowing softly.

It was becoming ethereal out here, the mists rising off of the various bodies of water around town and moving into the neighborhoods. It was a familiar sight in the fall and winter months around Seattle and the surrounding area. Still, it never failed to be spooky or unsettling.

I perked up when we turned off of Lake City Way and onto a street that was heading up into the hills surrounding the top of the lake. Some residential hills...

"Yeah, we're almost there," he said when I sat up a little. "My place isn't much to write home about," he said, heaving a big sigh, and before he could say or do anything else, I cut in.

"I'm sure its fine," I said tonelessly. "I don't have a home to write to anyway."

He grunted, his hands tightening on the steering wheel, causing it to make a noise somewhere between a creak and a squeak. I felt myself tense but tried to ignore it and pretend it didn't worry me.

Little things like that always worried me, especially coming from Devin. It was like I could feel his annoyance or displeasure radiating off of him and I didn't want to aggravate it. I didn't want to draw any attention when that happened.

I wanted to sigh, but I didn't dare – in fact, I held my breath, letting it out slowly, so very slowly, tense and waiting but for what? Blackjack wasn't Devin. He wasn't going to hurt me. He was here helping me... for now. Only time would tell if he would want or expect anything in return.

Men usually did. Nothing was ever really done out of kindness. It was almost always transactional in nature and the currency was usually sex... but I wasn't getting that vibe from Blackjack for now. I was grateful for that, but I definitely didn't expect it to last. Maybe only as long as the bruises. Devin tended to keep his hands off of me until they'd faded to barely yellow and were covered by makeup.

I wondered for a fraction of a second if that was it, or if Blackjack honestly found me attractive at all? I know it wasn't *fair* thinking like that, but he looked to be a man who was used to life being unfair. I think we maybe held that in common.

He slowed the truck and I perked up a bit as he turned the wheel in a sweeping curve into a wide, flat concrete driveway in front of a garage.

"Here we go," he said, pulling to a stop and throwing the gearshift up into "park." He turned off the truck and the noise of the blasting heat suddenly cut, and everything just fell into a sudden, deafening silence.

I stared at him in the dark. The floodlights off the corner of his garage had turned on via motion sensor and illuminated things well enough. I jumped slightly when it clicked off and suddenly the sound sort of just gradually returned... or at least I started to notice things again. Things like the ticking of the cooling engine, the rub of his coat against the seat's upholstery as he reached for the inside door handle on his side. You know, the little things.

"Stay right here a minute," he said. "I'm going to bring your things in and move a couple of things then I'll be out to get you."

"Okay," I murmured, and I hated how small it came out.

"You're alright," he said. "I just didn't have time to do anything before I ran out to get you, so hang tight."

I nodded and low-key hated it even more that he'd heard whatever in my voice, too.

He shut his door, the motion light flicking back on, and popped open the back door to the big crew cab on his side to grab some of my things before he went around the front of the truck. He took the path by the garage to his front door, and I followed him with my eyes, just trying to take it all in.

There was a flag hanging off to one side of his porch, red with some yellow and white. Not an American flag, that was clear, but I couldn't tell in the dark and the way it hung limp what it was supposed to be. Something military, maybe? I think I saw an eagle's foot, but I somehow doubted it was Boy Scout related and that was the only thing I could pull from memory that was any kind of eagle related right now.

Like, didn't they have an eagle scout rank or something?

"Just breathe," I told myself, my voice loud in the quiet, out in the driveway as I tried to quell my racing thoughts.

He came back out a moment later with a big bag of trash and threw it into the bin by the garage before coming over to my side of the truck. He went to the back door first and gathered up the rest of my things.

"Okay, c'mon," he said, and I opened my door. He was just suddenly there, and I froze for half a second before his hand appeared, tote bag handles hanging off his arm, as he still held out one of his long fingers and large hands for me to grab onto as I got out of the truck. I slid to the ground, superficially holding onto his hand as I didn't really need it, but I didn't want to offend him, either.

"This way," he said leading me to the front door of his house.

I followed at a relatively close distance, the quiet unnerving, the mist muffling everything and the cold night so still, so very still, it scared me to be quite honest. I had never been a fan of the dark and the night. Nothing good had really ever happened to me at night as a child, and I sort of felt that way again now…

Like a child afraid of the dark. Hurt from the betrayal of the people she was supposed to count on the most failing her time and time again. Alone… God the prospect of being alone was so soul crushingly intense. I batted it away as I stepped through the door and *yikes.*

His house was a *mess.* Like, holy shit. There were piles of stuff everywhere and it looked like he hadn't dusted the place in at least twenty years. There were drifts of animal hair stuck to things and blowing like dust bunny tumbleweeds, but I didn't see a dog or a cat or anything.

"Um, you have a dog?" I asked, and he set my things down in a relatively clear corner between the bay window and the fireplace.

"Ah, no… no, he died last year," he said. "He was an old man. A Husky."

"Ah," I said. That did explain the hair, but last *year?*

"I'll uh, get some sheets and blankets out of the closet. The couch will have to do tonight. Maybe for the rest of the week until I can get the guest room back together."

"Okay." I nodded. "Thank you."

"No problem," he said. "I'll uh, be right back."

He left and I went and dug through some of my bags of stuff looking for a pair of leggings and an oversized tee or something to sleep in.

The living room was a couch backed up to the window, a blanket tacked up over it, and piles of random stuff in it that had been there so long the sun was bleaching the color from it.

I tried not to judge, I really, did... but some of this was *yikes* and I wasn't even getting a good look at it during the daytime. I didn't quite know what to expect come morning.

Blackjack returned a moment later with sheets and blankets in his arms and I asked, "Do you have someplace I can change?"

"Uh, yeah... the uh bathroom out here doesn't work so my bedroom and the bathroom in it is your option."

"Okay." I went past him and down the hallway toward the light under the door at the end.

The bedroom was lit, the ceiling fan above the king-sized bed circling lazily and holy *yikes*! Cluttered didn't even begin to cover it in here. The room was just *trashed*. I think his laundry was everywhere but *in* the dresser. The bed was unkempt, and despite the fact he didn't smoke in the house the room sort of reeked of unwashed laundry and stale cigarette smoke.

The bathroom was just as bad. I don't think the toilet had been scrubbed in God knows how long and I was almost afraid to touch the toilet seat to put it down to use it.

There were his and her sinks, and every bit of counter space was littered with trash – mostly empty or half or lower bottles of beer. It appeared only one side worked. The shower looked like it worked but it wasn't clean, and the deep jetted tub was bone dry and had a layer of dust in the bottom.

There were rust stains and the floor? Well, it was a lovely tan tile, but the grout was definitely not supposed to be that dark. I didn't think anything short of the harshest chemicals and probably a steam mop would get that clean and yeah – it did vaguely smell like a men's room in here.

Gross.

Okay, I was judging, but it was *really* hard not to. Like, oh my God.

I changed swiftly and kept my socks on. I didn't want to walk on these floors barefoot – yeah, it was that bad. Still, by the looks of it, his bedroom was the cleanest room in the house.

I was worried, stressed, and suddenly it hit home – *what was I doing?*

Oh my God, oh my God, oh my God... what had I gotten myself into? Just what the hell was I doing? Just what was I going to do?

"Ember? You, uh, you doing okay?"

I jumped up from the edge of his bed where I'd sat down and called out, "Yes! Sorry! I'm coming."

I edged out of his room into the hallway where he waited and he touched under my chin with gentle fingertips, turning my face into the light from his room. He looked me over, brow furrowed and said, "That's going to be a hell of a shiner."

I tried to laugh it off and said, "Won't be my first."

His scowl deepened.

"I gotta go to work in the morning," he said, turning to lead me back up the hallway. "When I get home, I'll uh try to straighten some things up for you. I guess I got a little behind on chores."

I could hear the discomfort about the state of things in his voice, but I tried to simply shrug things off as them being no big deal.

"We all get a little behind sometimes," I murmured. "I'm grateful you're letting me stay tonight and I promise to figure something out in the morning. Even if I have to try and go back home."

"Where's that?" he asked.

"Yelm," I said quietly. "I'd rather not, but... but it might be my only option."

I cleared my throat, and he stopped me beside the couch. "Nothing has to be decided today," he said, and I set my wad of clothes on top of my jumble of stuff.

He pulled back the blankets on the couch which he had made up with sheets and things just like a bed and I nodded.

"Thank you," I murmured, and he nodded.

"I'm glad you called me," he said, and I nodded.

"I'm glad you answered."

"I told you I would," he declared, and I smiled taking a seat on the edge of the couch.

"In you go," he said, and I swung my legs up. He tucked me in and said, "Goodnight, darlin'."

"Goodnight," I called, and he stopped at the hall and hit the switch there, cutting out the light that was on past the wall in the kitchen.

I closed my eyes and settled and cried myself to sleep.

"COME ON, put your arms around me."

"Mm?" I was half-asleep, and gentle hands guided my arms around a solid set of shoulders and a neck covered in long, damp hair.

"There you go." An arm went beneath my knees, and I was hoisted into the air. I held on, the shock of being airborne and floating across the laminate floor startling me.

"What are you doing?" I asked, voice tight with surprise.

"Take it easy, darlin'. I got you."

He kicked open his bedroom door and marched up to the side of the bed and set me on it, pulling the blankets back over me and tucking me in as he'd done only hours earlier.

"One of us might as well be comfortable," he muttered and with a final press of his hands, tucking the blankets around me tight, he left the room, shutting the door tight behind him and the light out in the hallway with it.

I was so tired; I simply accepted it and went back to sleep.

4

*B*lackjack...

I dragged my ass into work and vaguely wondered *just what the fuck was I doing?*

I did a bunch of under the table shit so it wouldn't fuck with my government disability check for being a vet. I'd earned that shit by fire and blood, and I wasn't about to let it slide – still, it wasn't enough to pay the fuckin' bills. Especially living on this side of the mountains and shit, so I had to make ends meet somehow.

Today it was helping Glass and his crew on a house out in Ballard.

When I got there, Glass was the only man on scene and he raised an eyebrow as I walked up, tool belt in one hand, toolbox in the other.

"Didn't expect you in until later," he declared, and I shrugged one shoulder.

"Yeah, well..." I trailed off. Not wanting to get into it but he bucked up a bit and I knew he was going to make it a thing.

"Same girl as the overpass a few months back, huh?" he asked.

I frowned and said, "Mav is just out there tellin' all my fuckin' business to everyone, huh?"

Glass scowled and as I set down my shit on the sidewalk and asked me, "What the fuck you talkin' about, you dumbass? You sent the text to all of us."

"What?" I demanded, and I pulled out my phone which hadn't started going off yet. It was still too early for that. I had a flood of missed texts from the fuckin' club group chat and I squeezed my eyes shut and tried not to visibly cringe from it.

Fuck me.

"Well, shit," I muttered.

"Ah. Ah-ha. Not so slick after all," he accused, and I shrugged.

"I was in a hurry," I said with a shrug, scrolling through and scanning what everyone had to say about it.

"She alright?" he asked when I shoved my phone into my pocket.

I shrugged my shoulders again, and I told the truth... "I don't know, man. Only time will tell."

"Fair enough," he grunted with a nod. "Can't really do anything about it while her douche boyfriend is on law enforcement's radar," he said.

"Right?" I nodded.

"You thinkin' about keepin' her?" he asked with a shitty grin, and I shook my head.

"You fuckin' crazy?" I asked and he barked a laugh. I had a reputation for keeping my solitude. I wasn't about to wreck my streak on that.

Besides, I had a gut feeling that Ember was the kind of girl that deserved way better than the likes of me.

"Hey." I looked over from where I lifted my toolbox back over the bed of my truck. Mace was walking up the sidewalk at me and gave him a chin lift.

"What's up?" I asked.

"Before you go, Raven wanted me to give you this," he said. He handed me a white-and-green tube, and I looked at it.

"What the hell is this for?" I asked.

He was walking backward up the sidewalk and called back, "Bruising! It's supposed to work wonders on it!"

I frowned slightly and called to him, "You aren't telling secrets, are you?"

"Hell no! You sent the text about it to my phone!" He gave me an intense look, the *not my burner* hanging in the air between us unspoken. He had a point. I didn't like it, and I didn't *have* to like it… but he had a point. I sighed and put the tube of whatever whatsit in the pocket of my Carhartt jacket as I popped the back door to my truck to set my tool belt inside.

When I got home, Ember was nowhere in sight. I frowned and went down the hallway and opened up the door into my room and found her just where I'd left her – snug in my bed.

I felt my shoulders ease from their stiff, on guard posture and I went over to her. She moved, swiping her fingers under her eyes and cringed slightly as I sat down on the edge of the bed.

"Hey," I said softly and she sniffed.

"Hey," she warbled back, and I instantly felt a little guilty but I couldn't tell you why.

"You been here all day?" I asked gently, and she nodded miserably. She wouldn't look at me and I put my hand over the covers on her shoulder, half on her back and rubbed her up and down through the blankets.

"You eat anything?" I asked and she shook her head.

"Not really all that hungry," she said, and I nodded.

"I'm going to get in the kitchen and fix some dinner," I said, and I tried my best to sound kindly even though it was far from natural.

"Okay," she murmured.

"While I do, I want you to get yourself up and get a shower. Find something clean to put on and put some of this on your bruises." I handed her the tube out of my pocket and she reached out a hand from underneath the covers and took it.

"What is it?" she asked.

"Some kind of goop," I said with a laugh. "A medic friend of mine swears by it for bruising. She sent it along with one of my bros for you."

"I don't understand..." she said and looked a bit frightened or at the very least taken aback. I smiled and rubbed up and down her back hoping I was somehow coming across as soothing.

"I let my president of my club know I was coming to get you from the hospital last night and I might be out of club business for the week – except I accidentally sent the text to the whole crew. I'm sorry. I didn't mean to put your business out there. I should have been more careful."

She pushed up into a sitting position, her long dark brown hair sleep mussed and even with the spectacular spangle of bruising around one eye and across her face she wasn't anything short of beautiful. Made me want to hurt the guy all the more.

"Did you... did you just *apologize* to me?" she asked.

I nodded. "I can admit when I'm wrong. Doesn't happen very often," I said giving her a reckless grin. "But when it does, I got no problem saying as much."

I got up and went into my bathroom, feeling her eyes watch my every movement. I started up the shower for her and pulled down a couple of clean towels – unsure if she was a two-towel kind of a girl or not. You know, one for her hair and one for the rest of her – especially with all of that long brown hair.

"Give that a second to heat up. Come on, let's get you something clean and comfortable to put on. I'll cook dinner and then I'll get to work on putting the guest room back together."

"You don't have to do all that just for me," she tried to protest.

I just looked at her, wan and sad, tired and clearly depressed, and I just held out a hand and said, "Come on."

She stood up and followed me hugging herself, and I dropped the hand and went out into the living room, turning to the left to go into the kitchen – the sunroom just beyond it and in its own sort of shambles. The floor half done. I really needed to finish it... I probably should call one of the guys for help to get it done but I was notoriously bad at asking for any kind of assistance with anything. I liked my solitude. I liked being able to handle shit on my own. It just was the way I'd always been.

Ember padded in her socks over to the pile of her belongings and rooted through things to find some clean clothes like I'd asked her to. She was good at taking suggestions, and I filed that away into the back of my mind. I liked a woman that was pliable. It felt good to take care of someone but too often I'd been burned, giving a woman my all only for her to go off and cheat or burn me and I wasn't about that shit anymore.

It was just plain better to be alone and while I had no problem helping Ember out – mostly because I couldn't get that image of her climbing over the railing on that fuckin' overpass out of my head, and I'd been that sort of desperate, I'd been that sort of guilty and hurt and had someone intervene for me... that was where that shit ended for me.

I didn't want to take advantage or whatever. I just wanted to pay it forward. I owed it to the guy that'd kept me going.

She paused at the mouth of the hallway, her arms loaded with stuff, and I waited to see if she would turn and say something, but she didn't. Just ghosted back toward my room and shut the door – which was a habit for me. It'd been to keep Nanook and the cats out, but as they'd all gradually gotten old and passed, I hadn't replaced them, the club taking up too much of my time for me to own any animals.

I did the dishes and pulled some shit out of my fridge to make up some dinner, firing up the gas stove and throwing a quick marinade together of spices and apple juice for the pork chops while I got some hot water going for some instant potatoes.

Yeah, it wasn't super grand or anything, but it was quick and would allow me to get to some of the shit that needed getting to around here. Shit that I'd put off for far too long considering I hadn't really had the time or reason to do anything with it.

I sighed and poured myself a shot of Jack and downed it to unwind and loosen up. I didn't have to wait for very long for Ember to reappear. She took a fuckin' tactical shower, that one. In and out inside ten minutes.

"Hey," I greeted her and she hugged herself and said, "Hi. Um, where do you want me to put my used towels?"

"You cold?" I asked, reaching out for the one she held onto, the other wrapped in a turban on her head.

"Yeah, a little," she confessed with a nervous laugh.

"I'll turn up the heat," I said and she looked surprised and blurted out, "You don't have to do that! I can put on a sweatshirt."

I dumped the towel into the top of the washer in its open closet in the kitchen and with a shrug said, "Why not both? Go on, now."

She went into the living room and put her stuff away, taking a seat on the couch to pull out some lotion or hand cream or whatever. She sat on the edge of the couch and used it on her skin before pulling on a sweatshirt and a pair of fluffier socks on over the thin regular socks she had on her feet.

Her expression was somehow hollow and far away, and I flashed back on the image of her collapsing on the other side of that railing, the safe side, and just falling the fuck apart.

I turned up the heat and realized I was still wearing my jacket and hell yeah; the house was cold. I shed the coat and went over to the hall closet just across from the front door, hanging it up inside beside my leather jacket and cut.

I went over and sat down on the couch beside Ember and looked at her.

"Want to talk about anything?" I asked, and she looked at me, dropping the tube of whatever lotion down into the bag by her feet. It smelled like a rich peppermint buttercream over here and I liked it.

"Honestly, I don't know what's wrong with me," she murmured. "All I want to do is sleep."

I got up and bent down, lifting her feet by hooking my hand under her ankles, lifting them and turning her on the couch and tucking her in. I grabbed the remote off the coffee table and switched on the big wall mounted television for her, putting the remote in her hands.

"It's all good, darlin'. You're safe, and I think your body finally knows it even if your mind hasn't quite caught up. You take as much time as you need and rest. You probably need it."

"Why are you being so nice to me?" she asked, her eyes brimming and turning luminous. I looked away, suddenly feeling like I'd been caught or something.

I gave a shrug and mumbled something to the effect of, "Isn't it about time somebody was?"

She didn't answer, which was a good thing. The question had been one of those rhetorical ones anyway.

Truth was, I didn't know except it was who I was; it was what I did and what I stood for. What I'd always stood for from the moment I'd joined the Corps and hell, probably even before that.

At my heart, I was a big damn hero... a piece of shit and not always great at it, but that was my job. My duty. To protect those who couldn't protect themselves and to save those who couldn't always save themselves.

...and it bothered me that something about Ember felt so different from business as usual on that front. It felt incredibly different, and I didn't know why.

5

*E*mber...

"Thank you," I murmured as he handed me down a plate. He sat next to me on the couch with a gusty sigh and nodded silently, putting a forkful of food into his mouth and chewing.

I took a bite of my own and had to smile at how he'd cut up my meat for me. Like I was a child or something. I don't know why, but I didn't find it to be overbearing or obnoxious... rather I found it to be sweet. Even though the shadow of a thought crossed my mind that he might have done it to keep a knife out of my hand. But then I glanced at his plate, and no – I guess it was just the way he did things. His meat was all pre-cut too.

I took a bite and *wow*... it was really good.

"Mmm," I hummed in appreciation and he looked over at me, giving me a bit of side-eye and asked, "What else you have to eat today?"

It sounded reserved, like I was in trouble or something and I sort of clammed up and without speaking just shook my head a little. I mean, he'd already asked me what I'd eaten when he got home and I'd told him I hadn't...

He grunted in consternation and chewed through another bite, swallowing and asking me; "You drink anything?"

"No," I said and I know it sounded small. The disappointment in his tone striking me in the heart.

"What do you want?" he asked, getting to his feet. "I have water, orange juice, and iced tea."

"Oh, um, some orange juice, please?" I didn't look at him, the way he was looming while simply just standing there unnerving.

"Okay, I'll be right back." He went into the kitchen and returned a moment later with a tall glass of orange juice and a big bottle of Intelligent Water brand bottled water in the other.

"Here." He handed both down to me.

I set my plate in my lap and took them both and murmured, "Thank you."

"I don't got any rules for you staying here but one," he said, taking up his plate again and continuing to eat.

I paused and waited, watching him warily as he finished his bite to continue.

"While you're here for however long, you'll eat three square meals a day and get your requisite amount of water in you. I'll do the math on that and get you one of those water bottles with the times and whatnot on it if you need that to help you."

I gave a sort of incredulous little laugh, I mean... *what?*

"I mean it, Ember. You need to take care of yourself."

"Why?" I asked and I almost immediately clapped a hand over my mouth as soon as the sound issued forth.

"What do you mean 'why?'" he demanded.

"I... I don't know," I said and shuddered at the sternness in his tone.

"Sorry," he said. "You're fine." His tone gentled and I wanted to believe him but I was still guarded. Tense and wary. He grunted and thrusting out his chin in the direction of my plate said, "Keep eating."

I put a bite into my mouth and chewed automatically and it was really very good. The pork perfectly spiced and flavorful. Still, my nerves jangled, and I fought to keep my breathing even.

I didn't know what was wrong with me other than... other than I was scared. I know it wasn't right of me, but I couldn't help it. I sat saddened by that fact. That Blackjack hadn't been anything but kind to me and yet here we sat side by side and I couldn't stop flinching every time he made a sudden movement.

He didn't apologize, which he had no reason to – this was purely a 'me' problem. Neither did he berate me, though. He didn't say anything like 'stop it' or tell me I was being dumb or any of that stuff. He just ate his meal in silence seated calmly next to me and eventually when I finished my own meal a bite or two after him, he just silently held out a hand for my plate and fork.

"Thank you," I murmured and he gave a single nod and got up, going back into the kitchen. I thought he would start an immediate clean up, but he didn't. Instead, he went down the hall and I heard a door open.

"You need any help?" I called.

"No, just stay there and watch some TV or something. Try to relax. I got this."

It felt wrong to settle back on the couch and pull the blankets back over me. Felt somehow worse still as I reached for the little remote and turned things on. I found a show about ghost stories on one of the streaming services he had and settled in, closing my eyes and listening more than anything, jumping and body tightening as things thumped, crashing and tumbling in the room Blackjack had gone into as he swore with venom and cursed whatever object he wrestled with six ways to Sunday.

I gritted my teeth and stared intently at the mouth of the hallway, my heartbeat throbbing in my temple and chest feeling like it was constricted as I waited for him to appear and draw a bead on me with that ire.

He came back out a while later and with a bit of a frustrated grin gave his head a slight shake and declared, "Sorry, but it's the couch for at least one more night darlin'."

"Oh, I don't mind at all," I said, pushing myself up to a sitting position, and he looked across the expanse of the living room floor open between us and said, "Yeah, well I do. I got work in the morning, so I'm gonna have to say goodnight. Drink your water for me."

"Okay," I said a little taken aback as he shut off some lights, turned around, and went up the hallway to his own room. I heard the door open and shut and I turned onto my side facing the television from where I'd settled back down.

I huddled there and closed my eyes, and sleep took its sweet time coming.

When I woke, I wasn't on the couch but rather tucked into Blackjack's bed all over again, surrounded by his smell and a sense of calm and safety. I was confused about that last part given that when I was awake and he was here, I tended to be so damn jumpy. I couldn't figure that one out so I just shoved it aside and forced myself to sit up. I groaned, my body aching and feeling abused... which I guess it had been, by Devin. I rubbed the sleep from my eyes, my bladder protesting and sat on the edge of the bed for a minute and sighed.

There would be no going back to sleep like I had yesterday. I'd slept the whole damn night and day away, only to eat dinner and to sleep some more. Now it was like my body was sick to death of the act of sleeping while my mind? My mind just wanted to go back to it.

Nothing hurt when you were asleep. I didn't have to think about anything while I slept, either... and lord knows all I wanted to do right now was *sleep*, but I knew I was past that now. There would be no more sleep, no more rest, even though I could mentally just sleep for a thousand years if given the chance. My body had other ideas, though; and damn if I didn't take that as an almost personal betrayal.

An even worse one than getting my period every month at that.

"Come on, Ember," I groaned and stiffly got to my feet.

Everything fucking *hurt*.

Partially from the tousle with Devin two days ago and partially from just plain inactivity.

I dragged myself into Blackjack's disgusting bathroom and winced.

I wasn't sure how anyone could live like this and it made me wonder about him. I mean, on the surface it looked like he had it together – so why all of this?

I mean, I don't think this bathroom had had a proper cleaning *this year*, and I wasn't sure if his kitchen floor had been scrubbed like *ever*.

I shook my head and swallowed hard, used the bathroom, flushed and made a face at the stains in the toilet and shook my head.

Well...

He had saved me, twice over now. Maybe I could save his house... I mean, did he even own any cleaning products?

I looked under the bathroom sink and found some. Relatively new at that – like he'd had the intentions of cleaning had bought the supplies like a normal person, and then had just... forgot.

The whole house was going to be a monumental, days-long undertaking but I had to start somewhere. I guess that somewhere came down to what I just couldn't live without being clean and the easy answer to that was the kitchen followed by the bathroom but that kitchen floor was literally so yikes I couldn't even.

Well... maybe...

I went out to the kitchen and surveyed the disaster of it and yeah, no, yep... I couldn't start with the kitchen. I was better off starting with the bathroom.

I had to give him credit where credit was due, though. As filthy as the kitchen floor was, the food preparation surfaces; countertops, stove, et cetera, were *immaculate*. Like I was relieved by that, I couldn't tell you how much I was relieved by that, but it made the state of the floor and even the rest of the house just that much more confusing.

"Okay, let's see..." I murmured to myself and I started snooping for more cleaning products. I found a trove under the kitchen sink, and some more in the closet thing that held the washing machine and dryer in the kitchen and even a few *more* things in the pantry.

I had more than enough to do what needed doing I just needed a bucket for the mop water...

I went door to door in the messy, dusty, cluttered house and found said mop bucket in what Blackjack had declared the defunct bathroom that didn't work. It was in the bathtub, the shower curtain rod laying at an angle in the bottom of the tub and propped against the wall.

"Okay, then." I raised my eyebrows and checked under the bathroom sink and felt a surge of satisfaction. *Jackpot.* It was a whole unopened *gallon* of floor cleaner. *Fabulous,* I thought to myself.

I tied up my hair and retrieved the bucket and said floor cleaner and retreated through the decrepit clutter back to Blackjack's master bath...

"Okay, we're starting with the bathroom," I said to no one. "Now where to start *in here?*"

God, this was going to be a daunting task.

lackjack...

"You okay, bro?"

I looked up frowning from my phone and the several unread and unanswered texts I'd sent checking on Ember.

"She's not answering her phone," I said. "Probably sleeping."

Mace frowned at me slightly and asked, "She sleeping a lot?"

I nodded. "Didn't get up at all yesterday, didn't drink, didn't eat until I put dinner in front of her. I wanted to check on her but she's not answering."

He nodded slowly and said, "Sounds like she's depressed and can you blame her?" he asked.

I shook my head. "No."

"You worried she's done something to herself?" Glass asked and I shook my head.

"Honestly, I don't know," I said. "I don't think so but considering everything..." I trailed off and Glass nodded.

"You need to get the fuck outta here, *go*, man. I won't fault you for it."

I nodded, and he said, "No work tomorrow, and I'm gonna be letting the rest of these guys go early today anyway."

I frowned. "Why?" I asked and Mace laughed and Glass rolled his eyes.

"Don't you pay attention to the news or the weather?" Glass demanded.

"Fuck no," I grated.

"Late season storm is going to come through," Mace said. "Looks like it's going to be a blower."

"Shit, it *is* late," I said.

"They're saying widespread power outages and downed limbs and trees so I want everyone off the roads and able to stock up at the store and shit if they need to. I already got Cadence and Mark prepped as best I could. I'm going to weather the storm at her place with them."

"You fix her fireplace yet?" I asked and he shook his head.

"No, not yet. That's going to be a big summer project."

I nodded. "Hit me up. I'll help you out."

"Appreciate it, now get you gone, motherfucker. Stop at the store and check on your girl."

"She's not my girl," I said. "I don't want that. I'm just helping her out for a minute."

Mace and Glass traded a look and Mace said, "Right... because this kind of thing has, historically, gone that way for just about every fuckin' guy in the club that's found themselves in this kind of thing."

"Yeah, shut up," I said. "You're the princess in your relationship. Your woman saved *you*, remember?"

"Damn straight she did," he said with a grin.

Glass had a strange look on his face and I scowled.

"What?"

He shook his head. "Nothin' man. Nothin'."

"Bullshit," I declared.

"Guess you ain't all that worried after all then," he said.

"Why you say that?" I demanded, getting irritated.

"You're still here," Mace said, and I flipped him off.

"Yeah, yeah," I declared and I hefted my tool belt and lunchbox and turned up the block where my truck was parked. The boys were laughing behind my back, but I was in a sour mood. I'd like to blame it on their fuckery and razzing, but no...

No, I was worried about Angel – er, Ember. Why wasn't she answering her phone?

I tossed my shit in the back seat of my truck and made for home. There was really only one way to find out.

I needed to stop at the store, but I skipped it. The nagging feeling that something was wrong driving me right to my door. I threw the truck in park and walked around to my front door, keying it open and going inside.

It was quiet except for this weird rhythmic swishing sound and the odd sniff from Ember emanating from the kitchen.

I went for the sound and stopped cold in the entryway to the kitchen and the sight of her on her knees on a folded towel scrubbing the fucking floor like some sort of scullery maid. It pissed me off. She wasn't here to clean my fuckin' house. She was here to get a break from the shit she'd been going through and to heal.

"What the fuck are you doing?" I blurted without thinking and her head whipped up and she stared at me in mute panic, her wild blue-green eyes wide and red rimmed, face slicked with tears hands as red as her eyes as she let go of the scrub brush.

"I can't get the grout clean no matter how hard I scrub," she said and then her voice cracked. "I'm sorry!"

I didn't even think about it, I moved forward and she flinched and reared back. I put my hands out and slowed down.

"Easy," I said. "I'm not mad." She hiccupped and tried to get some breaths in around her crying and I moved forward slowly. She didn't move, and I got down on her level and hugged her. She slumped over my arm, hers coming up to hug it as she melted the fuck down and I had no idea why. I seriously doubted it had anything to do with the goddamned floor, though.

"Easy," I soothed. "Easy there, darlin'. What's going on?" I asked. "How come you haven't answered your phone?"

"Oh, God what time is it? Did you leave work early?" she cried, and I shook my head.

49

"Mm-mm, how about you answer me first?" I asked.

She calmed down a little and looked up at me stricken and said, "Devin's out of jail."

"Ah." I nodded. "Started blowing up your phone?" I asked.

"Yeah," she said. "I turned it off. I was afraid he would find me."

"Find you?" I asked.

"Yeah," she said. "Paranoid and stupid, I know, but it just wouldn't shut up and I don't know…"

"Right, well, let him come on over. I'll blow his fucking head off for you, gladly."

She sniffed and laughed a little awkwardly and I smoothed some of her hair that was loose from her messy bun out of her face.

"Now back to my first question…" I said gently.

"What?" she asked. I gave her an awkward little grin.

"What the fuck are you doin'?"

"Oh, um, I got bored so I'm cleaning your house?" she answered and pulled away from me. I let her go and didn't like the itch I got in my palms to put my hands on her again.

I shook my head and said, "You ain't gotta do that."

"Oh, no, I know," she said… "I want to."

I snorted.

"Bullshit, nobody wants to clean up this fuckin' sty. Not even me. How you think it got this way?" I sighed. I wasn't proud of it. Far from it. Just sometimes things got to be too much and I just… I don't know. Powered down. Went to auxiliary power only like some kind of a fuckin' cyborg and shit just didn't get done and by the time I could get to shit it was like I was paralyzed and didn't know where to fuckin' start.

"Why are you home so early if not for me not answering my phone?" she asked guiltily, changing the subject.

"Storm's coming. Boss told us to get the fuck out, stock up at the store if we needed to and to go home before it starts blowing."

"Oh," she said faintly.

"So come on," I said getting to my feet and holding a hand down to her. "Let's hit the store and get something to eat. I want to try and get the bolts to fix that fuckin' bed so I can get you off the couch. It's no place for a woman."

She reached up and took my hand and I hauled her slight frame to her feet. She was too thin, likely a byproduct of too much fuckin' stress. I cursed myself for adding to it and not taking any away. I was bad at this where women were concerned. Usually, it was fellow soldiers or men I helped deal with their problems. This… this was a particular challenge I didn't quite know how to deal with.

She looked up at me, all wide blue-green eyes framed by wisps of her deep, dark brown hair and for the first time I noticed she had a smattering of pale freckles across her even paler cheeks and nose.

She was adorable, seemed so sweet, and I didn't understand dude's fuckin' deal.

"You want me to go with you?" she asked and I nodded.

"You need to get out of the house," I said, and she nodded.

"I'll go change," she said. I nodded and let her rummage through her bags out front in the living room. I took myself down the hall to my room to take a leak and hit the switch for the overhead light and the ceiling fan in my room.

Nothing was out of place in here, except my bed was neatly made, which wasn't completely typical. Sometimes I flipped the blankets down into some semblance of made but usually not.

I went into my bathroom and flipped on the light and couldn't stop the disbelieving, "Huh," that came out of my mouth.

The bathroom in here never fuckin' looked so good.

I mean, it sparkled in places I didn't think *could* sparkle. The floor was clean and it smelled nice. Like *actually* nice, above and beyond the cleaning products she'd used. A three-wick candle sat partially burned down between the his and her sinks that I think I'd only ever used the one side and the towels were neatly hung. My bathroom rugs were missing, but the floor was scrubbed and looked so nice I actually checked my boots before stepping on it.

I stopped short in front of the toilet and lifted the lid and the seat and the water was a deep blue and the bowl white.

I'm not proud to admit the fact I didn't think that bowl would ever come clean from the stains and I felt some serious soul-crushing guilt at picturing Ember cleaning that rancid mess.

I didn't deserve this. I didn't deserve nice things, clean things like this.

What the fuck?

I used the bathroom and flushed, and self-consciously lowered the seat and lid before making my way out into my room as she poked her head in.

"You cleaned my bathroom?" I asked.

"Yeah." She nodded, clutching her clean clothes to her chest, and I shook my head. "Mad at me?" she asked and she cringed.

"Fuck no, I feel guilty as hell, though. I didn't bring you here to clean my house."

"No, I know that," she said and gave a bit of a nervous laugh. "I just really needed something to do, and I thought I could help."

I pursed my lips and nodded without looking at her, my hands on my hips.

"You want in here to change?" I asked.

"You mind?" she asked back and I moved toward her.

She quickly stood aside, and I said, "No, I don't mind," as I passed her. She ducked into the bathroom and shut the door and I looked around my room, and I mean really looked. Mostly it was just a lot of clothes, some old military equipment like packs and bags, and a bunch of stacked and random ammo cans.

Yeah, I was one of those guys... post military, owned a fuck ton of guns and ammo should the shit ever go down.

I went down to the kitchen and looked around and sighed. She was working her ass off in here and I realized she'd taken the brace thing off her wrist. I went snooping around and found it on the cluttered kitchen table and sighed, picking it up.

The door to the bathroom scraped open from the depths of my room down the hall and her light tread tapped against the laminate flooring coming up the hall.

I turned with the brace in my hand and waved at her to gimme her wrist.

"You need to keep this on," I said and she obediently held out her arm with its fresh ring of bruises around her delicate wrist.

"It was in the way," she said feebly.

"Mm." I sighed, thinking about her and what she'd said, how she'd just needed something to *do*.

As I slipped the black soft cast brace thing back on her arm, which was still swollen looking and carefully worked the straps, I asked her, "What do you do for work or whatever?"

"I'm a checker at a grocery store. I want to get into the bakery and cake decorating but my store doesn't have any openings."

"I hate to be blunt, but you still have a job?"

She nodded quickly as I worked the straps doing and undoing them, tightening them up to give her support incrementally.

"I'm union, and the chain and the union are being really good to me. Told me to tell them where I settled and that when I was, they would transfer me to the closest store that needed it."

I made an incredulous scoffing noise; I couldn't believe it. A citizen corporation actually doing right by one of their employees? Be still my racing fuckin' heart.

I said as much to her and she snorted a bit of a laugh and she asked softly, "A little cynical, don't you think?"

"But am I wrong?" I asked softly, and she averted her gaze. I let her hand go and studied her. She was still on the ragged edge, a tightness around her eyes, her shoulders hunched and posture guarded and tight.

"No, I guess not," she said and she sounded sad. I silently cursed myself. I was supposed to be making things better, not worse, but breaking shit and killing the enemy – those were the concepts I understood and the toolkit I had at my disposal.

Don't get me wrong, motherfucker was fixin' to die, just not any time soon. Too much heat with him out here acting the fuckin' fool and on the pigs' radar.

"We'll get your number changed and we'll look and see what's around here when it comes to your grocery chain or whatever. Rome wasn't built in a day, darlin'. Slow and steady."

She looked up at me, her injured arm cradled against her chest and she nodded.

"That better?" I asked. "Too tight? Not tight enough?"

"Oh, no… it's perfect."

"Okay." I gave a nod. "Come on, let's go."

We went to the hardware store first; of course, they didn't have what I was fuckin' looking for to fix that fucking bed. I wasn't quite ready to admit defeat on it though. Not yet.

Next, we hit the grocery store, by the time we were done in there it was gusting bad enough and I was tired enough of dealing with shit we hit a drive-thru on the way home for tonight's dinner.

The whole time we were out, Ember was practically up my ass, sticking close to me like glue and I wondered what that was about. Half the time she seemed half terrified of me and the other half she was so close to me, we were practically wearing the same clothes.

Once home, we sat on the couch and ate our food. After that, she waved me off and said, "I want to clean the fridge before we put anything in it." Which was fair but fuck if she was going to do it.

"We'll do it together," I said, and she nodded. I went and dragged the trash can over.

We cleaned out the fridge and her version and my version were clearly two different things. I thought she meant just ding out the old shit and put the new shit away. No, she meant take literally *ever-fuck-ing-thing* out to the bare shelves and wash the inside of the thing before loading things back in.

Not gonna lie, it needed it. I didn't want to do it, but I didn't want to upset her or piss on her fuckin' efforts, either.

Seemed like she'd had a lifetime of that shit.

I was curious about her, and I wanted to ask questions, but I was half afraid I'd accidentally take off a scab or straight up open some old wounds.

She worked hard, and I took over from her on the regular when she got frustrated with not being able to use her hand and wrist. I'd bought some bags of Epsom salts at the store for her. They'd worked some wonders on me when I was stiff as hell so I figured what could it hurt? Plus, she'd put all that work in on my bathroom. She should be the first to enjoy the fruits of her labor.

I straightened up after wiping out the last of the fridge and eyed the overflowing trash can and the half full trash bag beside it.

"I'm going to take this shit out," I said. "Grab a quick shower."

"I don't know how you like things to go, but I think I can get it all put away for the most part from memory. Just don't get mad if I misplace stuff," she said with a shrug and I stopped.

"I'll never get mad over something so stupid," I said with a shake of my head. "If I'm mad about anything, it's that I let this place get this bad and I brought you into it. You deserve better than this."

She smiled up at me a little sadly and said, "You helped me, now let me help you... please?"

I chuckled a little and gave her a half-strength smile.

"This isn't a quid pro quo, darlin'. I helped you because I like helping people. It's not transactional. You don't owe me anything." I stretched and turned to go up the hall and as I disappeared around the corner, I could swear I heard her say, "That's where you're wrong... I owe you *everything*."

I pretended like I didn't hear... I mean, it was some serious food for thought.

Don't get attached, Clint. I told myself. *She's not a lost puppy. She's a human being... and everybody fuckin' leaves you eventually. Remember that.*

I went into my bedroom and looked around, and picked up my fuckin' laundry, sorting through the piles, before I even thought about getting undressed and getting in the shower.

I couldn't let her clean my place. This had definitely gone on long enough. It was time for me to man up some and do the whole lead by example.

How could I expect her to pick up the pieces when clearly, I wasn't?

Fuck.

*E*mber...
 I finished putting everything away and groaned looking at the kitchen floor. I swear to fucking God, it was going to be the bane of my existence. I looked around and twitched my nose sniffing, taking in just the sheer number of things that still needed to be done. It was a monumental undertaking for sure.

"Hey." His voice was soft but that didn't stop me from screaming and pulling my limbs in to protect my chest as I bent at the waist. He laughed at first but it wasn't malicious, just... uncomfortable, I guess? The look on his face and in those brown eyes of his were a wincing apologetic.

"Shit, I'm sorry," he said.

"It's okay!" I blurted quickly. "Just scared the shit out of me!"

"I can see that," he said and shook his head. "Okay, you're done for tonight. You need to relax. Grab your things and come with me."

"What?" I asked.

"Grab whatever you're going to sleep in and come with me," he said slowly.

I did as he asked, grabbing fresh house clothes and following him down the hall where I could hear the rush of water coming from his bathroom. He let me in and a bath was going. He went over to the big corner tub with its jets – which had been a bitch and was totally disgusting to clean, but I had managed to do it – and he measured out a big two cup measuring cup of bath salts out of a blue bag and he scattered it in the filling water.

"In you go," he said. "I'll leave you alone."

He passed me by as I stared at the bath and the already flickering candle I'd dug out of my things and he hit the light right before he shut the door behind him.

I blinked and lowered my armful of things to the counter between the bathroom sinks.

I took advantage of the offering before me with deep gratitude, undressing and stepping into the steaming water with a hiss.

Too hot, but only just so.

I turned down the temp to almost all the way cold and gritted my teeth against the sting against my feet and ankles as I swished the water into a more bearable temp before equalizing it again to as close to perfect as I could get it.

I could hear Blackjack outside the bathroom talking to someone, likely on the phone, but I couldn't make out what he was saying which was good. I didn't want to invade his privacy when he seemed to be so cognizant of mine.

I closed my eyes and listened to him without trying to pick out words, just the rich timbre of his voice. He had a good voice, smooth and melodic without trying to be. Rich, not quite deep and bass but just on the edge before the lower range. I don't know what they called that. It wasn't worth turning on my phone to look it up, either. Hell, I didn't even know where my phone *was* at the moment.

I cuddled down into the steamy bath and let the warmth of it soothe my aches. It was nice in here, now that the bathroom was clean, and I tried to decide where and what to start with tomorrow. Tackling the kitchen floor had been an abject failure on my part. I think I'd been a little ambitious with that one...

I startled, the water sloshing as I drew in my arms and legs, hiding myself and reflexively scrunching back into the corner of the tub that I occupied when the light touch fell at my shoulder.

"Easy darlin'! Easy… it's just me."

"What are you doing?" I asked, alarmed.

"It got quiet in here, I knocked and when there was no answer…" he looked slightly amused, his dark brown eyes fixed on mine, his gaze studiously doing no wandering lower. I appreciated that.

"Did I fall asleep?" I asked.

"Yeah." His smile was a bit rueful. "Hang on a minute, let's get you out of there."

He got up and I craned my neck up and back, watching him take one of the big bath towels off the shelf above the toilet. He unfurled it and came back over, looming slightly over me but still not looking, his head turned to the side as he held open the towel.

I sat frozen in the tepid water for several heartbeats and he said gently, "Haven't got all night, darlin'. If you'd rather I just fuck off, I am more than happy to do that. I just thought it might be nice to have someone take care of you for a change."

Oh…

"That's sweet of you," I murmured, and I bit my bottom lip. I wanted to tell him *'I've got it, I can take care of myself,'* but at the same time…

"Ember," he said gently. "You alright?"

"I'm fine!" I said quickly, and I forced myself to move, standing up. He kept his eyes closed and held out a hand when my foot slipped a little and made a rubbing screech against the bottom of the tub and I took it saying "Ow!" when my wrist protested. I had reached out with my dominant hand, the sprained one.

"Easy," he said. "It's not that big of a hurry."

I swallowed hard and stepped over the deep lip of the tub and he let my hand go when I gave him a quiet "Okay," and he knew I was firm. He kept his eyes shut and took up the side of the towel he'd dropped to reach for me and I held still hugging myself and shivering slightly. He enveloped me in the big soft fluffy thing and opened his eyes to meet mine.

"Not so bad, was it?" he asked.

"No," I murmured softly as he rubbed my back and shoulders through the material.

"You drink your water today?" he asked, and I smiled and huffed a bit of a laugh.

"Most of it, I think."

"You gotta work on that for me," he said, stepping away and letting me wind the towel proper around me.

"How come?" I asked and he smirked and said, "Staying hydrated is good for you and leads to all sorts of good things for the body. It will help you heal faster."

"Okay," I said, not completely sold on the assertion.

"I'll go get you a fresh bottle while you get ready for bed," he said, and I nodded. He left, shutting the bathroom door and I blinked stupidly for a few seconds. That'd been an odd exchange but still... nice.

I couldn't remember the last time I felt cared for and I had to admit a certain amount of wariness from it. Like, *what did he want in return?*

I stepped out into the cluttered bedroom and found it... less cluttered? Things at least moved around and sorted a bit better. By things, I mostly meant laundry. He returned and held out a big bottle of Intelligent Water out as I came out of the bathroom and I took it.

"Thank you," I murmured, and he raised an eyebrow at me. I gave a bit of a shy little laugh and cracked the seal on it and drank some and he nodded satisfied.

He jerked his head past him and I nodded and said, "Goodnight, Blackjack."

He smiled and said, "Goodnight, darlin'," and the softness of his tone and the affectionate little endearment felt good. Like he had just rubbed silk all down my back.

I would be lying if I didn't say I felt some attraction but... *but who would want a broken thing like you?* I wondered and the thought was one of those intrusive ones that hurt, but couldn't be silenced... I mean, it was a valid point.

I went out to the living room and sighed, sitting on the edge of the couch and drinking some more water before tucking myself beneath the blankets.

I looked at my phone on top of one of my bags of stuff and sighed. The wind was picking up outside, which I was glad for the white noise of it. I had a hard time falling asleep anyway though. Worry overtaking me at the thought of Devin and his string of nasty texts and threatening voicemails. He was big mad and promising to find me.

I would feel better when I could get my number changed, like Blackjack had suggested. I felt safe here, for the time being, but I couldn't help but wonder if or when Devin ever found me just what would happen.

I hunkered down under the blankets and wound up crying myself to sleep again, my panic making rest feel so very far away.

8

*B*lackjack...

I'd put her in a bath and started straightening up my room. I spent a little while at it, only a few minutes really, then with a sigh I stopped. Thinking about what she'd told me, I went out into the living room, finding her phone and turning it on. I was curious, and I didn't want to upset her by talking about it or whatever. I just wanted to scope things out and see what kind of shit she'd been dealing with and stewing on while I'd been out of the house.

I was glad the thing was on silent when it finished booting up because after it had, it buzzed in my hand relentlessly like a hive of angry hornets with all the text and voicemail notifications.

Did this loser motherfucker not have a life? Did he not have anything better to do?

I stood in the living room and scrolled through his texts and the limitless attempts at gaslighting at first, then his toddler tantrum calling her every name in the book, before more gaslighting trying to lay the blame for his bullshit at her feet, before taking a swing and a miss at some really vile threats.

I flicked over to her voicemail and started playing some, holding the phone to my ear and shaking my head at the vitriol and just plain shit that was spewing out of the earpiece.

No wonder she'd been driven fuckin' crazy and had wound up on that overpass. *Jesus fucking Christ!*

It was while I was swiping through the automated transcriptions of some of those voicemails that Devin's number flashed on the screen with the angry devil emojis to either side of it.

I answered and put the phone to my ear walking back toward my room where Ember was secluded in my bathroom and listened as he launched into one of his petulant tirades.

"You need to get your ass home, *now,* you little bitch!" he snarled into my ear, and I felt a slow, nasty little creeping smile lift the corners of my lips as I let him go on. "You better bet your ass there are gonna be consequences this time but I'll still fucking forgive you."

"Oh, how magnanimous of you," I said dryly.

"Who the fuck is this?" he demanded.

"The new man in her life," I said which wasn't exactly the truth but wasn't a lie either. "A *real* one," I declared, flopping down on my bed, and leaning back up against the headboard.

"This is how this is gonna go," I told him. "You're going to fuck off, and I mean *all the way off* and never darken Ember's door again. In exchange for this, I might let you keep your fuckin' hands for laying them on her. You get what I'm saying, or do I need to spell that shit out any clearer?"

"Just who the fuck do you think you are? You stupid, asshair!" he sputtered over the line.

"I'm the most dangerous thing you've ever come across in your life," I said. "I'm Ember's guardian angel – for now. You might want to mind your fuckin' manners and your fuckin' tongue in her direction or I'll cut it out too if you don't. I can go from guardian angel to avenging angel in two seconds flat and after going through your text messages and your voicemail's I've met – no, scratch that. I've *exceeded* the level of bullshit I'm willing to put up with from you already. This is your final warning, bro. Leave her alone, stop fucking with her, or I'm coming to pay a visit."

I ended the call on him and turned off her phone, closing my eyes and resting my head back against the wall with a sigh as I untensed muscles a group at a time and breathed through my seething anger. I was in that place where I was so beyond pissed the fuck off, I was *calm*. Which, unironically, was the place I found myself in when I was overseas killing a bunch of enemy combatants. I'd killed men for a lot less than what ol' boy'd done where Ember was concerned. I'd also killed men for a lot worse. Things that still haunted me to this day and that would haunt me forever. Things that I'd never be able to scrub from my mind no matter how many pills I took and no matter how much booze I swilled.

I lived with horrors that were too much to put into movies or on television that played out real-time in my PTSD-fueled nightmares.

Shit that there was no cure for and demons that I battled daily... except right now. Right now, my demons and I were cuddle buddies as I contemplated just how long I needed to wait and just how I would get Devin where I wanted him to try some violence out on him and see how he'd like it.

It didn't take long for my thoughts to drift to the woman behind the closed door to my right. I sighed out and tried to calm down and thought about her. About her wrecked and devastated expression on that fuckin' overpass that tore at my heart in my dreams almost as much as the in-country shit did.

I felt bone weary for a minute. The fight to keep going could, at times, be exhausting... likewise, I didn't feel like I was doing a very good job of holding things up for Ember. Some of that was my own insecurities getting to me, even though I would never admit that shit out loud. I jolted slightly and looked/ at my phone. Some time had elapsed. Like more than me just resting my eyes for a few seconds and Ember hadn't stirred – at least I don't think.

Shit.

I worried about her but had the presence of mind to put her turned off phone back from where I'd ferreted it out before I went to check on her.

I tapped on the bathroom door and called out, "Ember?"

No answer.

I tapped again.

Nothing.

With a tight feeling in my chest, I opened the door. She was sound asleep in the tub. I stopped, one foot in the door and let my eyes slide over her. The way she was turned I could see some of her back, and the bogus nickname she'd given me when we'd first met didn't seem so bogus anymore. She had these delicate long and narrow angel wings tattooed from her shoulders to her hips with these thin lines of 'thread' stringed at random with these 'pearls' stitching them to her skin back and forth between them like lacing a corset.

The art was *beautifully* done in light blues and lavenders with subtle grays but all of it soft and dreamlike, none of it harsh or over saturated.

I banished the thought of what it would look like to make those wings flutter with every thrust and buried them deep as I went to kneel at the side of the big tub.

"Ember," I murmured softly not wanting to startle her, but there was no dice. The woman was a world-class sleeper. I'd learned that the second time I'd carried her to my bed, and she hadn't even stirred.

I dipped my hand into the water and winced some, it was cool. Far too cool, how did she sleep in it like this?

"Ember?" I ventured again and still nothing. I reached out and touched her shoulder lightly at first, petting her soft skin in a gentle caress, running the backs of my knuckles up and down her shoulder lightly until she jerked, and scrunched back into the corner. Those vivid eyes of hers flying open and pinning me where I knelt.

"Easy darlin'! Easy… it's just me." I soothed.

"What are you doing?" She demanded.

"It got quiet in here, I knocked and when there was no answer…" I shook my head and got up and worked on getting her out of the bath. I was taking liberties drying her off and caring for her but… but it felt good. Like I was making some kind of a difference and as selfish as it was, I needed that.

The wind was picking up outside as I left her to her own devices, fighting the rising erection in my pants and questioning if I weren't just another flavor of predatory piece of shit for it. I went out to the kitchen and rummaged in the plastic wrap of one of my cases of water to retrieve a bottle for her.

She wasn't taking care of herself, and I knew it was soon, but I wanted her to find that strength I knew was in there and I wanted her to get back on her feet – I wanted to tell her the same thing one of my old Drill Instructors had told me... *"I won't give up on you until long after you give up on yourself, so get up! Come on, now, Princess, let's move!"*

Just with someone as delicate and beautiful as Ember, I didn't think the screaming at her until she broke approach was the one to take. Especially given the girl flinched at her own shadow.

I came back into my bedroom as she exited the bathroom and held the bottle out to her.

She took it with a wan little smile and a chuckle and while I didn't want to be too domineering, I couldn't resist it when she was so sweet and pliable. I simply raised an eyebrow and crossed my arms and she giggled a little and cracked the seal on the bottle, opening it up and taking several small sips and then when I didn't let up, drinking deeply of it. I lowered my eyebrow and relaxed my shoulders in silent approval and not trusting myself, simply jerked my head in indication that she was free to go – which she was *always* free to go.

Everything was on her time, on her schedule, on her to decide her level of comfort.

"Goodnight, Blackjack," she murmured and it almost sounded reluctant. Like she didn't want to go but I needed her to. I had self-control, and a lot of it, but it wasn't completely infinite...

"Goodnight, darlin'," I said as she moved past me and when she'd slipped out of the portal to my bedroom, I closed the door firmly behind her and sighed.

I didn't do anything other than get changed and go to bed myself, sighing as I settled into my too-big bed and listened to the wind howl and the rain patter the roof above my head. It lulled me, and I went out pretty quick... not even realizing that one touch of her soft skin and a look from those fantasy-colored eyes of hers had soothed the rage enough that I wasn't even thinking about her dipshit ex. All I could think about as I fell asleep was her.

It was still dark when I jolted back awake again and at first, I couldn't tell you why. I sat up in the extreme dark of my room, the weather still raging outside and as the covers slipped, I realized that it was cold as fuck in here, for one and for two, it was entirely *too* quiet.

"Aw, fuck!" I muttered and threw back the blankets. I got up and shivered and knew that the power was out – but my thoughts weren't immediately about myself they were on Ember.

I went out and up the hall, grabbing a flashlight out of the inside of the hall closet door. I had a shoe organizer thing hanging on the inside of the door full of emergency supplies. Candles, flashlights, a handgun, a box of ammo, extra mags, that sort of thing. I clicked on the flashlight and swept it in her direction. She put up a hand as she huddled on the couch and shivered and I sighed.

"You alright?" I asked.

"Yeah, just cold," she said sleepily.

"How long you been awake?" I asked.

"I don't know," she said. "There was a big boom outside and sparks… that was a while ago. I fell back asleep."

I grunted and reached down a hand and said, "Come on."

She took it and I hauled her to her feet and turned her in the direction of my room, walking behind her hands on her shoulders. She went obediently before me and I massaged her neck slightly as we went.

"In you go," I ordered when we stopped beside my bed and she crawled up into it adorably and scooted over to make room for me. I got in and laid on my back and lifted an arm and told her, "You can come here if you want."

She practically dove into my side and cuddled in and I chuckled, covering us both up and holding her tight.

She laid her head on my shoulder and I massaged the back of her neck and head through her silky soft hair. I turned my head without thinking about it and pressed my lips to her forehead and she let out this little contented sigh and her body went lax against mine.

It was one of those moments, you know? One of those absolute, singularly perfect fuckin' moments that when they happened, they burned themselves into your brain, branding your memory forever more with the mark of just sheer... *fuck*. I took a deep, deep breath, letting it out slow and closing my eyes.

"Thank you," she said, her voice small, and I didn't have any other response than to kiss her forehead once again.

9

Ember...

I woke up warm and protected by the curve of Black-jack's body.

"Yeah, still no power here. We're warm and just getting up," he said. "Could use some hot coffee and a hot meal – what's it lookin' like out there?"

I could hear the buzz of conversation through his phone, another man saying, "*Fen's out of power at the farm, the club's out, Mav's out, Dump Truck's out, Mace says the backup apartments are out – it's a damn mess.*"

"At this point, it'd be a shorter list of who *does* have power," I said.

"*You ain't lyin'. I have it, and Deac does but he's up on Cap Hill in that tiny ass apartment so that's out.*"

"Even if Squatch and Nine have it, fuck that noise – their place is a hot mess. No way am I bringing Ember there." He stroked down my arm beneath the blankets and I craned my head back and looked up. Blackjack gave me a smirk as the other guy laughed on the other end of the line.

"*Major's place is too small, I guess that leaves mine. You all are welcome to come down,*" he said. "*I've got plenty of room, electricity, a working kitchen and the grill – just bring some meat outta your freezer or whatever.*"

"Roger that," Blackjack said. "We'll mobilize when we can."

"No hurry, brother. Might want to put a chainsaw in the back of your truck. I can't speak to the condition of the road leading up to my place. Might be some downed trees or limbs."

"Copy, we'll see you when we see you along with anyone else showing up."

"Yep, drive safe."

"Will do, brother."

He ended the call and looked down at me and I smiled and reluctantly began to pull away.

"Where you going?" he asked and gave me a little squeeze around the middle. "You don't have to go anywhere on my account."

"Oh, um, I wasn't," I said, laughing nervously. "Just need to go to the bathroom."

He searched my face and raised that eyebrow and I felt pinned to the spot with that dark gaze.

"Ember…" he said finally, and I jumped just a bit at my name. "Talk to me," he said gently and I slipped free of his hold and he let me go.

"About what?" I asked, sitting up on the edge of his really comfy bed. I was trying to feign innocence with my tone and inflection but I studiously was looking anywhere but those deep brown eyes that I seriously thought could see right through me.

His hand found my hip, thumb caressing my lower back through my scoop necked sweatshirt.

"About what you're thinking; how you're feeling," he said.

"Does it matter?" I asked softly, and I felt my shoulders drop.

"A great deal," he said. "But if you're not comfortable, you don't have to talk to me."

I twisted, my lower back popping and I made a groan of appreciation at some of the stiffness leaving it as I got in a good stretch on top of the satisfying pops. Blackjack grinned and said, "I'd kill to be able to do that, but let's not get off the subject."

I sighed and shook my head and said, "I don't want to be depressive or a bummer."

He snorted, "You just been through hell and gone, darlin'. There's

69

no reason for you to be all sunshine and fuckin' rainbows. I don't care for that fake ass shit. I care about seein' you get healthy again."

"Why?" I asked, curious.

He cocked his head and considered me and said, "I'm here to suck out the poison."

"What?" I asked, giving an incredulous laugh. Like – *what?*

"You've been in this toxic environment for so long, the poison seeping into your heart and your mind, and I'm here to suck out the poison just as if you'd been snake bit by that motherfucker."

"I don't understand..." I mean I *did* understand the analogy but I didn't understand *why* he would want to do such a thing.

"What don't you understand?" he asked.

"Why you would want to do such a thing," I answered honestly. I mean, what was the harm in that? Of course, the truth didn't have much of a track record in serving me well, so...

He sighed and rubbed his lips together and said, "In the beginning, when you were on the overpass... I stopped you and tried to get you through it because someone did the same thing for me, once."

"Okay," I said cautiously.

"Another vet, an old-timer from the Vietnam War," he said. "He died a couple years ago but I promised if I ever was put in the same position that he was in with me I would do something about it and truth be told, I think he maybe had a thing or two to do with me spotting you up there."

I swallowed hard but didn't say anything. Finally, I croaked out, "And when I called from the hospital?"

"My work wasn't – and still isn't done, darlin'. I know a calling when I feel it." He smoothed his thumb back and forth against my lower back and I closed my eyes and just soaked in the nice touch.

"I don't know what to do or where to go from here," I confessed. "I mean, I know I can't stay here forever and—"

"Shh," he said. "I know I've told you Rome wasn't built in a day and you're perfectly good."

"I just don't know what to do," I said lamely. I closed my eyes and felt my face grow hot as the panic stirred in my stomach and chest and turned things sour. "In some ways it was so much easier when I had someone to *tell me* what to do…"

I palmed my face sighing, frustrated with myself and my absolute inability to just *get it together!*

"Hey," he murmured. "Come here."

I laid back down and he put the blankets back over me and pulled me back into him.

"Now we're just going to chill here, just like this, until you feel calmer and ready to take on the day… and then we're going to get up, head down to Cipher's and we'll spend some time with my club. I think it might do you some good. We'll get around other people for a while, have a hot meal, and when the power comes back on? We'll come home and start working on getting everything sorted out. One step at a time. I promise."

I swallowed hard and relaxed a bit and conceded, because it all sounded very nice, orderly, and like a good plan.

"Okay," I agreed.

"Good girl," he murmured, and he pressed his lips into the top of my shoulder. "Sorry," he apologized immediately. "I was already hugging you, and it seemed like the thing to do but I don't want to make you any kind of uncomfortable. Nothing is going to happen here without your consent."

"No, it's fine," I said. "I know I probably shouldn't… but I *really* miss being cuddled and affectionate. More than anything else."

He chuckled and said, "I didn't realize how much I've missed it too. If you need a hug or whatever, I can provide that. Just have to tell me."

"Okay," I said.

We were silent for a long time and after drawing a deep breath that came out as a long, drawn-out sigh of certainty he told me, "You're going to be okay, Ember. I'm sure of it."

I tried not to shoot him down, but my thought to that was, *I'm glad one of us is.*

CIPHER LIVED SOMEWHERE DOWN near Gig Harbor which was a long way from Seattle. I hadn't been this far from the city in I don't know how long.

"I never really got my license," I was telling Blackjack as he piloted the big old work truck down the interstate through the city.

"How come?" he asked.

I took a deep breath and let it out slowly and said, "When I was fifteen, my dad wouldn't let me take the classes or teach me. My home life wasn't... wasn't great," I said. "I was constantly getting in trouble for pretty much everything and it got to the point that I was in trouble for things I wasn't even doing like all the time and so I sort of gave up and figured if I was constantly going to be busted for it, I might as well find out what it was actually like so I started drinking, experimenting with drugs and the like."

I stared out the window at the passing scenery.

"Okay, well, I guess that's glossing over it, really. I wasn't even home for my dad to teach me how to drive or to take the classes. My dad's solution to me being a teenager was to send me to some teen bootcamp thing when I got caught out at a party underage drinking after sneaking out one night. I was pretty much locked up when I was supposed to be learning how to drive and doing other normal things like that."

"Sounds like your dad's headed for a nursing home in his ripe old age," Blackjack remarked dryly.

I snorted a laugh. "He's got my little sister Jaime to take care of him. I was in that place until I was nineteen. Couldn't leave when I thought I was aged out and could get out on my own. My dad did something or other with the courts to declare me crazy or some shit to keep me in longer. I was totally prepared to get out at eighteen. I was pretty much prepared to be homeless but somehow, some way, he got them to keep me and when I was nineteen and finally got out, it was with my GED. I toughed it out at home for a few months, started working for the grocery chain I still work for and got out and an apartment with a roommate as soon as I could."

"Yeah?" he asked curiously.

"Yeah. Then I met Devin and the rest is sort of history."

"Hmm." He sounded thoughtful but didn't say anything else.

"What's your story?" I asked.

He sniffed, and I studied his profile as he drove. He was hot. Like, the more I looked at him, the hotter he got. His jaw clenched for a second and he said, "Joined the Marines a bit late. Was nineteen, almost twenty. Did a couple of tours, got blown up and shot a couple of times… came home with some issues. Some physical, a lot more mental. Bounced around from dead-end job to dead-end job – ended up on disability through the VA. The house I live in now was my dad's. He died a few years ago. I haven't really made it mine yet." His hands creaked against the steering wheel and he didn't go on.

I thought about that and it struck me to ask, "How old are you?"

"Forty-three, why?"

I blinked, a little stupidly.

"Really?" I asked.

"Yeah, why?" he asked.

"I wouldn't have put you outside your early thirties," I said.

"Huh." He looked a little proud of that and I smiled and turned to look out the window at Elliott Bay passing by.

I said, "Maybe we could help each other?"

I caught him smirking a bit when I turned back to him when he was quiet for too long and he said, "I'm listening."

"I'll help you with your house and making it yours while you help me with… well… *me*."

He looked thoughtful and nodded slowly and almost impercep- tibly said, "Let me think about it."

I nodded, slightly disappointed he didn't jump on it more, mostly because the whole thinking about it played on my insecurities and made me worry.

"Okay," I said, and we fell into silence as we slipped out of the city, through more industrial areas, then further past the airport, through suburbs before rejoining thick traffic through the city of Tacoma.

The Tacoma Narrows Bridge was a sight to behold as we went

over it and once over it, we finally felt free of so much cityscape and urban sprawl.

The trees rose to either side of the highway dark green against a leaden sky and I thought *how Pacific Northwest Gothic*. I dreamed up imaginary stories of ghostly hitchhiking women and Sasquatch walking just inside the tree line, in the heart of the deepest shadows, watching the traffic rush by.

We turned off the highway and wound down through long tree-lined lanes and pulled up behind another car, a tree across the road. A man, *huge*, stood outside of an SUV's driver's side door in a leather jacket and jeans, leaning heavily on a copper pipe cane a woman was getting out of the passenger side, her long brown hair braided in a French braid and likewise, was she in a leather jacket meant for riding.

"Looks like we aren't the first to the party," Blackjack commented dryly, and he pulled up behind the SUV and put his truck in park. "Just a little fashionably late, or whatever."

"You know them?" I asked.

"Yeah, that's Dump Truck and Little Bird."

"Oh," I said and he opened up his door.

"You can get out if you want," he said. I unfastened my seatbelt slowly as he called out, "Hope you weren't waitin' here long!"

"Yeah, no," the man he'd called Dump Truck called back. "Just pulled up like two minutes ago. Passed you on the freeway back in Tacoma.

"Aw, shit. I didn't even notice!" Blackjack chuckled and went to the back of his truck.

"This might be more 'n what you brought can handle," Dump Truck said critically, limping back to where we were. I slipped out of the passenger seat and to the ground.

"Hi," the woman Blackjack had called Little Bird greeted me.

"Hi," I said softly. "I'm Ember."

"Kestrel," she said. "But everyone calls me Little Bird."

"Nice to meet you, Little Bird. I used to be called Angel, but I don't know if I like it anymore," I said with a shrug. "Ember will do just fine."

"Nice to meet you, Ember," she murmured and smiled.

"You girls either get in one of the cars or stand way back," the giant of a man ordered.

"If you please," Blackjack agreed, handing one chainsaw to Dump Truck and taking up the smaller of the two.

"Would rather you not get hit with any flying anything," Dump Truck grunted.

"You sure you're going to be alright?" Little Bird asked quietly, going to what I had to assume was her man.

"Leg hurts," he said. "But it's not gonna give out on me if that's what you're asking. I'm solid, baby."

"Okay," she said, and she stood on her tiptoes and hand on his arm to steady herself he leaned down to kiss her.

"Go on and stand way back, please."

"Okay," she agreed and she jerked her head at me and said, "Let's sit in mine for a front-row seat. Gotta like a free show of manly men doing manly things." She winked at me and I giggled. She went around to the driver's seat and I went to the passenger door of her car and we got in.

"Wow, it's cold," I said and shuddered.

She blasted the heat and shivered herself.

"Cold temps with as humid as it is it's apt to feel ten degrees colder than it actually is," she said.

"I guess so," I said. "I don't really know how all that works." I gave an awkward little laugh. I didn't really do the whole social thing well. Usually, I had to be worried that Devin was going to bite my head off and grill me about the entire conversation later and the anxiety from that fizzed in my veins even though I knew, logically, I never had to answer to him ever again. There were mixed emotions with that. Fear, sadness, and worst of all the feelings of being abandoned even though I knew I was the one doing the leaving – which wasn't that weird?

"Ember?"

"Hmm?" I asked and tore my gaze from where I'd been staring off into space to focus on Little Bird's face. She was extremely pretty, like could be a model kind of pretty, but that pretty face was pinched with something that was a cross between empathy and concern.

"I'm sorry, what?" I asked.

She smiled kindly and said, "You know, if it's one thing DT has taught me, it's that it's okay to not be okay sometimes."

I gave a sheepish bit of a shrug and cringed shyly.

"It's that obvious, huh?" I asked.

She laughed a tiny bit and said, "A little."

"So… um… you're the girl he met a month or so back?" she asked after a time.

"Yeah, uh… the one on the freeway?" I eked out and again with that kind smile.

We both jumped when the chainsaws whined and started lopping off limbs to the tree blocking the roadway.

"Sorry!" I immediately cried, figuring my jumping caused her to, too.

"Oh, no, it's fine! I jumped too. It wasn't you!"

We both tittered nervous laughter and Little Bird sighed.

"Look, I'm honestly glad that I was the first to meet you out of any of the other old ladies… I think we might have the most in common."

"Really?" I asked. "And the other *what?* I mean, you're not *old*…"

She laughed again and her smile was infectious as she grinned and said, "Whoa boy, we have a lot of catching you up to do before you meet the rest of the guys and gals. Okay. First things first, they call the women attached to any given brother an Old Lady and likewise, Dump Truck out there is my Old Man."

"Okay."

"They have a lot of weird terms like, I'm Dump Truck's property – which I know sounds really, *really* bad on its face, but I promise, it's not! They just have different definitions for things than Citizens do."

"Okay, I think I'm going to need a glossary of terms," I said laughing, and she giggled and said, "I'll get right on that for you. Seriously."

We chatted, she caught me up and promised that she and no one else would expect me to remember all of it – but she especially warned me not to ask anyone how they got their road name, which I assumed was their nickname but I asked just to be sure.

"Yes," she said. "It's considered the height of rudeness and I strongly caution against it. Like, if you slip up it's not the end of the world but these guys don't tend to trust easy and you're new."

I nodded and stared out the front window at Blackjack working his saw through a thick branch, cutting it into chunks, DT lifting and chucking them off to the side of the road.

"To be honest, Tic-Tac is the only one that would give you a ration of shit over it but he's been sort of put on a time-out over in Eastern Washington."

"How come?" I asked.

"I can't answer that. That's club business and we aren't supposed to know," she said, putting her hand to her chest. "But they're men and we're women, and by God, we *always* know, right?"

"Right!" I rolled my eyes and she grinned.

"Anyway... my story is I met the big guy out there a few years ago standing in line at the bookstore. He paid for my book and he was supposed to be a one-night stand."

"Oh, shit, really?" I asked.

"Yeah," she stuttered a laugh. "Except I was getting married – not for love or anything. It was an arranged marriage."

I looked over at her like she was crazy and asked, "Are those even legal in America?"

She laughed and nodded. "Unfortunately, yes. Anyway, my husband was an abusive prick and finally..." she stared back out the windshield at Dump Truck and her gaze became dreamy. "Finally, I broke. I couldn't take it anymore and I called DT and begged him to come and get me and he did."

"That's so romantic!" I said, and I felt so sappy but seriously, that was one of the most beautiful things I'd ever heard!

She shook her head. "It is *now*, looking back on it, but it wasn't then. I was so broken and fucked up. I got a hold of one of his guns one night and was working up the nerve to pull the trigger with it pointed at my head when thankfully he woke up and stopped me."

"Oh, my God," I said taken aback.

She nodded and didn't look proud of it but she looked at me and said, "So it's okay not to be okay but another thing DT likes to tell me..."

"Yeah?" I asked.

"This too shall pass," she said. "'It may pass like a motherfucking kidney stone – but it'll pass.'"

I chuckled at that and nodded and said, "I'm... I'm trying, but it's hard."

"Healing is the hardest thing anybody *can* do," she said and she looked Blackjack over. "But if anyone can show you the way, I think it's BJ. He's done it himself something like a thousand times. He's a good guy. Will drop everything at a moment's notice to come and help one of the other guys. He's helped us with the house more times than I even care to count. I'm glad he was the one to find you. Just understand he can sometimes be a little rough around the edges. I think it's all the crayons. Does something to their heads."

"Crayons?" I asked.

She laughed. "Sorry. Military joke. Supposedly a Marine's favorite snack. Here, watch this..." she rolled down her window and called out, "Hey, Blackjack!"

"Yeah?" he called, his eyes swinging over to me once his chainsaw was safely stopped.

"What's a Marine's favorite snack?" she called out.

"Crayons!" he called out, dead serious. "Only Crayola though – none of those cheap-ass RoseArt or whatever."

"Your favorite color?" she called out.

"I like the green ones!" he called back. "They always taste best."

She howled with laughter as my mouth dropped open. He sounded dead serious! He caught my eye and gave me a wink before the chainsaw whined back to life and Little Bird rolled up the window to drown it out.

"This is going to be a serious learning curve, isn't it?" I asked.

"Welcome to The Life," she said smiling and the way she said it? *The Life* was definitely in capital letters.

"Oh boy," I said, and she said, "You're gonna be fine."

I met her brown eyes, and they were warm and liquid and instead of my first thought being *I'm glad somebody thinks so,* I actually thought, *yeah, maybe I am...*

It was like a ray of light had broken through the clouds. Feeble, not very bright, but *something... you know?*

10

*B*lackjack...

Cipher met us on the other side of the tree with his own, bigger chainsaw than even what I had. As soon as we cleared enough of the tree to get Dump Truck's rig through, we sent him and the girls to Cipher's house to rest his leg and get the girls settled.

Meanwhile, we worked to clear the road, waving a crew that came up on us off to tackle a different mess.

Whether we had 'permission' or not, this was good Douglas Fir and we would be filling the back of my truck and Cipher's with big ol' chunks of it to cure and burn next year or whatever. Free firewood? Fuck yeah. Call it the cost of busting this big bitch up and clearing the road.

It wasn't much longer after we'd told the crew to piss off some more of our guys showed up and pitched in.

Mace and Raven showed up, and Major too. Marisol and Maverick were the last to show up and as soon as they did, we sent Raven and Marisol on up the rest of the way to the house.

DT came back down and pitched back in saying he'd be fucked if he would sit around a gaggle of fuckin' women but we all knew he was a big damn softie. I mean, the fucker read romance novels with his woman but he read that shit even before she'd come along. In fact, I knew they'd had something to do with them meeting in the first place. It was DT's favorite story to tell anymore, on the rare occasion he got fuckin' drunk.

We filled the back of my truck, the back of Cipher's and then agreed there was no way we should let any fuckin' bit of this shit go to waste, so we went on up to the house, dumped off, and made something like three more trips to get it up there.

"Man, you get that fireplace swapped out to a wood-burning stove, I'll hook you up with some of this shit, as much as you wanna cart up your way." Cipher said.

"I planned on it this summer, man. I don't like not being totally self-sufficient."

"I get it, bro, but we're your fuckin' unit now and you don't have to be," Major said and shot me a salute. I just laughed. He'd been Army – but you know, ain't nobody perfect.

"So, anything we ought to know about this girl you got shacked up with you?" Major asked, half yanking my chain.

"She's pretty," Cipher and DT said in unison.

I rolled my eyes.

"She's fragile, so try not to flirt with her too hard or crowd her or nothin'," I said. "I don't know what we're gonna do yet. We're working it out, though."

"It's a good thing you're doing," DT said, and I nodded.

"Agreed," Maverick declared.

"Man, I'm fuckin' starvin'," Cipher put in and I sighed and looked around, grateful for the change of subject.

"Last load?" I asked.

"Last load," Cipher agreed and we all cut up and pitched rounds into the beds of our trucks.

"Mav," I called when we were through, all of us sweating and chests heaving.

"Yeah?"

"Mind if I get you to ride with me?" I asked.

"Sure thing, bro."

"Cipher, take our phones with you?" I asked. Everyone sort of froze up, but Cipher came over and took our phones, Mav looking at me kind of curious.

"What's on your mind?" he asked as we climbed into my truck.

I got into my truck and I moved Ember's one bag she brought to the back seat and I turned sighing and settling in. I didn't start talking until our doors were shut.

"Ember's ex – he's a big damn problem and what he did? What he's done and what he's pulling? I'd like for the heat to wear off him, you know, let law enforcement have their turn and when all is said and done with that and I've bided my time a little more, I'd like to—" I cleared my throat and he nodded slowly.

Mav wasn't stupid. He knew what I was asking.

"He the reason she was up on that overpass in the first place?"

"Yeah," I said, piloting us over wet asphalt coated in pine needles and wincing thinking about Mace and Major on their bikes bringing up the rear. It was as bad if not worse than fucking grass clippings on the roadway. We crept along, way under speed to make sure everyone was good and stayed good.

I guess it let me and Mav have this conversation, so there was that.

"He gets her so wound up, threatens her six ways to Sunday, has her gaslit to within an inch of her life and he would have beat the hell out of her this last time if the neighbors hadn't phoned it in."

"You sure she won't go back to him?" he asked.

"I don't think so," I said honestly.

"Something here?" he asked, and I shook my head.

"Just friends," I said. "She needs some time to heal and figure shit out before anything like that."

He nodded slowly and said, "You do what you gotta do." "You loop anyone in on it, make it Fen and no one else. Gotta do something to keep that Berserker Bloodlust of his in check and he's nothing if not a master at his fuckin' craft."

I huffed out an ironic laugh at that. I mean, Mav wasn't lyin'. Even with Aspen there to sooth that fucker's rage and pain – which she did admirably, Fen was one crazy ass motherfucker and he could only quell whatever demons he had inside for so long.

I wasn't any stranger to that notion but I mainly kept my shit to the odd bar or fistfight. Fen? Fen straight up needed to *kill* something on the regular. The goats sometimes did the trick but he fuckin' loved dealing out street justice when the occasion called for it.

"You ain't even seen the bruises and you're turning Fen loose on this to help me out?" I asked.

"You complaining?" he demanded.

"Not a fuckin' bit," I said.

"Didn't think so," he said, giving me a devil may care sort of grin.

"Thanks," I said. "You read the texts or heard the voicemails you'd be totally comfortable with that choice.

"Blackjack, I don't *need* to read any texts or hear any voicemails. My dude, if you say it's bad, then it's fuckin' bad. You've never brought anything like this to me before. Hopefully, you never will again… but if you say this is the solution to the particular problem? Fuckin' have at. You sound like you got a solid plan. You know the golden rule."

I nodded. "That I do," I said and neither one of us was going to say that shit aloud and jinx the fuck out of my mission. The golden rule among us? *Don't get caught.*

Cipher's place was fuckin huge for just one fucking guy, but if Fen's place, which was definitely in a more populated center, didn't work out for us or got overrun – Cipher's place was our 'Plan B' come the zombie apocalypse or invasion by a foreign world power.

Truthfully, the older I got the more I was becoming all about my creature comforts and in that vein? Cipher's place was actually my *first* choice. While Fen did have the goats for meat, and plenty of land for growing things, Cipher's place had a well, land to sustain a grow operation, a better defensible position and we *could* conceivably get a bunch of goats moved this way if need be.

The main thing Cipher's place had that Fen's didn't was the solar panels and its ability to run exclusively off-grid fully powered with electricity which meant hot water and the place was like a *seven fucking bedroom house*, with a four car separate outbuilding garage and was pretty much a doomsday prepper's paradise.

Cipher was even more paranoid than my paranoid fuckin' ass, and it was beautiful.

I knew all of what he had going on up here, because out of anyone in this club he and I were likely the most alike and as such? I'd spent more time up here than on my own place helping him install shit and fortify others.

He had two shipping container underground bunkers on the property, both used to house non-perishable stores. He had enough MREs in one to feed a whole fuckin' company for a fuckin' week – breakfast, lunch, and dinner.

His place was pretty fuckin' ship shape and hence why we were using it today. If it were anything else, we probably would have met up at Fen's but Fen didn't have the indoor space in the winter to keep the lot of us warm. Cipher didn't have that problem. Yeah, his house would probably end up running more in an auxiliary capacity if the power outage dragged on longer than a week, but it rarely went on that long in this area. That was more out toward the coast where it could be out a week or more.

We shook as much of the man-glitter that was the sawdust we were sporting from our labor off of ourselves before we entered the house, but some things couldn't be fixed without a shower or a load of laundry.

"Hey, our triumphant heroes return!" Raven crowed as we came in the front door.

"Soup's on, boys," Marisol declared and Maverick scoffed.

"Boys? *Boys?*"

"We're men," Cipher declared.

"Men in tights?" Ember squeaked and we all just stopped for a second, the laughter delayed at the old movie joke.

"We should fuckin' watch that high," Major declared.

"I'm down," I said and winked at Ember who was sort of half huddled on the end of one of the kitchen's bar stools.

"Blackjack, you worked hardest," Dump Truck declared. "You should get dibs on a hot shower. Go warm up, man."

I nodded. When the big man spoke something like that, we all listened.

"You good?" I asked, putting a light hand to the small of Ember's back and handing her, her bag from the truck, mine an old Marine Corps rucksack rescued from an Army/Navy Surplus outfit downtown.

"Yeah, I'm good," she said and I gave her a nod and turned to head up the hall.

"Y'know, no one'll be offended if you opted to shower with a friend," Cipher cracked in her direction and I glanced back over my shoulder to see her turn as bright as a cherry tomato.

She looked up the hallway at me eyes wide and I chuckled and waved at her. She looked confused, torn almost, and then glanced away, turning a brighter shade of red as the rest of the boys had a laugh at her expense.

I made a mental note to check in on her later and went into the bathroom to wash up and change.

I'd be lying if I said I wasn't low-key disappointed that she didn't come and join me but way too soon if you fuckin' asked me.

I stopped cold at the thought and looked at myself in the mirror above the bathroom sink. Everything about Cipher's place was modern perfection. Like something out of a sci-fi movie. Clean, straight lines. Pristine surfaces. Easy to clean surfaces... this bathroom was no exception with its glass subway tile walls and a mirror taking up the entire wall from shower stall to door chair rail height to ceiling.

I stood under the bright white LED lighting and stared into my own eyes and wondered to myself *what the fuck?*

Why her? What the hell was it that I would think something like that even at a time like this?

Because she spoke to me without words. Something broken in her touched the broken in me and there was a deep and abiding unspoken understanding there and it was heady as hell...

I knew why, even if I didn't want to admit it to myself and I knew I was fighting it but shit if I shouldn't be asking myself *'why?'* on that too.

"Fuck," I muttered, dispassionately, and I pulled my shirt off over my head. I paused, looking at the faded white scars against the pale skin of my ribs.

A stab wound here; a shrapnel wound there. I'd been lucky with both. The fuckin' stab wound hadn't even been in service to my country. No, that'd been a jilted piece of pussy that'd had it in her head that she actually meant something to me when she'd meant nothing at all.

A lesson in *'don't stick your dick in crazy'* that I'd learned the hard way.

She'd been going for my kidneys but she'd failed. The knife had gone in both clean and deep but by the grace of some higher power, she'd missed everything vital and had pulled the knife out clean.

She'd been subdued before she'd gotten the chance to strike a second time and man, that had been a mess.

A lot of the boys had figured she wanted to do me like that then that'd meant she wanted to fight like a man and thus the club rule of *'no women, no children'* need not apply in this instance.

Ultimately, it'd been left to me what to do. I'd let it go to the citizen justice system. She'd been put away for it at the Purdy Correctional Center for Women and as soon as her time was up, she'd have an escort out of state with a strong warning not to bring her ass back here or it'd be the last thing she did.

That'd been six years ago. She had priors for other shit and it was going to be awhile yet before she saw the outside. Part of that was, by my understanding, from not being able to stay her ass out of trouble on the inside. Constant fights and a few rapes. Bitch had been one hell of a wild ride but I tried to keep my wild rides to my Harley from now on.

Ember may have been mental, but it by far wasn't the same kind of mental as that crazy bitch. No, all of Ember's troubles were something that I believed whole heartedly was shit that was done to her. A result of trauma, repeated abuse and trauma.

It was pretty clear to me, after what she'd told me in the truck about her family, that when she'd finally hooked up with Devin, she'd stayed so long because she'd been lost, unable to cope, and to an extent Devin had offered her a love that felt at least normal to her. Comfortable. Like *home*.

Made me want to kick her daddy's ass something special.

I may yet, depending on what else I found out.

Devin for sure was going to lose a piece or two off his hide for his part in her pain. I'd make sure of it.

I spent a minute under the hot water, just letting it thaw me out and pound the back of my head as I braced forearms against the shower wall and let my thoughts race, trying to get them to stop and settle on anything other than those wide and beautiful blue-green eyes that haunted not only every waking moment – but every sleeping one I had anymore as well.

11

*E*mber...

Word got around throughout the club from what I could gather and the energy shifted in the house. It quickly became what everyone was calling an 'apocalypse dry run' party. Pretty soon, more and more people started showing up. After Blackjack got out of the shower, I brought him a bowl of hot soup. Cipher started a fire in the living room fireplace for us girls.

We had made a variety of soups in the kitchen, enough, I thought, to feed a small army and maybe that wasn't quite off the mark. There was a certain chain of command among the men; the uniform of choice being their black leather jackets and dirty yet still colorful vests.

More women joined us. A woman named Kinzleigh and another named Cadence with her teenage son.

There were pouts when a man named Fenris showed up without his lady, who everyone called Aspen, but rather was accompanied by another man who was bald but sported a long, ginger beard that the first thought I had to describe it was 'wizard's beard.'

When Blackjack had emerged from the shower, he'd done so in a faded black tee shirt that clung to him like a second skin and equally snug and form fitting jeans. His hair half up in a knot, his jacket and vest dangling from one hand, the other taken up with his military backpack. He'd set his cache of items at the end of the couch near my bag but had shrugged into his jacket and motorcycle vest with purpose. Like it was its own sort of body armor.

I tried not to look too hard at him, people were already making suppositions about us, and I felt guilty about it.

I knew full well everyone here knew...

Knew that I was the crazy girl that had almost jumped off an overpass. Knew that I was some kind of pathetic headcase that Blackjack was taking pity on and I was at such odds, such war within myself at the light jabs about wanting him. It was... I don't know. It felt like a vicious mockery. You know? Mostly because the voices in my head were relentless in pointing out that I wasn't worth it. That I was just a poor dumb project.

Not worth the effort... unfaithful, disloyal, a stupid fucking whore for even thinking about it.

Still, I brought him some stew to be nice, and I smiled in the face of all the looks and played dumb with my expression that there was any interest or whatever on my part. I knew there was no way it could go anywhere.

Anytime anyone came to talk to me, I tried to be quiet, stay polite, and say as little as possible, keeping myself small. I don't know if I was shy, per se, but I was definitely afraid. Afraid of saying or doing something to embarrass Blackjack or myself even more than I felt like I already had.

I didn't like this feeling. I didn't like feeling like I was alone in this room full of people. I didn't like listening to their laughter and their chatter and being too afraid to join in. I didn't like listening to their stories and not being able to relate. I didn't know what to do, honestly, or how to act, and so I just sort of sat like a sad, lonely little wallflower my gaze pinging between the people speaking, smiling and laughing along whenever I caught someone looking in my direction.

Checking on me?

It certainly looked to be so, but it could also just be my overactive imagination. Probably, more likely, making sure the crazy girl wasn't totally insane which, yep. I felt like I ticked that box. *Fuck my life...*

With the arrival of the man with the long red wizard's beard, the alcohol began to flow. Some stuff called *mead*, which was wine-like but I'd never heard of it before. I took a sip and it was really good but it didn't taste like grapes.

"Okay, but what is it?" I asked.

"Mead!" several people cried.

Blackjack raised his glass to me a little imperceptibly, and I gave him a crooked smile and took a sip from my own again. He turned and went out the sliding glass door onto the back deck while Little Bird took pity on me.

"I think she's asking what it's made out of."

"Yeah, I know," the man said. "It's just honey, yeast, and water," he explained. "This one's been aged in an old whiskey barrel which is where it gets it's oaky finish."

"It's really good," I said smiling and then said, "but the way you make that sound it comes it other flavors?"

"Oh yeah, you can add all kinds of fruit and shit to it to make things," he said. "I even added a bunch of spices and made a Taco Meat flavored mead before."

"Why would you do that? What the fuck?" one of the other guys demanded.

"What?" wizard beard asked, his blue eyes crinkling at the corners with happy as he shrugged his shoulders.

"Ruin a perfectly good mead like that," Raven said making a face.

"I didn't ruin it!" he cried.

"Who would even buy that?" Marisol asked looking kind of affronted.

"Lots of people! Most of them said they liked to cook with it."

Marisol's face changed from affronted and disgusted to considering for a moment before crushing right back down into a frown before she muttered something dismissively in Spanish.

Several of the guys standing around got a good laugh over whatever it was while a bunch of us just looked confused and wizard beard said, "I don't get it."

"Don't worry about it, man. You're good," Maverick said laughing.

"So, what got you into making this stuff?" I asked. It was probably the most comfortable I'd felt thus far. I appreciated learning new things, especially when someone seemed so passionate about it.

"Just something to do at home, a new hobby," he said. "At first."

"Jon's being modest," Fenris declared.

"Not really," Jon said, shrugging one shoulder. "I was just sort of exploring my heritage and then people said I was really good at it and it just sort of went from there."

"Where did it go?" I asked curiously.

"Jon owns and runs one of the best mead making operations in the states," Dump Truck declared.

"Psh! *The best*," Fenris declared.

"Arguably," Jon said grinning, a shine of pride in his blue eyes. "There are a lot of good places out there besides mine."

"Quit being so modest, bro. You've earned your accolades," Fenris declared and a rowdy cheer swept through the room. I jumped at the loud noise and laughed.

"Wish you had more time and a bike," Fenris finished with a wink.

Jon laughed. "Maybe someday," he said.

It wasn't long after that, most of the guys went outside to join the bonfire that was getting going in the firepit in the back yard and left us girls warm, safe, and fed in the living room with the cheery fire and in our comfiest pajamas which most of the ladies had changed into by now.

"You should let me braid your hair," Raven said, eyeing me with a smile.

I laughed and finished off the mead in my glass and said, "What?"

I mean, I'd heard her, but still.

"Yeah!" Little Bird declared.

"You should go take a hot shower, put some comfy clothes on, and let Raven braid your hair like she said," Kinzleigh declared and came over with a bottle, filling my glass with a red almost fizzy liquid.

I blinked and asked, "What is this?" and smelled it.

"It's a mead mixed with hard apple cider and some other fruits," Raven said. "Jon makes it. It's called 'You Have My Sword' and it's a session mead."

I sipped and it was *really* good! Lightly carbonated and effervescent on the tongue with an apple flavor and some kind of berry. I asked, "What am I tasting with the apple?"

"Blueberries!" Raven crowed, and I smiled.

"This is all really good," I declared.

"I don't know how he doesn't think so, or that there is anything better out there." Kinzleigh rolled her eyes. "Best stuff I've ever tried."

"He's just modest," Little Bird declared.

"I think it's a little bit of Impostor Syndrome, myself," Raven said.

"What's that?" I asked.

"It's when someone believes that they're really not as good at something as they are and that doesn't believe their success is deserved. Like a writer whose books sell really well, but they just chalk it up to luck versus skill," Little Bird explained.

"Oh, I can see how that might apply."

"Jon's earned every bit of his success in the industry through hard work and the like and yes, he's phenomenally talented – but he's worked his *ass* off to get where he is," Raven declared.

I nodded and took another drink of the sword stuff in my glass.

"I think Blackjack might be like that, too," I murmured absently.

"Oh yeah?" Marisol asked, and it was almost like she was pouncing on what I'd said to turn the conversation to him. She and Kinz traded a knowing look that set my teeth on edge and made me instantly regret letting the words leave my mouth.

"You should let me braid your hair—"

Raven tried to change the subject but Marisol wouldn't let her.

"No, no. I want to hear this," she said and fixed me with a look that was neutral at best, but I suddenly felt like a spotlight had been trained on me. How many times had I been here? Pinned by a gaze, by unspoken expectations? Waiting for me to speak, knowing that no matter what came out of my mouth it was going to be the wrong thing but also knowing the coming confrontation, the screaming, the yelling, the degradation was fast approaching like a runaway freight train and there was no such thing as getting out of its path.

"I – I – don't know what you want me to say," I stammered because I didn't, and I knew that in and of itself was going to be the wrong thing to say, that the best I could expect was disappointment at the answer and continued prying.

"I think all of us want to know just what's going on between you and Blackjack," Kinz said, waggling her eyebrows suggestively and my gaze swung back to Marisol who was looking at me, her dark eyes cold and calculating like she was waiting for me to confess, but confess what? I didn't do anything! I… I just asked for help… because I was too stupid to leave when this had all begun with Devin.

I flashed back to Devin and the argument that had started it all. I mean, I could recognize that now. To the endless back and forth and how the longer we talked, the more I tried to placate him, the more upset and worked up he got until I was pinned up against the wall with him screaming in my face as I cringed and shut my eyes waiting for the blow and it'd fallen… just not on me that first time. No, he'd punched the wall next to my head. Put a big old hole in the plaster with his fist and I'd just skidded down the wall to the floor and cried while he'd fucked off out of the apartment to God knows where.

I'd cried for a long time and worried incessantly until he'd come back and then we'd both cried together while he'd waxed eloquent about how he'd *never* gotten so worked up before me and how I just drove him so crazy because he loved me so much. How it was my fault – and I'd believed him. Hook, line, and sinker; I'd swallowed his bullshit whole.

It was a song and a dance I'd heard before from my own father.

I don't want to send you away, Ember – but you're making me do this, sweetheart. It's for your own good.

I was so desperate not to be abandoned like that again, that I would have done anything and everything to make it up to Devin; and so, I had. I'd made myself smaller, jumped on every small criticism and had swung wildly in the opposite direction, breaking my back I was so swift to bend over backward to please him and keep him happy thinking that his happiness would lead to my own happiness... but that's not how that worked, was it?

That wasn't how any of that had worked.

Devin... Devin just took and took and took until there wasn't anything left and I was so hollow, so empty, and sitting tucked on the floor in the corner of the monstrous wrap around sectional couch with my fuzzy blanket around my shoulders in front of a blazing fire, with a glass of alcohol in my hand – I felt colder than I'd ever felt in my life and my panicked mind screamed at me: *'Why are you even here!? You should have just jumped! Nobody's going to love you like you want. No one is going to love you like you need? What's even the point?'*

...and it wasn't wrong.

There was a slight clamor of voices from the couch around and behind me and I looked down, letting my hair fall and hide my face as the world narrowed down to one panicked point and I struggled to breathe past the lump in my throat as Raven and Little Bird began to quarrel with Marisol and Kinzleigh.

A light hand fell on my shoulder and I jumped and closed my eyes.

I knew what Marisol and Kinz were driving at – they wanted to know how deep things were between me and Blackjack. If we were boning or not, and it hit me sideways that I *wished*. How much I really liked him and how it would be nice to be with someone as caring and compassionate for a change...

...but that couldn't happen. That wouldn't happen. Not when he looked at me, with those shadows in his dark eyes. Shadows of pity... because the voices in the back of my mind were right. I was pathetic, and who wanted a pathetic headcase like me?

Certainly not a guy like him who had his shit together. His own home, a good job, a chosen family who clearly cared about him. I mean, Marisol and Kinz didn't have a claim on him or anything, they had men of their own!

No, I believed they didn't think I was good enough and I wasn't and I wouldn't dream of overstepping or of making him uncomfortable, even in his own home and maybe I was overreacting, I didn't know. All I could do was sit here silently and try to get a grip and not embarrass myself any further – but it was hard, because no matter how much I tried, I couldn't seem to get my eyes to stop leaking.

12

*B*lackjack...

When I came out from my shower, Ember slipped off her stool and brought me a bowl of hot stew after I set my shit down with hers.

"Thanks," I said with a half-smile and a nod of appreciation.

"You're welcome," she murmured.

She went over to her bag and took up her fuzzy throw blanket that was this girly pastel purple with feathers on it, wrapping it around her shoulders and sitting on the floor in the crook of the sectional's corner bend. Little Bird was perched on the couch itself and most of the thing was taken up by Dump Truck's big frame, his head in Little Bird's lap, his bad leg outstretched and a paperback of some romance novel or other in his big hands as he read.

Little Bird lifted her own book in her hands and went back to reading as I shoveled a mouthful of the rich stew into my face.

It was good, the beef tender, the vegetables perfect, and only the slightest edge of bitterness from whatever beer it'd been steeped in.

"Where's Cipher at?" I asked.

"Getting a fire going out back," Jon answered, putting a spoonful of stew in his face.

"Was starting to wonder if you were ever gonna get out of there, man." Mace winked at me and passed me up in the direction of the bathroom with his own pack likely holding a change of clothes.

"I like long showers," I said with a shrug.

I caught Ember's eye and raised one of my own and asked, "You good?" She nodded, and I lowered the brow and asked after another bite of stew, "You got your water?" She lifted it out of her bag beside her and held it up. I smirked. "You drinkin' it?" She rolled her eyes and unscrewed the cap and took a big mouthful and swallowed.

I gave a nod as Fish cried out, "Woah! Foul! Water in the presence of this greatness?" while he stood at the kitchen island and poured a stemless wine glass of golden liquid.

"Ooh, Jon brought party favors?" I asked.

"Fuck yeah!" Jon answered, his smile bursting forth from his eyes. Jon was one of those dudes that when he smiled, he did it with his whole fuckin' face. It was kind of great, but not something a straight dude told another straight dude without calling some shit into question so I kept my mouth shut.

Fish handed me a rocks glass with a bunch of mead in it and handed Ember the stemless wineglass. She sniffed it.

"What is it?" she asked.

"Mead!" a bunch of these fucks called back jovially and I snorted, slipping away and going outside to catch up with Cipher.

I found him, Glass, and Mav out at the burn pit. Cipher was getting it going.

"Hey," Mav called in greeting.

"Hey, am I barging in on anything?" I asked, taking a sip of the Oak Barrel in my glass. Perfect balance of sweet and oaky. Gotta love it.

"Nah," Mav answered.

"You good?" Cipher asked.

"Me? Yeah. Just a little crowded in there for my tastes."

Cipher grunted. He got it. He liked his solitude, too. Maybe not as much as I did, but still.

"How's the girl doing?" Glass asked.

I gave a shrug.

"Ember? Okay, I guess. She's getting an education in mead at the moment. Don't think she's ever encountered it out in the wild."

Cipher and Mav chuckled. Jon and Fen made their way down along with Fish after a little while of us boys shooting the shit.

"What's up, what's up?" Jon asked.

"Nothin'," Cipher answered as we stood around staring into the licking flames. It was already dark out here. It got dark at like 4 o'clock in the winter here though. So far north there was like only four hours of fuckin' daylight during the worst of the winter months. Add all the overcast days in the rain it was a depressive's worst nightmare. Not me, though. I sorta loved all the rain.

Major and DT came down after a while and Major lit up a joint and passed it, then got another one going and passed it the other way.

We stood around smoking, drinking, and bullshitting for a while when the subject got back to Ember. Fen was the one to bring it up...

"So, you want a hand dealing with the fool that tuned up that girl in there?" he asked.

"He's already way ahead of you," Maverick said and Fen nodded.

Jon frowned. "What girl?"

"Ember," I said and took a hit off one of the joints and passed it. I spoke through holding my breath. "The one that didn't know what mead was." I blew out my breath and he looked at me and then to Fen and then back to me.

"What happened?" he asked.

Jon was a friend of the club, a good guy, and trustworthy. I looked to Mav who gave a nod that it was safe to speak on it and told Jon how I met her, and how we reconnected.

"Shit, I thought that brace thing was for carpal tunnel or some shit."

"Lighting kind of sucks in the house, but you didn't notice the shadow under all that makeup on her cheekbone?" Cipher asked.

"Nah, guess I didn't," Jon said. He frowned and looked at me. "You boys need an alibi, you were at the meadery with me, helping out. That's my story and I'm sticking to it. You just let me know the times you need covered."

Fen nodded, staring into the flames looking every bit the Viking fuckin' warrior he was. He flicked those blue eyes to mine across the fire and we both nodded at each other.

"See, that's just one more reason yet to love you, Jon," Maverick declared through holding in a lungful of green smoke.

We all stood outside shooting the shit until a light tread from the direction of the house fell on the terraced steps leading down from below the back deck.

"Sorry," Little Bird murmured. "I hate to interrupt but..." and she looked at me. "Ember's crying."

"Shit," I swore, and I downed the rest of what was in my glass and handed it to the hand nearest me that would take it. "What happened?"

"Marisol was prying and Kinz – I don't know if she realized it was bothering her so much and she just started crying and now she can't stop."

Maverick swore in Russian behind me and Fish echoed, cursing in American but fuck if I knew if they said the same thing.

"She's probably just overwhelmed," Little Bird said, keeping pace with me.

"I got it," I said. I turned to Mav and Fish and said, "Hold up, we all go in there it's just liable to upset her more. Let me bring her out, get her some fresh air and go from there."

"Kestrel," Dump Truck intoned and held out his hand to his woman. She went to him without a word and stayed there, Mav and Fish a little more reluctantly going back to the fire. I wasn't going to yell at their women – they were their property; not mine, and as such, they were theirs to handle.

I went up the steps on the back deck. If I were younger, I would have taken them two at a time, but my knees, hips, and back wouldn't let me do that shit anymore. Didn't mean I wasn't quick about it, just not as quick as *I* would like.

I slipped inside the back slider and traversed the kitchen and dining room into the living room where Raven and Cadence were consoling a silently weeping Ember; Marisol and Kinz looking on a mixture of baffled and worried on their faces. Kinz almost looked like she was ready to cry herself, but I knew by now she wouldn't. Not in front of the lot of us. That wasn't her way. Marisol would get pissed off and double or triple down to save face. She'd had to be hard growing up, and I was afraid being the sort of part time friends, part time enemies that she could be with Dahlia didn't do shit to improve anything for her. Dahlia was her own sort of messed up and broken – but so were all of us.

Still, getting a girl riled up like this was more Dahlia's speed. I expected more out of Marisol. She didn't need to pick up the slack for Dahlia while our errant little flower was in fucking time-out specifically for causing this kind of fuckin' drama. *With Kinz, no less!* Not even a couple months ago! Like, what the fuck?

"Mav wants to talk to you," I told Marisol and I jerked my head behind me toward the slider. She paled beneath her permanently golden complexion and nodded, moving in that direction.

"Am I in trouble too?" Kinz asked.

"You think you should be, you probably are. Might want to go with Marisol."

"What did I do?" she asked plaintively, but her eyes were swimming a little.

"Take that up with your man and the pres," I told her.

She took an intrepid breath and nodded and followed Marisol.

I got down to Ember's level, and she stared at me wide-eyed.

"What happened?" I asked her, fixing her with a level steady gaze.

"N-nothing," she stuttered.

I swiped a thumb lightly through the tear tracks and muddied makeup on her face and held up the pad of that thumb where she could see it.

"This isn't nothing," I said. "Now either you can tell me or one of these two will – you got your choice, darlin'." I kept my tone soft, tried to be careful with her so I didn't tip her over the edge she was riding into a worse tizzy than she already had herself worked up into.

She stared at me, mute. Those eyes of hers bouncing between

mine, searching my face and with how wide open those windows to her soul were, I could see the fear.

"Come on, up you go," I murmured, and I helped her to her feet.

"Where are we going?" she asked.

"Get some air, you look like the walls are closing in." She swallowed hard and followed me out onto the deck. It was a way enough away from the firepit that though we might be visible if we kept it down no one would be the wiser about what we were talking about.

"Ain't no one out here that can hear but you and me... so what's going on."

"Nothing!" she insisted but she wouldn't look at me now. Instead, she stared down at the near distant flickering fire and I waited her out. She shivered lightly in just her sock feet and thin blanket wrapped around her shoulders which were covered by little more than a tee and I took a deep breath and let it out in a sigh that came out way more impatient sounding than I wanted it to.

She flinched and I hated that, but I couldn't fix it if I didn't know what was broken so I needed her to talk to me.

"Ember..." I tried and her face contorted.

"They kept poking, poking, *poking!*" she finally blurted. "I know they didn't mean anything by it but..." her voice faltered, and she exhaled, making a frustrated and exasperated noise that I knew had nothing to do with me. Honestly, I didn't think it had anything to do with the rest of the girls, either. I think it had more to do with Ember, and that she was frustrated or mad at herself... but I still didn't know why. I didn't know the root of the problem, and the only way to know was for her to communicate and *tell* me.

"Poking about what?" I asked gently. I didn't know, there were too many things it could be. Her past, why she didn't leave sooner, what she was doing up on that overpass...

"You! Alright?" she hissed. "They wanted to know if anything was going on with *you!* And I didn't know what to say! I didn't know how to tell them!"

"Tell them what, darlin'?" I asked, even more confused, not less.

She took a breath, started to speak, stopped, opened her mouth again, and her face contorted in the most anguished expression I'd ever seen on another person. Worse than even when she'd been up on that overpass, over the railing, ready to throw herself onto the freeway below.

"Hey," I said steady, gently, and I captured her by her unhurt wrist and pulled her into me. I put my arms around her, palming the back of her head and pressing her face to my chest, tucking my chin over the top of her head and I didn't know if it was too much, or just the right thing to do or what, but she finally *broke* – and it wasn't cleanly.

No, she put her arms around me, sucked in the biggest, deepest breath she could take and she *lost it*, sagging against me and just fucking *bawling*.

There it is, I thought at the rush of her tears. *The dam finally gave way.*

I knew a cathartic cry when I heard it, but I'd never been this up close and personal with one before. I didn't really know what to do, except a voice told me *steadfast Marine*, and so that's what I did. I stood steadfast, held her tight and just let her fucking lose her shit against me.

"My room, I changed the sheets today. It has a bathroom. You guys stay there tonight and take as much time as she needs." I looked down over the railing and gave a nod down at Cipher and he lifted his chin back. I glanced toward the fire and the ring of faces illuminated by it and saw guilt on Marisol's while Kinz looked absolutely crushed.

Fish had a good one with her. She was tough, but she had a heart of gold.

"Come on, darlin'. Let's get you someplace quiet," I murmured against her ear and all Ember could muster was a sniff and a hitching breath.

I tucked her in hard against my side and took us inside and turned her toward the stairs off the kitchen leading down into the big, finished basement master suite that Cipher had created for himself.

"What are we doing?" she asked, her voice sounding as wretched as a cat in the rain looked.

"Getting you someplace quiet, where you can calm down. Where you're safe for the rest of the night."

"I'm not going to do anything," she murmured, and I took a step back and asked the closed network system to turn on the lights down here. The lights came on and Ember winced.

"System! Lights, fifty percent."

The lights dimmed and yet she still grimaced.

"Come sit." I sat her down on the edge of the freshly made bed and sat down with her, unzipping my combat boots and nudging the heel off with my toes.

"Take your time, darlin', but you gotta let me in."

I straightened and looked at her and waited until she looked a measure calmer and asked her, "Now, what has you so worked up about those two being foolish?"

"It wasn't them; it was *me*," she insisted.

"Whatever the case, why are you upset about them poking their nose into what's going on with me?"

She looked away, attempting to hide behind her hair and I let her if it would help her find her voice.

"I know that you're low on trust, baby, *super low,* but I promise – as cliché as it sounds – you can trust me."

"I'm embarrassed," she said. "Mortified."

"Okay."

"They can tell I like you and I know it's stupid, and it's probably some psychological thing and that there's absolutely no way you could possibly feel the same way about some stupid, crazy bitch that tried to jump off a bridge and let herself be abused and all the other shit that's fucking wrong with me but it was nice for a second to try and pretend I was something just a little bit more than a pity case and—"

I did the only thing I could think of to silence the rush of sewage that was coming out of her mouth about herself. I touched the side of her face and forced her to look at me and covered her mouth with mine.

"Mm!" she made a muffled noise of surprise and I kept everything solid, stern, and in control as I took the absolute poison from her lips and breathed her insecurities in a sigh against her mouth.

I kissed her into a state of too stunned to speak and when I pulled back, I did it with a slightly crooked smile and said, "Don't talk about the girl I like that way. It upsets me."

"I-I'm sorry," she stammered and I nodded once and said, "Apology accepted, darlin', but we gotta work on that among other things, okay?"

"O-o-okay."

"Okay," I murmured firmly. "We're good on that, yeah?"

"Yeah, um, I guess so."

"Good."

13

*E*mber...

"Good," he murmured and his voice was as steady as a rock and the word held such a finality to it, it was like it had magically sort of flipped some internal switch and things just sort of calmed down. Like, I didn't quite feel like my mind was on fire as much. My train of thought wasn't out of control, barreling down the tracks at a breakneck speed like it had been. I no longer felt as though I were frantically pulling back on the throttle and it was just... *stuck.*

We sat side by side just looking at each other, and with the panic no longer seizing me up I felt... exhausted. Empty. Just so tired...

"You steady?" he asked.

"Yeah, I think so," I whispered back.

"Okay, what do you need?"

I blinked stupidly. I mean, I understood the question but...

"What?"

"What do you think you need right now?"

"Um, nothing?"

He smiled, and said, "We both know that's not true. I just don't think you're used to ever getting it. From what you've told me, it sounds like you've only ever been denied, denied, denied... it's a wonder you trust anyone at all and a pity what's been done to you all at the same time." He reached out and touched my forehead lightly with the tip of his middle finger, chasing my hair out of my face and behind my ear with a gentle, careful touch that left my heart cracked wide open and crying on the inside with relief.

I think I'd always wanted to be touched like that by someone. Comforted, comforting...

I stared at him in open mouthed wonder as he stripped me to a sort of bare and vulnerable with his words and I felt so scared and sensitive and... all I wanted was to lay down. To have him hold me and to fall asleep.

"Ah, there you go," he said and smiled slightly.

"What?" I asked.

"You just thought of something, there behind your eyes, I saw it."

"You did?" I asked, swallowing hard.

"I did. What's that thought?" he asked.

I didn't say anything. It was like the words just stuck in my throat and I couldn't speak them out loud.

"Oh, come on, darlin'," he said with a smile that was so personal and so precious and enough to set my heart to racing in my chest. "You're doing so good. Just tell me what you want so I can make it happen for you."

"I-I-I would like a m-million dollars," I said meekly, and he laughed. It was a good sound and brought a giggle out of me and I calmed again.

"She's got jokes," he said appreciatively. "But sorry, I'm a broke son of a bitch so you'll just have to tell me what else you want. Something maybe in my power this time."

I took a deep breath and said, "I want to go to bed. I want you to hold me while I fall asleep and not let me go."

His lips curved up, and he nodded slowly.

"That's what you need?" he asked softly and I nodded maybe a little too quickly and he leaned in pressing his lips to my forehead. My eyes slipped shut, and I sagged with relief as though a burden had been lifted.

"Good girl," he whispered against my forehead and he leaned back. "Not so bad, was it?"

"N-no," I muttered and it was a lie and he knew it because he called me out gently.

"Bullshit, that was way harder for you that it had a right to be, but you know what? I'm proud of you." He stood up, and I looked up at him blinking stupidly as my brain processed what he'd just said before catching up that he was going to the door at the bottom of the stairs.

"Where are you going?" I blurted, fear seizing me that I'd just shared something that was really fucking hard for me to ask, to admit out loud, and then here he was just... leaving.

"Relax, darlin'. I'm just going up to get our stuff, okay? I'll be right back down with it and then I'll help you get ready for bed."

"Okay," I whispered and he disappeared through the door, closing it behind him.

I bit my lips together and waited, looking around down here. It was vast, finished, and really nice... a bathroom, a big closet, the bed, and a big television mounted to the wall, but eerily, there were no windows.

I waited, practically holding my breath and hated that I worried whether he would return but a few moments later, I heard his tread on the stairs and he returned, his pack over his shoulder and my bag hanging from his opposite hand.

"Okay," he said. "Come on, let's get your face scrubbed off and your teeth brushed and all that good stuff. Hm?"

I stood up, a little awkwardly not sure what I was supposed to do or how any of this was supposed to go but knowing that I was liking this... it was soothing, and I would take it right now. The fallout could be dealt with tomorrow morning.

He set down his pack by the foot of the bed and reached out a hand to me and led me to the bathroom, letting it go to switch on the light.

"Okay, here you go." He handed me my bag. "Teeth brushed, face scrubbed, and pajamas, darlin'. Bring your hairbrush out to me when you're done."

"Why?" I asked.

"So that I can brush your hair before bed, not so I can paddle you with it. I would never hit you without your consent – if you're ever even into that sort of thing." He winked at me and I blushed to the roots of my hair.

"I don't understand how being hit could ever be a part of someone's good time," I said honestly. "I think I've been abused enough."

He nodded thoughtfully. "Duly noted."

"What is?" I asked quickly.

"That you equate impact with abuse," he said.

"You don't?" I asked.

"Depends on the context, the prior negotiations, and whether there's consent," he answered me honestly and I just blinked at him, stupidly.

"You're into all that?" I asked.

"Not exactly," he answered.

"What exactly, then?"

He fixed me with a firm look and said, "Wash your face, brush your teeth, change your clothes and bring out your stuff and your hairbrush to me. Absolutely nothing is going to happen tonight except I am going to brush your hair before bed and hold you tight while we both get some much-needed rest."

"Okay," I murmured.

He gave me a nod and said, "Take your time," before shutting me into the bathroom.

I turned to face the mirror and groaned at the muddled and gross tracks of mascara running down my face in the melted rivulets of a mind burning in absolute hellfire.

I did what he told me to do, in the order he told me to do it, and I took my time.

When I opened the bathroom door, I found him laid out on the big bed down here, feet crossed at the ankle in a pair of black lounge pants. He was bare chested and lean, one arm up behind his head the remote to the television in his hand as he surfed for something to put on through what looked like one of the educational documentary type channels I loved. One with all the true crime and paranormal shows my secretly gothic little weirdo heart could desire.

The same service that I liked best on his television back at his place.

"What is it you always got going on?" he asked.

"I've been watching *Ghost Woods*," I said. He scrolled to it and turned it on.

"I don't know how you can fall asleep to this shit and all those murder docs," he said with a smile and a sparkle of good humor in his eyes.

I shrugged. "Most of the narrators on these shows put me right out," I said. "Bill Curtis, I'm only good for like five minutes to his voice."

He put down the remote and gestured to me to come to him. I set my bag next to his and climbed up on the bed. He pushed himself up into a sitting position and held his hand out for the brush.

"You're sure?" I asked. I don't think I had met a man yet that had ever...

"If I wasn't sure, I wouldn't have asked, darlin'."

Oh. Fair point, well made.

I handed him the brush.

"Come sit between my legs," he said, and I did, as he leaned back against the headboard.

"This is a really big guest room," I murmured as he gathered my hair off my shoulders. I had run out of warmer options for PJs and was down to a summertime tank top and sleep short set – which now that I would be sleeping with Blackjack, I couldn't say I was sorry. He put off a lot of heat. I think it was a guy thing because Devin... I closed my eyes and took a cleansing breath. I didn't want to think about him right now, but he had too. Put off a lot of heat, I mean.

I kept my eyes closed and just concentrated on the feeling of his long finger, rough hands gathering my hair. He took his time, as though he was luxuriating in the feeling of the strands spilling through his fingers like water. Finally, I felt the bristles of the brush against my scalp as he lightly and carefully pulled it through my long hair.

Oh, that was nice...

My scalp began to tingle in a wash over my shoulders and down my back with each gentle, steady pull of the brush and slowly but surely, I felt my muscles that I hadn't even known I'd been holding tense begin to unknot.

I was relaxing, to the point I didn't even notice when he'd left off brushing my hair and instead had moved my hair over my shoulder so that he could knead them, digging thumbs into the tight little muscles at the base of my skull, where my neck attached, and moving them down, down, down incrementally, until he reached that sweet spot between my shoulders, fingers kneading my traps forcing a groan of grateful pleasure from between my lips.

"Hm." The sound he made was both thoughtful and pleased, as though he filed this information away for later use and yet he didn't give up. Just kept thoughtfully and gently prying the tension from me by loosening one tight muscle at a time until I was all but practically asleep while sitting up.

"System, turn the lights out please?" His melodic voice was firm, but not loud and I opened my eyes to find that open or closed, it made no difference. He had turned off the television and the room was plunged thoroughly into darkness.

"Here, come lay down, beautiful," he murmured, and he pulled me down, against his chest. I settled at his side and lay my cheek on the swell of his chest as his arms went around me.

"There we go," he said and he pulled the blankets up to his hand with his foot and then over us the rest of the way.

He sighed out in something like contentment and asked, "Is that a little bit better?"

"It's a lot bit better," I said and yawned, sleepily. He chuckled and kissed the top of my head, squeezing me a little tighter.

"Goodnight, little darlin'," he murmured, and I didn't even have the energy to respond. I was already halfway asleep.

14

*B*lackjack...

I woke a bit stiff from not having moved the entire night... but oddly more deeply rested than I had been in a while. I'd slept hard in addition to deep, apparently and I don't think I was alone in that. It seemed Ember had too.

She was still curled up on me like a sleepy little kitten, adorably hugging me like I was her favorite stuffy in the world and I had some thoughts and feelings about that. Mostly to the tune of uncertainty of just what I was getting into.

I mean, I by no means was the best pick in the world... better than her last ol' man, for sure, but I had my own problems and I worried that I wouldn't be good enough for her. Worried that even though, as much as I wanted her, to want her the way that I did was nothing but pure selfishness and truth be told, I didn't think there was anything the woman could say to disavow me of that notion.

I laid with her in the quiet dark of Cipher's secret basement bedroom bunker.

I thought I was paranoid? I ain't have nothing on him.

"Mm..." Ember shifted in her sleep against me, and I held her just a little bit tighter and whispered, "Shhh," soothingly, kissing the top of her head. Her hair like silk beneath my lips and fragrant with the smell of juicy green apples; a byproduct of her shampoo choice that made me smile. Her hold on me tightened and then loosened as her body stiffened and her leg slipped off from where it'd been over both of mine.

She stretched, long and lean like a cat against my side, sucking in a shuddering breath and yawning in the dark of the room.

I asked the closed-circuit system, "System? Turn on the lights, twenty-five percent."

The lights came up and Ember made a noise of protest; "Mm!" Burying her face in my shoulder and whining slightly at the intrusion of the light. I chuckled. I could already hear people moving around above us.

"Time to wake up, darlin'," I murmured.

"I don't want to!" She pouted and I couldn't help but chuckle again. I pressed lips to her hair again and breathed her in and sighed, a mixture of contented and, well, discontent. I know, it sounded weird to me, too... but it made sense. I was content to just be here with her, like this, cuddled close in the warm nest of blankets – by the same token, I shared her discontent in having to rise. Trust me, there would be no shining.

"Up you go, darlin'. Get yourself a shower and into some warm comfortable clothes."

"What's the plan?" she asked and cuddled into me just that much more.

"Let's get out of here, head on home, and let me get to work on the house for us," I said.

"You going to let me help?" she asked.

"It's not your mess," I told her.

"Same goes for me," she pointed out stubbornly.

"What?" I asked.

"I'm not your mess. I'm my mess, but you've been helping me..."

"That's different," I said dismissively, effectively batting her argument from my mind. I mean, it was like comparing apples to oranges – false equivalency and all of that.

"Is it?" she pressed.

I looked down into her eyes and she raised an eyebrow at me. I smirked and said, "Alright. I'll entertain you. What's your reasoning?"

She rolled those beautiful blue-green eyes of hers hard enough I wondered if she checked out that perfect peach shaped ass of hers and I laughed. "Well?" I prompted.

"You rode up to the top of that overpass and picked up my mess, then did it again when you came and got me from the hospital. The least I could do is put in a little elbow grease on yours," she argued and I sighed.

She had a point, and even if I didn't exactly like it, I had to concede that many hands made for light work.

"Go take your shower," I murmured, my lips against her head again. I couldn't get enough of the sensation of her soft hair against my lips. Couldn't get enough of her sweet apple laden scent. She was magnificent and it was everything in me to hold off touching her, claiming her. I mean it took *everything* to unhand her and every bit of self-control I had to tell myself, *not until the time is right...*

She closed herself in the bathroom and almost as soon as the shower started up, there was a rap at the door at the bottom of the stairs. I sighed and got my own ass up and went to it, unlocking it and opening it up to Cipher standing at the bottom step.

"How's she doin'?" he asked.

"Good," I said, thought better of it and frowned slightly and said, "Better."

"Cool, that's cool. You guys sleep okay?"

"Yeah, man. Thanks for this. Really, I mean it. Any idea what made Mav's girl go full Dahlia last night?"

Cipher shook his head and said, "Probably some shit Dahlia put in her head about protecting shit while she was out – you know how D can be about that shit."

"Girl's messed up," I agreed. "Heart is in the right place most of the time, but she's gotta work on those issues."

Cipher nodded and didn't look happy. Dahlia had that effect on a lot of us lately. It was unfortunate. When she wasn't being a raging fucking cunt, she was something else. Witty, funny, zany, and a sparkle to her personality that was sometimes unmatched but *goddamn* did she let that chip ride her shoulder, and let her personal demons drag her down.

We could be forgiving but she'd drag Tic to hell with her given half a chance, and fuck if any of us knew why he was so willing to take the fuckin' trip with her.

Any other bitch he wouldn't look twice but there was just something about Dahlia… their crazies just sort of matched up and attracted one another like a pair of high-powered magnets and the effects lately had set off some sort of electromagnetic pulse that'd left us all exhausted with their fucking bullshit.

"I took a calculated risk bringing Ember around the club, thinking shit would be all good, since Dahlia and Tic were on… let's just call it a forced sabbatical." Cipher huffed a laugh and nodded as I finished, "I'm feeling some type of way that I fucked *that* up."

"Guilty?" Cipher asked, searching my face.

I shook my head, stopped, nodded, and said, "And pissed off."

"Mav isn't happy either. 'sol fucked up hard and she knows it. I think he spanked her ass damn near raw and she took it – she knows."

"Yeah," I nodded and didn't say anything about their dynamic. I knew Mav. It wasn't like he beat her – no one laid a hand on anyone without consent which was a sort of gray area. Still, Marisol *had* fucked up, even if her heart was in the right place. She'd not only really upset Ember which had caused drama – which all of us were fuckin' over by now – she'd made her ol' man look bad in the process. Which was double bad considering who her ol' man was.

It was a good thing it'd been kept in-house. Some dudes in other clubs could have and would have taken that as a sign of weakness on Mav's part. He was already having issues with some of *us* over his soft spot with Dahlia.

"Well, what's done is done," I said. "Ain't no going back or taking it back."

"Kinz had no clue and was a fuckin' mess. She was just following Marisol's lead."

I nodded. "I thought it had to be something like that," I said. "Kinz can be vicious but she ain't unless she has a really damn good reason."

"Right..." Cipher nodded thoughtfully on that and then with a gusty sigh dismissing the whole situation changed the subject and asked, "So, what're your plans for the rest of the day?"

"Going back to my place. Power or not, I can finish laying that floor and I need to clean it up. I can't ask Ember to live in my stye and she's going to clean it when I'm not there if I don't do it when I am..."

"Your power back on?" he asked.

I turned and went over to the nightstand and picked up my charging phone and looked at the alerts. My security system was back online so... "Yeah, looks like it."

"Cool, I'll come with you and help you finish that floor like I promised."

"Bro..." I said, and he gave me a look.

"Nah, it should have been done a couple months back, I'll help as much as I can today just let me grab some clean—"

"Oh!" the bathroom door had swung open, and then closed immediately.

"Shit, I forgot to mention, she showers like a dude," I said and Cipher and I shared a chuckle.

"Just a minute darlin', let Cipher grab some clothes and fuck off and I'll get you handled."

"O-okay."

Cipher got his shit together and fucked off back upstairs. I shut and locked the door for Ember's sake and went to the bathroom, tapping on the door with a knuckle twice. She opened up and stared up at me with those wide lovely eyes, her hair slicked back and hanging lank with water.

She had a towel wrapped around her but it was just a regular one and didn't do much to cover everything.

"Trade you places if you want," I said.

She nodded mutely and I went in as she slipped out past me.

We got our shit together. As for cleaning myself up, I just did the basics having showered the night before and when we were ready, we shouldered our bags and I went for the door to the hidden staircase. Ember's hand fell on mine stopping me and I looked over at her.

"Is everyone gone?" she asked anxiously.

I took my hand out from under hers and traced some of her still-wet hair out of her face, tucking it behind her ear.

"Nah," I said. "Cipher'll let 'em stay as long as they want. He's going to follow us back to our place and help me with that back room's floor. Get it done and get that dining table out of the kitchen."

"Okay," she said and rolled her lips together.

"I'm sorry the welcome wasn't up to standard, darlin'. I promise you it's been fixed and it won't happen again."

She bowed her head and something like a grimace flashed on her face and I sighed inwardly.

"I promise, and I mean it. It's not an empty one, baby."

She swallowed hard and nodded, again without looking and I'd nailed it. I kind of figured it was a song and dance she'd heard before and nothing had come of it. I bet she'd been so much fresh fuckin' meat in that place her daddy had stuck her. She didn't seem the rebellious type. She was so... fuckin' *perfect*. So eager to please, and I just didn't understand how she'd been so *overlooked*.

That's the problem, I thought as we went up the switchback staircase past the first floor of the house and up to the second. *She hadn't been overlooked; she was too pretty for that. She'd been shuffled aside out of convenience for her dad, it sounded like, and then she'd been through hell precisely because she couldn't be overlooked.*

Jealousy had probably been a lot of it.

I couldn't fathom anything else.

When we reached upstairs, people were milling around the kitchen and living room already in various states of dress, which was sort of club typical.

Raven and Little Bird came right over to Ember and Raven took her hand.

"Let me braid your hair? I didn't get to last night."

Ember looked to me and I nodded. She murmured, "Okay," and let the two lead her to the living room couch. Fen handed me a cup of coffee and Mav eyed me from over by what looked like a big pressure cooker full of oatmeal.

"We good, bro?" he asked, and I gave a nod.

"Everything'll be cool with a little time and distance," I told him affably and he nodded, looking relieved.

"No offense, then?"

"Not with me." I glanced into the living room where Ember looked tense but was forcing a good smile and nodding at the girls and what they were saying as they spoke in low and fervent tones. It looked like Raven and Little Bird were throwing support and Kinzleigh moved in a moment later and was doing the standup thing of apologizing.

Fish hovered nearby, a strange little smile on his lips as he looked Kinz over and I caught his eye. I gave a nod, and he gave a knowing nod back. Kinz looked like she was trying not to cry and my prior statement about her being one of the good ones stood strong.

I turned back to the guys in the kitchen and we all traded a look and shared a little nervous laughter.

"What's she like in her oatmeal, man?" DT asked and I raised my eyebrows.

"Your guess is as good as mine," I said. "Shit's just still too new."

Mav sighed, and it was a heavy thing and I looked at him. "Just breathe, bro. It can't rain all the time," I said and he nodded and I worried a bit. I shot a look to Glass Jaw who gave me a nod. Our president was *stressed,* and this kind of shit wasn't helping.

"How can I help, Mav?" I asked from behind the rim of my coffee mug as I swallowed, half wishing Cipher would hurry his fucking ass up so we could get out of here, knowing that we weren't going anywhere until Raven finished whatever elaborate Viking-esque hairstyle she was putting into my girl's hair.

Shit, I thought silently... *too fucking soon! Way too fucking soon to be calling her* mine.

"Nothing, man," Maverick said. "Just heavy is the head that wears the crown," he added with a crooked smile.

"Delegate, motherfucker," Dump Truck grunted and Fen, me, Fish, and Mace all grunted in agreement.

"Later," Mav said sharply with a pointed look in the girl's direction. I turned to Ember's eyes fixed on me and it was like a punch to the gut. She had a wise and calculating look in them as she appraised us all and I knew, I just knew... she had all of our moods down pat in an instant.

Most chicks thought that shit made them an empath, but I knew better. Had learned some things in therapy after getting home from in-country... therapy I'd needed. Therapy I hadn't gotten nearly enough of before I'd been cut off.

Empathetic, sure... but hypervigilant as a means of survival was the truth of it. She didn't know it, but her body was tense, ready to spring into flight, her fight-or-flight response triggered and her switch flipped into the permanently 'on' position. Her faultless politeness the third 'f' word of the fucked-up bunch – fawning. She placated like a motherfucker to avoid any more pain and I knew it.

Just how to break her of it in the gentlest ways possible?

I hadn't figured that out.

One day at a time, I guess.

15

*E*mber...

They finished the back room's floor. It had the most windows of any of the house and I couldn't tell if it was supposed to be the dining room or the sunroom or a combination of the two. At any rate, as soon as they were finished snapping the laminate in place, they cleaned it off and moved the table and chairs I had painstakingly cleaned off and dusted into place. That just opened up more kitchen floor space that needed scrubbed and I spent the majority of my day on hands and knees going at it until my fingers were raw, red, and tender around my nails from soaking in cleaner all day long.

The kitchen and dining room were complete though, and progress was made.

We ordered pizza, too tired to cook, and shared a six pack of beer, two apiece until it was gone. Cipher and Blackjack talked plans for the rest of the house and Cipher ended up leaving what felt like *really* late. The sky heavy and black outside. I looked at the clock and was surprised to find it was only a little after eight... the winters were so long and dark here and even though I'd lived in the area since I was a kid, minus the time I was trapped at that place when I was a teen in

Utah, it *still* managed to take me by surprise how long and deep and dark the winter nights could be here.

"Hey." I jumped slightly and Blackjack eased up behind me, pulling me back against his chest and cuddling me while we stood in the still-wrecked living room.

He and Cipher had tried to repair the guest bed but the broken frame now resided in the back of Blackjack's truck. A lost cause.

The mattress and box spring were stood on end, leaning against the wall as I surveyed the room.

"What's wrong?" he asked me, holding me lightly as I sagged back into him tiredly.

I don't want to stay in here... I thought. Out loud, I said, "Nothing."

"Mm-mm, darlin'. Don't lie to me... not to spare my feelings – all one of 'em I got left. Tell me what's up."

"I don't want to sleep in here," I murmured feeling guilt and something akin to shame. "I want to stay with you."

He nuzzled behind my ear and I shuddered, his breath warms against my skin, blushing down the side of my neck sending all sorts of tingles and good vibes through my system that felt like it was just begging to go haywire.

"That's the plan, darlin'. My bed is big and has been real lonely for a while and I like having you in it. So, come on. Let's get you a bath and relaxed and figure some things out you and I."

I stiffened at the last he had to say and asked, "Figure what out?" alarmed.

He chuckled and kissed my temple over the top of one of the fine braids against it.

Raven had done my hair into this sort of Viking throwback braided on the sides, the top teased into a sort of mohawk that made me look fierce. She and Little Bird talked about how they were making Viking costumes for the summer renaissance faire and how Fen and some of his friends were helping to make them shields so that all the girls could go as shield maidens. They wanted to include me, and it sounded like fun. Raven had taken my measurements when she was done with my hair and had written everything down and then had started on Fen's hair, teasing out the old braids that were starting to look the worse for wear so he could go shower and get them done fresh.

I was distracted by the light touch of Blackjack's lips against the side of my neck, and I closed my eyes, wanting to live in that light, pleasurable little touch.

"Like how many orgasms you're going to take for me, for one," he growled lightly next to my ear, and I about died. I felt my knees turn to jelly as he captured my earlobe with his teeth and the light snarl that he let out in my ear, the sensation of his warm breath against my neck, his hard chest at my back... *oh, God...*

"I..."

"Yes?" he asked.

"Um..." I couldn't think. Not with him standing so close, not with him being so warm and his hands so gentle as they traveled over my tee shirt and the hip of my leggings.

"You say stop? Everything stops," he whispered, misreading my lack of being able to word properly as indecision or protestations. "I just want to make you feel good, make you feel safe," he finished, and I swallowed hard.

"I don't think my legs will hold me," I finally got out, breathlessly.

"Not when I'm done with you, for sure," he said and I think I swallowed my tongue. He chuckled and it sounded dark, not like a foreboding type of dark, but rather decadent like rich dark chocolate spilled along ribs and the edge of a breast. Tantalizing, erotic, and I had to ask myself... *was I ready?* I mean, *was this too soon?*

I worried about it as he steered me around and through the door into the hallway, down it, and across – through the door to his bedroom which was still a bit dusty but perfectly neat. His laundry folded and put away, his dresser cleared off, and his bed ideally made.

Did it need a good vacuum, and the laminate, artificial hardwood floor mopped? Yes, but it was loads better in here, the oppressive clutter gone and the whole feel less burdensome and I didn't even remember at what point he'd found the time or did it.

...then it hit me.

He'd done it for *me*. That he certainly hadn't cared but he knew it bothered me, the clutter and the mess and he wanted me to stay. Wanted me to be comfortable in his space, and no one had ever done anything even remotely like it for me before.

He led me into the bathroom and started the tub, turning on the faucet and eyeing me expectantly.

"When did you find the time to clean your room like that?" I asked.

"While you were fixated on the floor in the kitchen," he said. "Cipher and I came in here with a couple trash bags and just did it."

I frowned.

"You threw it all away?"

He chuckled. "Not all of it, just the broken shit that I was never going to get around to repairing and the random shit that was just taking up space."

"Oh," I murmured.

"You getting undressed or you want me to undress you for you?" he asked, arching a brow and I blinked, hesitating as I processed what he'd said.

Oh...

"Um, sorry," I said and reached for the hem of my shirt.

He stood up from his seat on the edge of the tub and came over to me, stilling my hands with his and staring down at me.

"If you're not ready for this..." he left the sentence open ended and kept his warm brown eyes fixed on mine and I stared up into them, speechless.

"I'm..." I stopped.

He cocked his head and said, "Breathe, baby. Just take a deep breath and let it out slow and tell me when you're ready."

"I'm not used to this," I confessed and wow that was hard.

"Used to what?" he asked gently, and I tore my gaze from his, feeling like I was under a spotlight and totally exposed and wow was that an uncomfortable sensation.

"Take your time," he said gently and he didn't budge. I bit my lips together and finally worked up the courage to say.

"It's like you care about what I want, and I've just... I'm just not used to it. Nobody's ever really cared about what I want before."

"Oh, baby... this type of thing," he said smoothing his hands up and down my arms, his voice so low it was nearly lost in the rush of the water from the tub spout. "What I'd like to build with you, a true power exchange, it's about both of us and it's *all* about consent. I don't know why it's such a hard fuckin' concept for the dude bros out there but they don't get it. They'll never get it. Too fuckin' stupid is my bet."

I looked up at him and said, "I don't understand, power exchange?"

"Mm." He nodded. "A healthy power exchange is predicated on consent and respect. You hold the power and you give it to me to do with what I will in the trust that I will take care of you. Which I will spend as long as it takes to prove that I *will take care of you,* and that you're safe with me."

"I don't understand," I said again. "What do you get out of it?"

"Only the best natural high there is," he said with a boyish grin that melted my heart a little around its edges.

I swallowed hard. "And what do I get?" I asked, still unclear.

"A sense of safety for one, and hopefully a sense of empowerment. Your confidence back."

I gave a nervous laugh and said, "I could use some confidence."

He nodded and touched my cheek, stroking it with his thumb gently. I looked back into his eyes surprised and he cocked his head again and asked, "What's that look for, darlin'?"

He trailed his opposite hand down my arm from my shoulder and picked up my hand, bringing it up to his lips, keeping his eyes fixed on mine as he turned his face and pressed a kiss to my palm.

It was as though everything was happening incredibly fast, but the world slowed down to half its speed at the very same time.

I swallowed hard, and he took his mouth from my hand. I froze, the blood pounding in my temples and my cheeks heating as he slowly, ever so slowly, brought his lips to mine.

I closed my eyes right before they touched mine and he kissed me. A slight whimper escaping my throat as I swooned, yes *swooned* into him and put my arms around him.

His hands slipped beneath my shirt, kneading my lower back, the feeling of his rough hands against my skin causing my nipples to tighten against the soft material of my tee, which was pressed against his chest.

I hadn't even realized I'd molded myself to the front of his body and if that wasn't a testament to the attraction I struggled against, I don't know what was.

"I don't even know why you would want me," I whispered against his lips and he pulled back slightly.

"One, I don't want to hear you talk about yourself like that, ever – okay?"

"Yes, sir," I mumbled, cheeks heating, the words just coming out of me automatically and without thought. The smile that crossed his face at their utterance was something to behold, though.

"Good girl," he whispered and for whatever reason, those two small words of praise made me glow from the inside out.

"Second," he murmured. "You're beautiful, selfless, and so sweet... I don't know any man who wouldn't want you."

I swallowed hard and he took a slight step back, letting his hands sweep up my back, my waist exposed to the cooler air of the bathroom as he swept my shirt up with them.

"Arms up," he ordered gently, and I complied with only minor hesitation. He took my shirt and I covered my chest with my arms automatically, out of habit.

"You good?" he asked quietly.

"Yeah," I answered breathy, and I practically gulped as he went down to his knees in front of me, staring up at me as he hooked his fingers in the waistband of my old, bleach-stained leggings I used pretty much solely around the house and to clean in.

He kept our gazes locked as he took down my leggings and my panties with them. He stripped off my socks when he reached my ankles, rendering me nude but not uncomfortable. I mean, he wasn't even looking at me. His eyes still locked to mine, and somehow, some way, I felt more exposed from that than I did from my lack of clothing.

He put a hand to my hip, caressing it with his thumb and ordered me gently, "Get in. I'm right behind you."

I looked over at the rapidly filling tub and stepped over the high ledge. The water was just a little too hot but not bad.

"Might need to drain a little of that out," he said and I looked up and *oh, shit.* He was sliding his pants off and getting naked with me. He legitimately was going to be *right behind me* as in he was getting in with me!

I moved over and made room and shutting off the tap, I bit my bottom lip and pulled the drain letting some of the water out. He got in with me and more water displaced, but not bad, not yet. If he sat down things might get bad, but he seemed to have more patience than anyone I'd ever met and he waited.

"Okay," he murmured, and I stoppered the drain.

He sank into the water with me with and said, "Come here, let me hold you."

That sounded so nice, and I moved to comply with no resistance, sitting between his knees and leaning back into his chest as his arms went around me.

He kissed my shoulder and sighed with what sounded like contentment and we lounged for a moment before my nerves compelled me to ask... "How does all of what you're..." I groped for the word. "Um... proposing? Work?"

He chuckled and gave me a little squeeze and smacked another kiss to my shoulder and sighing said, "You need to see your worth, and build yourself back up. I'll set out clear expectations and boundaries and I expect you to do the same. Some of it, we'll play by ear... you're good, you get rewarded, you're bad and there will be consequences but I will never ever hit you," he rushed out before I could interrupt.

"I don't think corporal punishment is the way to go for you, not given your history. So, I will have to get creative."

"Okay," I said softly. My nerves were fizzing and I didn't know why other than the prospect of doing anything wrong and being punished scared the hell out of me.

I shifted slightly in his hold and he chuckled sympathetically and asked, "What is it?"

"I don't like the idea of being punished and not knowing what some of those things could be," I said and I felt him nod.

"Okay, it might be something like..." he trailed off sounding thoughtful. "Having you write lines," he suggested, and I felt myself go limp with relief.

"Oh," I said. "That doesn't sound so bad."

He kissed my temple and said, "No, not bad."

"Just don't put me in time out," I said and laughed. "I would hate that."

He laughed a little too and he said, "Then that's something that will go on the list for a transgression if it's big enough."

"Hey! No!" I cried. "You can't use that against me!"

He laughed a little, chest hitching beneath my back and said, "You're starting to catch on."

"Oh," I declared. "It's like that, is it?"

"Mm, part of it."

I giggled and relaxed a bit and Blackjack made a contented sound, not quite a sigh and not quite a moan but something in between.

His hands wandered over my skin beneath the water and he put his lips next to my ear after a while and said, voice low and sexy, somehow soothing, "I want you to be a good girl and do something for me."

"Yeah?" I asked, a bit breathy.

"Mm, I want you to lay back just like you are but I want you to close your eyes and listen to the sound of my voice."

"Alright," I said, and I closed my eyes.

"I want you to relax," he said. "Think about the last time you felt good, and I mean really good."

I listened to what he asked, and I thought about it, and I mean I really thought about it and I couldn't think of anything recent... I mean...

"Have you got it?" he asked.

"Yes," I murmured.

"You thinking about a man?" he asked.

"A boy," I answered truthfully.

"Mm, did he touch you like this?" he asked, hands gliding over my stomach, one up to press me back into him between my breasts the other resting atop my thigh.

"No," I murmured.

"Do you like it when I touch you like this?" he asked me, low and seductive, his hand creeping up my chest, warm and slick to rest on my throat.

I held no fear, trusting that this was just some sort of dark and dirty play that truthfully was thrilling as I answered him breathy and equally as truthfully as I had before, "*Yes.*"

His hand on my throat continued its smooth ascent, fingers capturing my chin thrusting my head back gently at an almost cruel angle as he captured my mouth with his and that cruelty held such a deliciously dirty edge it absolutely stole my breath away as his tongue teased the seam of my lips urging me silently to part them even as his other hand below the waterline did the same to my thighs.

I parted both willingly and whimpered as he stroked my pussy beneath the warm water in the tub.

I kissed him back, my tongue lashing out against his even as my hips rose begging silently for him to touch me deeper.

"Hmm, yeah," he whispered against my mouth, his middle finger finding that button and pressing firmly against it, swirling in a sensual circle, sending a flutter through the depths of my pussy.

I arched back against him and exhaled, my body melting from the attention his hand beneath my chin, stretching my head back but not hurting me, just holding me helpless against him as he played with my pussy and gazed down my body, admiringly.

"Look at you," he murmured, and my eyes rolled up to his face, the look on it, in his eyes as he gazed down the length of me.

"Exquisite," he went on to say. "A work of art. You're so fucking beautiful, baby. So sexy." He breathed out in a hiss between his teeth and I felt his cock stir at my lower back.

"You make me feel honored that you let me touch this body," he said and slipped his hand further between my legs, sliding a finger just inside me. I gasped and writhed against him and he smiled appreciatively.

"So responsive," he practically moaned. "Such a good little girl," he breathed. "You feel good, sweetheart? I keep working you like this, you going to come for me?"

I whimpered an affirmative, because good lord I was almost there from just the sound of his voice. His praise.

"Good girl," he breathed into my ear. "We're going to stay here, just like this for as long as it takes for you to get some relief, aren't we? Yes..."

I half moaned, half cried out, and he raised my chin just that much more. I dug nails and was only vaguely aware that it was into his knees or his thighs I couldn't see, I couldn't be sure, he held me fast and in such a way that I was open, incredibly vulnerable, his legs over mine, holding me open as he tortured my pussy so sweetly beneath the water.

I jerked in his arms, crying out, and his hand tightened on my throat just slightly. Not choking, just controlling.

"That's it, darlin', that's it. Ooo, so nice."

I closed my eyes, panting, my breath coming in short gasps, my body taut and on display for him and the *feelings* that he wrought, not just with his hands, but his voice, the emotions, the intensity of it all, I came so swiftly, so hard, I shut my eyes and struggled against the overwhelmingness of it, my body going from numb to hypersensitive so quickly and he didn't let up – he wouldn't let up and I very nearly panicked that he wouldn't stop fearing what would happen if things just kept going.

My hands flew between my legs, wrapping around his wrist and tugging even as his hand tightened on my jaw and he soothed me with his voice, "Shhh, let it happen baby, you're good, I've got you."

Too much! My panicked mind screamed and just when I thought I would cry, he stopped, his hand slipping away from between my legs and wrapping around my waist and holding me fast against him as he soothed with voice, petting me lightly with touch, as I trembled in his arms.

"Shh, good girl," he murmured. "Such a good girl... I'm so proud of you."

I panted, and whimpered and let him cuddle me, turning against him and putting my arm under and around him, pressing my thighs together as he held me fast and told me how proud of me that he was. That I let him push me, and asking if I was alright with a slight chuckle.

I laughed a bit nervously, feeling a little stupid now... vulnerable, and still a little scared... *over what? A freaking orgasm? The best orgasm of my life? What the fuck was that about?*

I went to move away and he held me a little tighter and said, "Shh, no. Stay with me, just for a little while longer and then we'll get you out and dried off so I can hold you some more, hmm?"

I liked the sound of that and forced myself to relax, still unsure where this riled and pent-up fear-energy was coming from.

"Shhh..." he soothed and pressed my head to his shoulder, kissing my forehead as I shivered against him – but not with cold. No, just with the remnants of whatever that had been! I don't think I had ever felt anything quite like it.

After things had calmed and I'd stilled in his arms, he chuckled and asked... "So, better than whatever you remembered?"

I bit my lips together and told the truth after taking a deep and cleansing breath, "Better than anything so far..."

He laughed a little then and hugged me lightly saying, "You have that exactly right, darlin'. Better than anything *so far...*"

Oh lord, I both liked the sound of that and found it daunting.

16

*B*lackjack...

God, I felt good, the feel of her in my arms, so supple, the way she was so pliable to my will and her perfect and sweet silent supplication... I was enjoying the fuck out of my top space, my dominant nature satisfied and happy. She was worth going slow with, savoring every moment, every touch, kiss, gasp, and moan. She soaked up the positive attention like a fucking sponge and it low-key pissed me off just how fuckin' starved she was for love and a gentle touch.

I didn't know exactly what I was feeling, I didn't think a broken bastard like me was even capable of love anymore; but she moved me in a way I hadn't been moved in a good long while. Like the broken in me somehow recognized the broken in her and our souls were reaching across the gap our individual bodies provided and were grasping at one another, pulling our physical forms together and I suddenly knew what people talked about when they said '*it was magnetic.*'

We got out of the tub, I whipped a towel over me drying off and secured it at my waist before I tended to her, her body much more relaxed, a languid look in her lust hooded eyes. She let her gaze wander over me, her sight lingering on my tattoos and wandering over me like I was some kind of work of art.

I could watch her look at me like that all night, but I was eager to touch her once more, so I wrapped her in a towel and rubbed her dry through the thick cloth while she giggled when I hit her ticklish spots.

"Hmm," she hummed out in appreciation and I could tell she was firmly in that glowing post-orgasm state, but it was more than that. She was so relaxed and natural, and I knew a sub in subspace when I saw it – though admittedly, it'd been a real damn long time. I tended to play careful and didn't go too far with what I'd coined as temporary playthings in my own head... and it'd been a while since I'd even indulged with one of *those*.

I looked at Ember now and I couldn't even imagine putting her in that box. She was too wonderful, too sweet, and thoroughly addictive... and more, but it was the more I tried to ignore for now, shoving the worries and concerns about her broken status to the back of my mind even as the voice back there cautioned me: *she's not a project.*

I led her to the bed and lifted the blankets and top sheet, stealing her towel and giving her adorable ass a pinch as she got into bed. She squeaked in surprise and squealed in a peal of laughter as I smiled and felt lighter than some fuckin' air at her response to my teasing.

I ditched our towels in the hamper and got in after her, telling the closed-circuit system that was like Cipher's to turn out the lights. He'd helped me install it after I'd expressed how I'd liked his. Sitting at my PC while I'd worked in here and Ember had tackled the Mount Everest sized task of my damn kitchen floor.

The lights went out, and I gathered her close, moving her hand to my cock.

"Hmm," she hummed in appreciation, stroking me and fuck, that felt good. I closed my eyes against the dark and focused on the feeling of her tucked into my side, her hand wrapped warm and soft around my hard cock, stroking me gently. The way her breath caught, the way it quickened, and the feel of her lips against my shoulder as she explored me by touch. God it was fantastic, her touch light and almost phantasmic as she felt me up root to tip and back down again, her orgasm loosening her up, the cover of night and the deep dark of my room making her bolder as she pushed herself up into a sitting position.

I held my breath, daring to dream, and then her mouth was on me. I vaguely regretted in that moment not undoing the careful tight braiding of her hair in the bath. I longed for the sweep of her silken apple scented hair across my body as she made love to me with her mouth, longed even more to gather all those silken locks into my fists and to massage her scalp as she blew me, but alas not this first time... I mean, I could always dare to dream that there would be more but for now? I had to make do with fisting the bottom sheet on one side of me and palming her hip with the hand closest to her.

Her skin was so soft, so warm, and she smelled so divine! The deep darkness of the room effectively blinding us both, enhancing the other senses, bringing them into peak performance and I lived for it. Her soft, wet mouth working its way down my shaft slowly and gently, the way she sucked me with just the right amount of pressure, her velvet tongue running circles around my head when she came to my tip.

Fuck, fuck, fuck! I loved the bold and carefree version of this woman! The way she stroked my shaft and sucked my head, the way she got her other hand involved to play with my balls. God, I could lay here and let her fucking to this to me forever but I couldn't do that to *her...* As phenomenal as it fucking felt, I just had never really been able to get off via a blowjob no matter how good and *Jesus, fuck,* she was really good!

"Mm, baby you suck me so good," I praised her. "You just keep right on going as long as you – ah! Want. I just won't get off from it and don't take that as a challenge – I just can't, never have, *oh, Christ!*"

She took me in all the way to the back of her throat and very nearly made a liar out of me right then and there, but nope – I didn't come and I didn't think I could even if I felt like I was right on that edge.

She went for a few more minutes, driving me crazy, edging me close and closer and I swore if she got on me to ride, I was going to shame myself and go far too quickly. It'd both been too long and she had me *right fucking there,* more masterfully than any woman I'd ever been with before and that included Dahlia, who was a professional at her craft.

No, the reason Ember was as hot if not hotter than her name was the fact that she was so sweet and innocent in her approach to sex. I mean, *clearly*, she knew what she was doing but her timid nature due to her just… brokenness at the hands of that asshole – I don't know, she was just about every man's fucking fantasy of an angel in the streets and right now a total succubus in the sheets.

Her jaw had to ache with how she'd sucked me and when she straightened, I lay panting, so hard it fucking hurt.

"Ah, God… thank you, baby," I murmured, and she shifted running her hands over my thighs and up my chest, feeling me out in the dark.

"Can I?" she asked and it was adorable.

"Can you what?"

"Um, it feels awkward saying it out loud," she said with a nervous laugh.

"Can you fuck me?" I asked, and I could hear the grin in my voice even as I felt it pull at the corners of my lips.

"I- well, I mean, yes…" she said, stumbling over her words but I could tell, fucking me wasn't what she had in her frame of mind.

"Mm, no you need to tell me," I said, and I played my hand over her soft skin. "I don't think you want to fuck me," I said caressing a breast, thumbing her nipple as she gasped lightly.

"I mean, I want you inside me," she said and she sounded so wistfully desperate it was adorable.

"Not the same as fucking," I said softly, buying myself some time to calm down, my boner was flagging and my balls ached, but I didn't want to blow my load inside two seconds so that was a sacrifice I was willing to make.

"No," she agreed.

"Passion… is that what you're after?" I asked.

"Not exactly that either," she whispered and I could tell by her voice, the low intimate pitch of it we were in a dangerous place for her. She was cracked wide open, exposed, and no good had ever come of that kind of thing for her before.

"Tell me what you need, darlin'," I said, and I knew what to expect, but it didn't make it any easier.

"I need someone to love me," she said and her voice cracked.

Someone... not 'you'... fair, I thought. She didn't want to ask too much of me.

"Climb up here, baby. I'll love you tonight," I murmured. I already knew I was fuckin' lying to myself as much as her. The way I felt looking into her eyes when I could see them, the way she felt against me in that bath and the way she carefully put a leg over me now and let me help settle her into position – no, I wouldn't love her just tonight. I was already in too deep; and that was before she even had the chance to lift my resurging cock off of my stomach.

I was already ensnared by her beauty, her strength, and her fiery will to live and I wanted to feed her namesake, pile on bits of praise and build her confidence and I wanted more than anything to watch her fucking *burn*, to watch her burst forth like a phoenix rising from the ashes and to *thrive* like never before and – *oh sweet fucking mother of – shit!*

She lowered herself over me, her hungry, tight, hot, and wet little pussy working me in to the absolute depths of her fucking soul and I was glad for the dark of the room and that we were limited to just sound, touch, and yeah, even smell and she smelled fucking *divine!* So good, womanly, bountiful, so wonderful that something inside of me just *overflowed* with so many emotions that again, I was glad for the deep dark. As much as I wanted to see her, I didn't want to appear weak but she made me so weak in the goddamn knees.

"Oh, *God*," she moaned and her hands found my chest as she rolled her hips and I felt my eyes roll back in my head.

It was tantric, it was magic, it was everything that any of the encounters I had ever had before with anyone else had been lacking.

"That's it, darlin'," I grunted. "Take your pleasure. Ride me. You feel so fuckin' good – *yes!*"

She had started careful and measured in her movements but the more I praised, and the more comfortable she became with that praise, the wilder and more organic those movements became. She was so warm and soft beneath my hands, her body like satin under my palms and hot and silky wet around my dick as she moved – I knew I was lost. Even before her fingertips dug into my chest, even before my balls grew tight and my cock twitched and even before she cried out and tightened up around me and I lost any shred of control I ever fucking had and spilled up inside her, my cock jerking and her fingers plunging through any barrier I could presume to put up and dipping into my beating heart in my breast.

She touched me more deeply than any woman that had gone before and that even included my very ex-wife.

I wrapped my arms around her as she collapsed over me, her face turning into the side of my neck and I whispered, *"Good girl,"* into her ear.

Both of us panted. I felt the mess of our mingling fluids and I couldn't be fucked about cleanup for several long minutes. Her legs trembled to either side of my hips and I asked, "You okay?"

She laughed and said, "I can't feel my legs, but other than that, I'm great." Then she gasped at a particularly savage muscle spasm in the top of one of her thighs.

"Okay," I said, "Over you go!" I spilled her onto her side, giggling, and slipped from her, my cock going soft in the transition.

"Oh, God!" she moaned and it wasn't exactly a good moan as I massaged the wicked attempt at cramping going on in her leg, barely heading it off at the pass before it seized up completely on her.

"Easy, I've got you," I said tenderly, massaging the muscle back into submission.

"You're too good to me," she said softly.

I chuckled, "No, I'm just doing the bare minimum," I told her.

"It's a lot more than that," she said disbelief in her voice and I had a bit of a sinking feeling because honestly, if it was? It wasn't by much. *The poor girl...*

"Stay there, I'll get us cleaned up."

I cleaned myself up, unworried about any diseases – if he'd given her something we both had it now and it was just one more reason to kill him. Ember was honest, even when it hurt her, and if she knowingly had something I would already know about it, too. Pregnancy was another thing I wasn't worried about. I'd had a vasectomy years ago.

I returned with a warm washcloth in one hand and a glass of cold water from the tap in the other.

"Sit up for me, darlin'," I ordered gently and from the dim light around the bathroom door I watched her cooperate. I handed her the glass, and she drank greedily as I passed the cloth between her legs. She squeaked and I had to say, "Ah!" when she tried to snap her legs closed. She let her knees fall open, and I wiped her down gently and thoroughly despite her squirming.

"You done?" I asked and she handed the glass back with very little water in the bottom. I polished that off, took it back in the bathroom and set it on the counter, and tossed the washcloth into one of the polished sinks.

Getting back into bed with her was the best thing after switching out the light. The way she fit herself against me, her leg just naturally finding its way over mine... perfection.

"I... I'm not on any birth control," she confessed. "I can get a 'Plan B' tomorrow—"

"Don't worry about it," I said. "I had a vasectomy a long time ago."

"Oh," she said and sounded relieved.

"Any kids?" she asked.

"No," I said.

"Oh..."

Silence for a minute.

"Why then? If you don't mind me asking..."

"I never mind you asking me anything, questions are how we learn. I was military and going through some serious pussy. I knew it was reversible or even if it wasn't, there were ways around it if I ever ended up with the right woman; and I thought I had for a minute."

"Oh?" she asked, and she sounded lethargic, sleepy.

"Mm," I grunted in confirmation, kissing her forehead and holding her a little closer, palming her thigh.

"What happened?" she asked.

"Asked her to marry me, we got hitched. I got deployed and came back. She came up pregnant and thought she was gonna pass it off as mine. I hadn't told her about the vasectomy. I knew it wasn't mine. I divorced her ass and never looked back, just went on the next deployment."

"Oh, I'm so sorry..." she murmured and her voice was heavy with a needless sorrow.

"Don't be. Everything that happened between then and now needed to," I said.

"Why?" she asked, voice tinged with confusion in the dark.

"Because it led me to you, darlin'. Now get some sleep."

"Yes, sir," she uttered with a yawn and I chuckled and pressed another kiss to her forehead thinking to myself, *so this is what happiness feels like...*

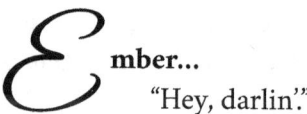mber...

"Hey, darlin'."

A light touch on my head, a gentle caress under my jaw, along the side of my neck. I winced slightly and pressed my blanket covered knuckles into my eyes and rubbed them.

"Hey." I yawned and then groaned, "What time is it?"

"Time to sit up," he said gently, his voice warm and tinged with affection.

I stretched, hard and there was a clatter near my feet and he said, "Oh!" and made a grab for something chuckling. I pushed myself up as he retrieved the plate of breakfast off the bed and picked up the table knife that'd slid half off of it. He brought it up to my lap and set it in it and retrieved a cup of coffee off the nightstand, pressing it into my hands.

"You did all this for me?" I asked and realized the scent of bacon was heavy on the air.

"Eat your breakfast, darlin', then take your time getting dressed and dress warm. I want to tackle the garage today if you don't mind," he said. He kissed my forehead and I blinked up at him, stunned stupid and watched him leave the bedroom.

I was in disbelief.

I looked down at the coffee in my hands and the plate in my lap and tried not to cry.

I mean... I'd never.

I ate my breakfast and drank my coffee and was grateful that my life had taken this strange and wonderful turn. When I got out of bed, I realized he had moved all of my things in here, my bags of clothes and the like. I didn't want to take for granted that he wanted me to integrate them into the dresser or one of the two closets in here, but curious I went to the dresser and opened and closed some drawers quietly.

Half of them had been emptied.

My, he'd had an industrious morning...

I felt a little odd; worried, like this was too good to be true or maybe, that things were moving way too fast, but... but at the same time this was a decidedly *different* feeling than when I'd first gotten together with Devin.

With Devin everything felt edgy and just *wrong* somehow, but he was being so *nice* and I ignored those feelings in favor of trusting what was before my eyes.

As soon as I was in the back of that police car being taken to the hospital, I had vowed *never* to fall prey to my own stupidity like that again and yet, here I was now and as I rooted through my bags and pulled out clothes to wear for the day, nude in Blackjack's bedroom only *days* into things even though it already felt like *years* I didn't feel the same apprehension that I had back then, with Devin. There was still apprehension, sure, but it was not the same.

This felt more, I don't know... manufactured? Like it was all thought and no heart whereas with Devin it was the exact opposite. All heart and no thought.

It was a curious thing.

One I tried to set aside in my overthinking mind to dissect later.

I found Blackjack through the door beside the front door that led into the musty and over-filled garage. He was sorting through some things, his jacket and cut on, the dim light from the bare bulb in the middle of things yellow and harsh.

"Hey," I called out, and he looked up and smiled and that *smile.*

"I put my dishes in the sink for now, I'll get them later if that's okay? The dishwasher was already running."

"It's fine," he declared with a chuckle. "Mind hitting the button right next to you to open this up? Looks like a doorbell."

I looked over and sure enough, there was an old doorbell button wired to the wall. I pressed it and the motor on the garage door ground to life, the door noisily trundling up.

"Wow, this is a lot of stuff," I declared.

"Yeah." Blackjack frowned. "This used to be my dad's place. He moved down to Oregon. His name's still on it, and the place is paid for – I just pay the property taxes and utilities on it by way of rent. It's left to me in his will and for all intents and purposes? It's *my* house but he left *a lot* of shit and it's only been up until recently that he's been cool with me getting rid of any of it."

"Ah," I murmured, a few things suddenly clicking.

"Yeah." Blackjack nodded. "Like yours, mine is a bit of a control freak."

I let out a breath surveying the jumble of boxes, totes and junk and said, "Where do we start?"

"I'm going to drop the tailgate on the truck, if you can post up by the door or someplace in the middle, I'm going to hand you shit. Anything I hand you, pitch it into the back of the truck and we'll make a dump run when it's full up," he said.

"Sounds like a good plan," I agreed.

We worked diligently and eventually, he passed me a five-gallon bucket that was brimming with rocks.

"Careful, this is heavy," he said and I took it and *yikes! Too much!* I set it down and frowned slightly at the rough chunks of stone in the bucket.

"These look like semi-precious of some kind, are you sure you want to get rid of these?" I asked.

"What am I gonna do with them?" he asked and passed me a milk crate that had a thick black cord piled on top. Through the loops I saw it.

"Oh, wow!" I cried and took the crate, setting it on the bucket. I moved the cord and got a little excited as I pulled up the rock tumbler.

It was heavy and the contents rattled. It was full of something.

"I know you're trying to ding this place out, but can I keep this?" I asked and looked up at him, holding my breath.

He stopped what he was doing and turned.

"What is it?" he asked.

"A rock tumbler and these are unprocessed – I don't know, something or other," I declared.

"You know how to work it?" he asked raising an eyebrow.

"Yeah," I said.

"If you can work it and you want to keep it, then yeah," he said.

"Where did you find this?" I asked.

"Over here, by me," he said and held out a hand to me. I straightened, leaving the bucket and the crate with its tumbler and barrels on top of it. I threaded my way through the weak pathway of junk and took Blackjack's rough, long fingered hand as he helped me step over a couple of more milk crates of what looked like auto parts of some kind.

"I'm trying to clear off and under this workbench right here," he said and he pointed on top of the thing. "That's where I found the crate, and under here was the first of what looks like a few random buckets and boxes," he said, stepping aside so I could look under the table.

"Oh!" I lunged a little excitedly at another crate hidden half behind one of the buckets and pulled on it, groaning a little and putting my back into it.

Blackjack laughed at me a little and said, "Here, let me do it."

"I've got it!" I cried and I did, but it was work. In the crate were old rusting coffee cans of raw rocks and faded plastic and woven bags of a plastic-like material of the various grits and polish needed to run the rock tumbler and smooth the stones.

"Everything's here!" I crowed. "I wonder why he left it." I looked up at him and he peered over my shoulder at the contents of the crates and buckets.

"I don't know. Your guess is as good as mine when it comes to my dad. He would do that shit, though. Get really into something and then all of a sudden just stop and move onto the next thing. Irritated the fuck out of my mom and was one of the reasons she ultimately divorced him and got remarried."

"Yeah?" I asked, sorting through the things and trying to identify what was what out of the rocks. It looked like there was some blue lace agate and some jasper. I wasn't sure about everything else. "Are you sure he wants to give this all up? There's a lot here!"

"He doesn't get a choice now. I'm not hauling it all the way down to Oregon and he's not fit enough to come get it. I love my dad, but I gotta get this place cleaned out. If you think you want it and that you could do something with all of it – by all means, you can have it, darlin'."

"Really?" I asked, twisting around and looking up at him.

"Really."

I chewed my bottom lip and nodded.

"I want it," I said. "I absolutely could polish it all up and do some stuff with it."

"Maybe start an online shop?" he asked with a nod. After a moment he said, "I'm surprised."

"What, that I know what all this is let alone that I know how to operate it?" I asked.

"Yeah."

I smiled and said, "We had this science teacher at the boarding school boot camp hybrid thing that my dad shipped me off to. One of the things we did was go out and do hard labor to build character, and learn to work together. We broke up rocks and then as part of our science classes we did some geology lessons and tumbled the stones and the like."

"Oh, shit. That sounds kind of shitty but you look happy about it," he said.

"Oh, parts of it *were* shitty," I said. "But I loved the learning and to watch the stones transform. One of the art teachers took the finished polished stones and showed us how to do wire wrapped jewelry out of it. I got really good at it. I guess it was one of the bright spots that was the dystopian hellscape that was that place." I made a face and Blackjack laughed a little.

"If it makes you happy, yeah. Keep it. Do whatever you want with it."

"Thank you," I said, looking over the small pile of things.

"Tell you what, we'll get this place cleaned up and dinged out and you can set up whatever you need to do right here."

I looked along the bench nodding slowly. There was an outlet right at bench height and an old shop sink next to it and I wondered out loud, "Does this thing work?"

"Don't know," he said. "Probably wouldn't take much to get it working, though."

"Water is a big part of the tumbling process, so it *would* be handy."

"Sure. We'll get it figured out."

"Okay." I smiled and got up, dusting off my knees.

He helped me over the crates and pulled me into him. I laughed and looked up at him and there was a strange look in his deep brown eyes as he searched my face. Something oh so serious, and yet undefinable. It didn't make me nervous though, in fact, if anything I gave me such a sense of peace.

"You know I just want you to know what it is to be happy for once, right?" he asked.

I smiled and nodded gently. "I know, and I'm working on that too... this is honestly the most content that I've felt in a while."

He smiled and lowered his mouth to mine and kissed me softly. I kissed him back, my arms twining around his neck and we just stood there for a little bit, his forehead pressed to mine, holding each other and speaking softly... and it was good.

It was really good.

~

THE DAYS BLED into one another, and before we knew it, the weekend was here, then it was over, and then it was almost midway through the following week, and then the next... and, well, you get the idea.

I had figured out the bus routes and had started at the new-to-me location of the grocery store chain that I'd previously checked at.

Blackjack wouldn't hear of me riding the bus after dark, and would have me wait, if need be, to pick me up on his way home from work, even if it was out of his way. I was grateful for that. As much as I wanted to feel normal, or empowered, or whatever, I wanted to feel safe and he made me feel safe.

I know, I know! It was probably ridiculously codependent of me, or something that any therapist would have a field day over – but baby steps, you know?

I was starting to feel better about things. More stable, and like I could start to climb out of the pit of confusion and despair I'd found myself in. We had gotten my number changed over that first weekend, which had given me back my music which helped *a lot,* and we'd cleaned up the rest of the garage to the tunes pouring from my phone which had made me happy.

At night, he touched me so gently and with such consideration. We didn't always have sex but when we did, it was the sweetest and most wonderful thing. I was quickly calming down and starting to feel content, so of course that would be when Devin showed up.

I had just finished my shift and was hurrying out to Blackjack and his waiting truck. I got in and he leaned over and captured my cheek gently with his palm, turning my face so his lips could find mine. I giggled and kissed him back in greeting and when I turned back to grab my seatbelt, I gasped.

"What's wrong?" he asked immediately, and I swallowed past the lump in my throat, my face hot, as I watched Devin disappear into the store.

"Please go," I said, and he scowled at me.

"Ember, what's the matter?" he asked.

"Just please go! Take us home!" I cried.

My phone rang and I fumbled it out of my jacket pocket. It was work, and I started to cry. I knew, I just knew...

"Hello?" I answered it and tried not to let my voice shake.

"Ember, it's Casey, have you gotten very far?" she asked innocently. *Shit! He knows!*

"Uh, yeah," I said. "Why?"

"Oh, your boyfriend is here. I'll tell him he just missed you."

Blackjack snatched the phone from my hand and said, "Yeah, no, *this* is her ol' man. You have no idea what you've just done. Put us on hold, tell the guy whatever you have to in order to get him to fuck off then get your manager on the line," he ordered.

He started his truck as I kept both my hands over my mouth to keep from keening in panic.

A few minutes later, Jordan, the store's manager came on the line.

"Ember, it's Jordan – I'm so sorry, we obviously didn't tell anyone about your situation and Casey didn't know."

"The fuck, Jordan?" Blackjack demanded as a sob bubbled out of me. "He knows she works there!"

"I know." Jordan sounded like he was at a loss.

"She's just a kid," I said, finally lowering my hands from my mouth.

I heard Jordan say piteously, "Oh, honey."

"Sorry not sorry, Jordan," Blackjack declared. "She quits. You can mail her last paycheck or do whatever the hell you do."

"No, I completely understand. I'll be calling an all staff meet—"

"I don't give a fuck what you do, just get Ember her money and give her a good fuckin' reference," he said. He hung up on him, swearing loudly as he threw my phone on the dash and piloted the big old work truck through the rain-soaked streets toward the hill that would take us up to his home.

I just cried, distraught.

"I don't know what to do," I said, and Blackjack shook his head.

Turning toward me and saying, "I got this. You let me worry about some things for now. Okay?"

"I'm so sorry," I whispered. "I'm so sorry!" I felt like it was all my fault somehow. That this whole time I had been somehow walking on thin ice and it had just cracked beneath me and I was plunging into frigid waters, the icy fear closing over my head making it impossible to breathe and the more panicked I became the more scared I became that Blackjack would be sick of my shit, of this shit, and would change his mind about me.

I knew that last thought was irrational but it was overwhelming in the face of seeing *that* face and knowing without a doubt that Devin was out there and still looking for me and that it would only be a matter of time before he had somehow found me and *what then?*

"It's okay, darlin'. Calm down." Blackjack threaded his fingers between mine and held my hand tight. "You're okay," he said. "He didn't see you. You're with me. You're *okay.*"

I couldn't describe the feeling I was having other than it really was like drowning while having my heart and my head in a vice at the same time and I just couldn't *breathe.*

Blackjack pulled into his driveway and threw the truck into 'park' and reached for me. Hauling me bodily across the bench seat and practically into his lap, crushing me to his chest, his hand in my hair, pressing my head over his heart as he pressed his lips to my hair and told me to breathe and to let it out at the same time.

"You cry, you scream, you have your fit, darlin'; for as long as you need," he said loudly over my choking and gasping panicked sobs and keening. "Then as soon as you're done, you gotta be done, okay? No unpacking and living here," he said and squeezed me tight.

"I've gotcha now," he said and I stopped trying to hold it all in, stopped trying to hold it back, and I just let the fear and the anger and the pain *destroy* me with the confidence that yes, this man would help me put it all back together. That it would take time, but his house was taking plenty of that, too…

18

*B*lackjack...

I was fuckin' pissed. Furious. I wanted to walk in there and beat the fuck out of him, pull out my gun and put him down like the fuckin' rabid ass animal that he was – but that wouldn't have done shit for my girl, who was my priority. Protecting her was my *top* priority, and as much as I wanted an immediate solution to that assclown, I needed to be patient.

As soon as her wailing had calmed to hiccupping sobs, I knew the storm of emotion that'd swamped her was almost petered out. Those hiccupping sobs turned to sniffles as I rocked her gently in the truck, and soon the pattering of the rain on the metal roof drowned even those out.

She made to sit up and pull away from me and I held her a little tighter and said, "Relax. Not just yet."

"Okay," she warbled weakly, but I could tell she was soaking up this comfort like a sponge. As far as love languages went, touch seemed to be hers and she couldn't get enough. She'd been deprived too long, for *so long*, and when that asshole had deigned to touch her toward the end there, it'd been to hit her.

"I guess I got lucky," she said with a bitter broken laugh.

"How's that?" I asked her.

"That we saw him but he didn't see me."

"Yeah, I think that technically *he* got lucky with that one. He said one word to you, I would have killed him."

"I wish you could," she said, and she was dead serious.

I grunted non-committedly. Our phones were on and near us. I didn't need to casually admit out loud that I was premeditating his unseemly demise.

"Sorry, that was really stupid and shitty of me to say," she said, pushing off of me. "I can be so dumb sometimes."

"Hey!" I said sternly, but I didn't bark at her. She jumped anyway and stared at me with wide, red-rimmed eyes.

Shit, all she had to do was *see* him at a distance and she was right back to being down on herself and trash talking herself like that.

"We'll deal with what you just said later. Right now, let's get you inside, cleaned up, and fed. In that order."

"Alright," she murmured and she looked like she deflated a little.

"Good girl," I murmured, and she perked just a little bit. "Wait there, let me get your door."

I got out, dragging my cut behind me off the seat from between us. She waited obediently as I swung into it and went around the front of my truck to get her door for her.

I opened it up and helped her down to the rev of an engine over the rainfall. I don't know what made my senses tingle. I don't know why I reacted the way I did, but I did, shoving her down, pulling my piece, and pointing as rounds popped off from the end of the drive.

I was vaguely aware of those rounds thunking into the siding of my house and one or two pinging off my truck as I shot back. I hit the car, one of the back windows shattering even as Ember screamed, her hands clapped over her ears. I dragged her up by her arm and dragged her back toward the front door of the house, barking orders at her to get up and *move, move, move!*

She complied, her panicked mind grabbing onto my words by some miracle as the car swung around out in the cul-de-sac and shot off like a rocket out to the street.

I swore and got the door unlocked and open cursing like a moth-erfucker and shoving Ember through.

"Stay away from the fuckin' window!" I yelled and she immediately plastered herself to the floor.

I got my phone out of the inside of my jacket and dialed.

I crouched down next to her and shoving my phone between my shoulder and my ear patted a hand over her.

"You hit?" I demanded, and she looked up at me. "Are you hit!?" I practically screamed and she cried back, "No! No, I'm okay! Are you?"

"I'm fine!" I said and put a lock on my fuckin' temper as best that I could.

"Fuck!" I shouted. I pulled the phone down and dialed Cipher since Mav hadn't picked up.

"Yo?" Cipher answered.

"Call the guys," I said. "Motherfucker just shot up my house!"

"What?" he demanded.

"Ember's ex just drove by my house and took shots at us in my fuckin' driveway, man!"

"On it." Cipher hung up on me.

"Just stay down for a few minutes, darlin'," I said low as she huddled in on herself and cried, trembling uncontrollably.

I heard fucking sirens.

Shit! One of the neighbors had to have called the cops.

"Well, this just got more complicated," I grunted and Ember looked up at me.

"What do you mean?" she asked.

"Nothing, baby. Just whatever the cops ask you, you tell 'em the truth. Okay?"

"What?" she asked.

"Just tell 'em the truth," I said, knowing in this case, there wasn't anything that could hurt me about the truth.

"I'm so sorry," she said. She was blanched a whiter shade of pale.

"Not your fault," I said. "It's mine for not noticing we had a tail."

I emptied and took apart my gun. They would take it. That was fine. I had plenty more.

"What happens now?" she asked, ashen.

"Now we wait," I said. "No matter what happens after that, you know I've got you," I said. "Right?" I fixed her gaze with mine and she nodded rapidly.

Blue and white lights lit up the outside of my place, strobing through the curtains across the front bay window.

"Civilian Cavalry is here," I remarked dryly as someone at the front door announced, "Police!"

"Yeah!" I called. "In here, nobody's hit! We're fine!" I had my gun in pieces on the ground and my hands up where the pigs could see them as they came into the house.

"Ma'am?" the one in front asked. "You alright?"

"Yeah!" Ember cried a little breathy.

"Neither one of us got hit," I declared. "I returned fire, gun's right here in pieces. Don't shoot me."

Fuck this was going to be a long night.

THE REAL CAVALRY took longer to show up just because of the fuckin' distance they had to work with. When they did show up, my house was officially a fuckin' crime scene out front and they were corralled by the bacon, which wasn't that a fuckin' joke.

I was hassled, but only minimally. They didn't really have a leg to stand on. I was a vet, legal to carry, and on my own property so they could fuck all the way off with their lectures and bullshit.

They were taking my favorite every day carry gun as evidence and for ballistics or whatever. They wanted to sweep the house for more weapons which is where the hassle came in. I didn't want to give them permission to search my place so they could overreach. Not that they would find anything if they did except a bunch of legally owned guns and ammo – I just wasn't keen on giving up any of my Fourth Amendment rights.

"...and you're sure it was your ex-boyfriend?" the cop asked.

"Who else could it be?" Ember demanded harshly.

The cop looked up from his notepad and directly at me and I made a rude noise, disgusted.

"You hear hoofbeats, you automatically think it's a zebra?" I demanded, and the cop scowled at me and looked back down at his notepad, scribbling something down.

Ember was staring at me plaintively, her hair bedraggled and hanging lank around her face, her shoulders wrapped in the blanket off the back of my couch. The heels of her hands were scraped and bloody and there was some blood seeping through the knee of her khaki work pants which didn't appear to have any holes in them but were dirty and wet from making contact with the driveway.

"I wouldn't recommend you stay here tonight," the cop said uselessly. Like, *no shit, Sherlock.* Jesus Christ.

"It's fine," I said. "We've got someplace to go, or did you miss the growing crowd of my brothers outside?" I asked.

The cop snapped his notebook closed, handed Ember a card and then came over to me and handed me one.

"Your case number, we'll be in touch if we find anything during the course of our investigation or if we need anything more from either of you."

"Pfft!" I scoffed. I knew that was a lie. This shit would get swept right under the rug and ignored except as maybe a catalyst to look into the club and dig deep trying to make this some type of gangland bullshit thing.

The heat had been up kinda high on the Sacred Hearts Prescription Drug Plan for a while but we'd finally gotten out from under that spotlight and now, here we were with a whole new one trained on us.

I looked to Ember who looked resigned.

Ol' boy was gonna die slow and in a lot of pain.

I was hoping sooner rather than later, but I would just have to wait and see about that.

As much as I was *not* a patient man in some aspects, on this I was going to be forced to be.

The cops were being sort of adamant that we should clear out tonight which made me want to dig my heels, but ultimately, I asked Ember what she wanted.

She looked up at me, her eyes glassy with shock, her body trembling from the adrenaline crash and said, "I don't want to run anymore."

I nodded and said, "That's my girl." I told the cops to get the fuck outta my house and let my boys in. That we were gonna be fine. Which we were. The likelihood of her ex-fuckboi pain in the ass trying to take another swing after that miss was minimal. Couple that with the fact that I knew Mav and the rest wouldn't be leaving? Yeah, there honestly weren't no place safer. If dipshit *did* pop back up tonight, he'd have a nasty surprise waiting for him. There would be more of us and a full show of force and it'd get ugly for him real damn quick.

"Hey." Cipher was one of the first of the guys through my front door. "I thought of something," he said without any preamble. "Let me see your girl's phone."

"Darlin'?" I looked down at her on one of my kitchen chairs. The cops had pulled it outta my back room and set it in the mouth of the kitchen where the living room laminate transitioned into the kitchen tile. I hand an arm around her shoulders and rubbed up and down her arm to try and help calm her shivering.

She handed her phone to Cipher without a word.

"Unlock it for me first, baby," he said with a reckless half-grin.

She did, and he went past us, wandering into the back room to sit at my table. Mav, Fen, and DT were in my living room, Deacon coming in the door behind Squatch, Nine and Major right behind him.

"Everybody showing up?" I asked and Mav threw me some chin.

"Fuck yeah, everybody's comin'," he declared.

"The fuck you think was gonna happen you put out the call someone shot up our boy's house?" Fenris demanded.

"Let me get Ember cleaned up and settled," I said. "Church?" I asked Mav.

"As soon as everybody gets here, I'll send somebody to come an' get you with the phones."

I nodded and helped Ember to her feet. She hissed, probably a little stiff from being shoved over and eating my driveway with her hands and knees.

"I'm going to clean up these scrapes and settle her in," I said and the guys nodded.

"Back room looks good," Dump Truck declared with a nod. He'd passed us and stood at the threshold through the kitchen.

I gave a nod.

"Thanks, man."

I took Ember back to our room, her things all sorted and put away, candles on the end tables and dresser, all being amassed a little at a time. When they were all lit, it was something magical in here and made making love to her all the sweeter. I hadn't really gone deep into making her mine, yet. She still needed time and healing and I was afraid at how far she'd come and how badly this incident would set her back.

"C'mere, let me have this," I murmured taking the blanket from around her shoulders and laying it atop the footlocker at the foot of my bed.

She wrapped her arms around my waist and buried her face in my chest and breathed in deeply. She didn't cry, but I think that was honestly the fact that she was just done plumb cried the fuck out and didn't have any reserves left.

"I was so scared you were going to get hurt," she said. Her voice cracking, the sound of it muffled against my chest... but her words reverberated through my ribs, resonating in my heart and echoing in its chambers. They suffused me with a warmth and determination that neither I nor she would ever be hurt by this son of a bitch. In her case, ever again.

"Everything's going to be okay, baby. I promise." I held her tight, pressing her head to my chest and kissing her hair. "Let's get you cleaned up and dressed for bed, okay?"

She breathed in a long slow deep breath and let it out in a

measured sigh, nodding.

"I'm exhausted," she said, and I nodded.

"I bet. Now come on now." I led her into the bathroom and worked the hidden button free on her khaki pants.

She shrugged out of her jacket and light hoodie beneath it, wincing as her raw and scraped hands made contact with the material. I wanted to get a look at the injuries I couldn't readily see, namely the nasty scrape on her knee.

I dropped her pants and went for the hem of her work polo before she could, gripping the hem and saying softly, "Arms up," as though I were undressing a child. Which to be fair, I had a suspicion that a lot of the shadow work and healing that Ember needed was in regard to nurturing her inner child – and yeah, that'd been a long talk with Raven and Deacon. I was a savage, crayon snacking, motherfucker whose main form of communication was a series of caveman grunts. I *was* a grunt. I did *not* come up with that all on my own.

Still, I knew when certain things were above my paygrade and the trauma that she'd gone through was so very different from mine.

Still, every time that I thought I couldn't fuckin' do something when it came to her, I flashed on that image of her precariously balanced on the edge of that big freeway sign, over the railing of that overpass, and I knew that I could. I had already done so much – I just needed to do a little bit more.

"Okay, darlin', hop up for me," I murmured backing her up against the edge of the bathroom counter. She winced, but complied, leaving a smear of blood from her hands on the edge of the counter which made me feel like an ass, but it was honestly the most comfortable I thought I could make the both of us while I cleaned her up.

"Just like that," I said gently and laid her hands atop her thighs palm up. "Good girl."

Her eyes fluttered shut and she seemed to relax just a little bit at the small praise as I got under the bathroom sink for the first aid med kit. I dug through it for some peroxide and clean gauze, setting out some triple anti-biotic ointment and some Band-aids I thought might work.

She sat still, wincing only a few times as I cleaned up her hand and she murmured, "I was really surprised Jordan was so okay with just being like 'nope, yep, you quit I get it,' rather than trying to talk me into staying or something."

"Nah," I said. "I met him the one time, and he was pretty decent. A corporate yes man, sure, but that's any manager to a degree. He seemed more human than humans deserve credit for lately."

She chuckled and it held a slight edge of bitterness, "Yeah, well, I don't much like the feeling of being unemployed."

"One thing at a time, darlin'. You been through a shock, and I know your mind is going a mile a minute, but this isn't something you need to think about *right now*."

She nodded, and I tipped her chin up with a gentle finger beneath it, she looked up at me, eyes a bit wide.

"I know you want to pay your own way, and you will. You'll get there and get caught up and all of that. Rome wasn't built in a day," I reminded her. "You got some really nice stuff going on out there in the garage with that rock setup, and you got rocks out there for *days*. Why don't you do an online store or something?"

It was something she had brought up and she *did* have all the supplies now. I'd insisted on her getting her wires and pliers and whatever she needed with a chunk of her first paycheck after getting back working again. To do something nice for herself, and it hadn't really cost much in the grand scheme of things.

She was quiet for a bit and finally conceded, "You're right. I probably don't need to worry about it or stress right now."

"There's a good girl," I said, smiling wide.

She smiled up at me and I brought my mouth to hers, kissing her softly, crumpling the Band-aid wrappers from her hand in my fist and getting ready to throw them in the bathroom trash.

"Hm, let's get that bra off you," I said.

"Okay."

"And into one of my tee shirts," I added.

She smiled a bit smugly. Most of the time, I wouldn't let her put anything on for bed if she'd let me get away with it. Even going so far as to argue the point. If she wasn't willing to bend or wasn't feeling it, the compromise had been to put her in one of my shirts because, let's face it, aside from your girl being nude up against you, the vision of her in your shirt and little of nothing else was the next best thing.

"Wait here," I murmured after unclasping and slipping her out of her bra. I ditched her clothes in the hamper and went out to my side of the dresser I pulled out one of my old military-reg tees, that brown that wasn't quite olive but wasn't quite brown either and returned to her. I helped her into it like a child and took pleasure in the simple act of caring for my woman.

I helped her off the counter, and she stood patiently waiting for me to tuck her in while I cleaned up and put everything away. Something that she constantly rode me about and she was right.

I appreciated how in such a scant few weeks she had improved my life so much around here, and even though I knew with the front of my brain, my own secret squirrel insecurities still played up and made me think, *I hope I do enough for her...*

I pulled the shirt down around her hips and she came in for another hug. I held her for a little while and just let her soak it up, while truth be told I soaked it up, too. Smoothing my hands over the soft material of the tee, feeling the warmth of her body radiating through it, and knowing that shit could have gone bad, *real* bad; and that if one of those bullets had had her name on it, there wasn't shit I'd be able to do about it.

I flashed back then, the vision playing out behind my eyelids of the ones a half a world away that I couldn't protect and that I couldn't save.

Ember's slim arms around, me, crushing me to her, did very little to repel the wave of guilt that rushed me in that moment, but they did give me a line to cling to, so that when it receded, I wasn't swept away and out to drown like I normally was when this type of shit hit me.

I cuddled her close and held her tight and let myself crack for just a split second, breathing in deep and blinking away my own tears before she could see them. I cleared my throat of the lump that was trying to root itself in it and said, "Come on, I'll lay down with you for a few minutes. Just until you fall asleep."

"I'd like that," she murmured and moved away just enough to let me take her into the bedroom and lift the blankets.

She climbed into the bed just as a knock fell at the door and I looked back to her. She smiled up at me bravely and said, "Go, don't leave them waiting. I can wait."

I nodded and leaned down, tucking her in and kissing her lightly on the lips.

"Try to get some sleep," I ordered and she nodded.

"I will."

I left her and it wasn't easy. Out in the hall, Fenris stood, and he looked like a tempest had taken up in his blue eyes.

"Church," he said and thrust a mixing bowl at me full of everyone's phones and burners. I nodded and took the bowl and dug my phones out dumping them in. I opened the door to one of the former guest rooms that was being transformed into a sort of office space for me and I set the bowl on the corner of the desk.

Once the door was shut and we were back in the hall Fen said, "This motherfucker is as good as dead, bro. I'll carve his ass up but good."

I nodded and said, "Something I need to know?" because it sure as hell sounded like some new shit had come to light.

"Cipher'll tell you. We're all here," he said. I nodded.

"Let's do it."

We went into my back room off the kitchen and I found the whole of my club, minus Tic of course, sitting or standing around my table.

"Just what the fuck happened?" Derry demanded and I could tell he was late to the party but that was alright – he was here.

I explained everything while Mav sat back in his seat looking thoughtful, doing the math and the calculations for shit way beyond just this situation.

"Well, this certainly fucks a whole lotta shit up," he said finally.

"How so?" Nine asked, and Major was like, "Man you need to slow down on hittin' the green. Cops are gonna be up our ass tryin' to blame this on gang shit or whatever. A beef with another club, some-thin'. They won't wanna chalk this shit up to a bitch ass ex-boyfriend."

We were all silent for a time and Mav heaved a sigh.

"Eastern Washington ain't in a position to take point. Idaho is our next best bet for getting the shit down over the border."

"Fuck, they're club but you trust Hemlock and his boys with that?" Derry asked.

"You know something we don't?" Glass demanded.

"Nah, not really," Derry said. "Those boys are survivalist types. Off-grid doomsday prepper keeping to themselves more than I ever seen anyone else in any other chapters of the club do. It rubbed my old P the wrong way—"

"Fuck your old P – he was a greedy bastard and a traitor to this club," Fenris said with some venom.

"I'm not saying he's not," Derry said looking thoughtful.

"Let me ask you somethin'," Mav said. "The misgivings over Idaho, are they *your* misgivings or it is just a ghost of loyalties past kind of a thing? Which, no one can or will fault you if it's the latter, bro."

Derry looked thoughtful. Like hella thoughtful, and finally said, "I guess it's the latter. Idaho may be secretive to a point and keep to their own but they've never done anything out of order and I can't say the same for my old chapter."

Mav inclined his head and the rest of us were thoughtful.

"Man, I'm sorry guys," I said, shaking my head. "I never imagined that this would turn into... well, *this*."

"It's a clusterfuck, for sure," Dump Truck declared. "But it's *our* clusterfuck now and ain't nobody around this table going to fault you for saving that girl and if they do and they wanna say it out loud, they can take me on if they want."

I looked across to him and gave a nod.

"So... what do we wanna do, boys?" Mav asked, sighing.

It was going to be a long fuckin' night the rate this was going, but all I kept telling myself was she was right down the hall, tucked into my bed, and as safe as she was gonna get with me and all of my brothers here.

19

*E*mber...

  I didn't even wake when he came to bed, and I woke long before he did. I lay beside him, watching him sleep, his face slack and losing the hard edge he maintained when he was awake. He was so tired he didn't even stir when I moved some of his long brown hair out of his face and pressed my lips to his forehead.

I got up, showered and dressed in comfortable clothes just to wear around the house, and I went out to the kitchen to make some coffee.

That's how I discovered there were still several of the men from his club around the house.

One was in the guest bedroom, the door left open to where I could see them. I found another crashed on the couch and Dump Truck was sitting at the table in the back dining room/sunroom off the kitchen reading a book.

"Hi," I said softly so as to not wake anyone else sleeping.

"Hey, how you doing, sweetheart?" he asked.

"Ah, I'm fine, I guess," I said, and he chuckled.

"Glad to hear it, glad to hear it," he said and put a strip of paper in the book to hold his place. I smiled when I realized it was some kind of romance novel.

"Is there coffee?" I asked and he took in a deep breath and stretched his massive arms way up over his head.

"No, but I would sure appreciate some. I'm sure some of the boys out front would too," he declared.

"How many of you are here?" I asked, a bit taken aback.

"Six," he said. "Two out front, me in here, you got Nine on the couch, Mace is racked out in the spare bedroom and Major's out back having a toke."

"Oh," I said. "You all stayed?"

"Damn right," he said with a nod.

"Thank you," I murmured.

"Don't mention it," he said. "You belong to Blackjack, that makes you family now."

The words suffused me with a warm glow and I smiled and nodded, trying not to get misty eyed or too emotional as I went over to get the coffee maker started.

I took coffee out back to Major and out front to Fenris and Derry. I let the others sleep and after making up a cup of my own, I slipped off to the garage to try and work on something, the stuff Blackjack had said about making my own pendants and things to sell online sticking with me.

I took a seat on the high stool at the workbench my rock tumbler and supplies resided on and under and sighed. My gaze wandered to the point of light coming through the garage door where a fresh bullet hole let it in. I shuddered and stared at it for a long time, listening to the two men talk outside of it. I couldn't make out a lot of their conversation but it was mostly about motorcycles and guns anyway that I could tell from the pieces of it my ears did snatch from the air.

I thought back to what Dump Truck had said in the kitchen... *You belong to Blackjack, that makes you family now...*

I mean, I felt like that should have scared me somehow, the idea of *belonging* to another man like property, especially after the way Devin had treated me as such but the way Devin treated me and the way Blackjack did – it was *worlds* of fucking difference!

Blackjack was kind, careful, wanted to know what I was thinking and feeling and took his time with me – and I wasn't just talking sexually. I meant in every aspect of our relationship. It felt so deep with him, so complete, and I knew beyond any shadow of a doubt that I could trust him. Because he had *never* let me down on anything big – at least not so far, and when it did come to the small stuff, if he did something that bothered me, he wouldn't let me pass it off or say that things were just fine and ignore it.

I'd actually garnered my first punishment that way. Had been made to sit at the table and write *'my feelings matter'* over and over again until I'd started to cry. I didn't even really know why I was crying! I mean, I wasn't hurt or upset… but he'd come to me when the sniffles had become too frequent as he'd worked in the kitchen to cook our dinner and he had crouched down and held me, and had ended the punishment once I'd affirmed that I wouldn't hide my feelings or brush them aside anymore for him or anyone else.

That I didn't have to do that anymore.

I sighed, and looked at the polished rocks that had come from the first tumbler, the one I'd found in the crate. The one I had finished only days ago. A shiny pile of tumbled rose quartz and amethyst sitting in two separate containers, sorted and waiting for me to do something with the silver, copper, and gold wire standing by.

I stared at everything in front of me and didn't really move. My thoughts consumed about how much I was beginning to love my new life and how very close I had come to losing it last night.

So very *close…*

I mean, it felt like a miracle that neither one of us had been hit.

I swung my attention back to that pinpoint of light coming through the small hole in the garage door and I fought not to crumble around the edges.

"Hey, darlin.'"

I jumped slightly and twisted in my seat toward the door leading from the garage out here into the house. Blackjack was standing at the top of the two wooden steps, his hair foaming around his face, shirtless, barefoot, the top button of his jeans undone looking absolutely *delicious*. Like one of the men that belonged on the cover of Dump

Truck's romance novels, only he was real and the smoldering look he held he had fixed on *me*.

"Hey," I said softly.

"What 'cha got going on up there?" he asked, coming into the garage and stepping lightly across the cleaned-out space to come touch me. I closed my eyes and relished the contact of his rough palm against the side of my neck, the way his thumb stroked under my jaw, and especially the way that when we were being playful? That hand would capture my throat and drag my mouth to his, or how his long fingers would snake up into the back of my hair and *grip*... God, I loved when he did that. My body responding automatically, losing tension, submitting to that insistent touch and how I knew to the bottom of my soul that it was okay and that I was safe with him.

"Baby?" he asked.

I smiled, knowing it was brittle, and said, "Nothing much, really. Was just thinking."

"Talk to me," he said, stepping into me, and he lightly threaded his fingers up into my hair beneath my messy bun and massaged my neck where it met the base of my skull, his gaze fixed on me, looking down from what felt like a great height with how he stood and I sat. Imperious, like all I need to was whisper my desire and he would go and fulfill it... but I didn't want him to go. At least, not right at the moment. No, I wanted desperately for him to stay. To stay and love me, which I knew was a little irrational given the circumstances.

"I feel like I almost lost you last night. Be it you or me that could have been shot... I feel like I was so close to losing everything on that overpass only to be given this almost miraculous opportunity in meeting you and he almost took it away last night."

"Yeah, well, your phone out here?" he asked.

I shook my head which was a little difficult with how he held the back of my neck but he let me do it.

"Well, it's going to be the last thing he ever does, darlin'. You just say the word and we'll disappear him."

"What word?" I asked. "Please? Because *please*... I don't want to lose everything now and I don't think he'll stop. Even if he *does* stop, I don't want him to move on to some other girl... I know, I shouldn't play God..."

"Hush, baby. It's not playing God. This is a fight between two men, he made his choice and declared war against a man that's well versed in it. That was his second mistake."

"Second? He's made so many I don't know what the first, third, or even billionth would be."

Blackjack chuckled and kissed my temple, putting his lips close to my ear and whispering, "His first was treating you like anything but the absolute goddess you are."

His voice was something low and primal and sent a shiver down my spine. He felt me move and his chuckle was low and dark, equally primal and decadent.

I swallowed hard, and he said, "I'm going to make you orgasm until you forget how to breathe and the only feeling you have is *free*."

I closed my eyes and told the truth, "I would like that very much."

He pressed his lips to my hairline and breathed me in before relinquishing his hold on my neck.

"Soon, I promise."

I smiled up at him and asked, "In the meantime, what happens now?"

"Now I let these guys go home to get some real fuckin' sleep if I can."

Which, in fact, he could not. Stubborn to the last, the boys wouldn't budge.

I made myself busy around the house with cleaning and regular chores. It was as clean as it could get, every room neat and orderly after a month of evenings and weekends spent working on it.

Blackjack's motorcycle could be pulled into the garage and *gasp* he could even work on it in there now. His tools and toolbox against the back wall and organized. We'd hung the peg board we'd found among the junk and had hung a bunch of his household tools and work tools on it. I'd even outlined them all in black marker so everything had its home.

I made dinner that night and he stood in the kitchen with me, each of us doing this well-choreographed dance of my cooking and his cleaning up after me so there would be less to do after dinner.

The meal was good, made better by company as it was decided that they would stay tonight, some trading out with others from the club after dinner and that if nothing happened or there wasn't anything suspicious, they would carve things down by the weekend.

I just wanted my peace to return.

I hadn't realized how in love with it I had become in such a short amount of time and I would do anything to have it back.

I was done being scared, and I was simply angry now. My rage simmering just below the surface, but not to the point any little thing set me off. No, this was a strange and especially concentrated anger that was tempered like fine steel by the knowledge that something *would* be done about it this time.

It may take time, and I may have some more bullshit to put up with in the interim, but Devin would be dealt with.

"I still feel like shit I didn't think to have Cipher check your fucking phone," Blackjack said unhappily.

"I didn't think about it either," I said as we sat around the table after dinner.

"Don't beat yourselves up too hard," Dump Truck said, as Blackjack's phone went off with a notification. He'd checked it every time today. His security system had caught everything. His cameras trained on the cul-de-sac, which had been another thing that he sort of regretted now. It meant that the police had more leads to go on and would be more involved dragging things out longer.

"Looks like someone's relief is here, boys," he said, looking at his phone as the chug of a motorcycle's engine filtered in from out front.

"If nobody minds, I'd like to get back home to my Little Bird." Dump Truck threw his wadded-up paper towel napkin on his plate and leaned back, stretching.

"No, man. Go. The rest of the watch change will be here any minute," Derry said.

"Good deal," he said and hoisted himself to his feet.

"Goodnight," I murmured. "Thank you."

"Anytime, sweetheart," he said and then stopped. "On second thought, let's not do that again, though. Okay?"

I giggled and nodded, agreeing. It still seemed so surreal still. My emotions still riding a roller coaster, and it was a sort of hell ride I wished I could get off of.

"Darlin', why don't you go on in, get a hot shower, and ready for bed for me, okay?" Blackjack requested gently.

I nodded and went to do as he asked, bidding everyone else a good night and an extra thanks for having stayed, most of them taking off of work to do so.

"The fuck are you doin' here?" I heard from the living room.

"I got word, rode all day to get here, the pass was a fuckin' mess." I looked over to the voice of a newcomer I didn't recognize. "You okay, bro?" the man was blond and curly headed with a straw goatee.

"Yeah, man. We're alright," Blackjack said hugging the blond man and pounding him on the back.

"Shit, is there food?" the man asked.

I silently dished him up a plate while he ran through hugging the rest of the club's men that I *did* know, like he hadn't seen any of them in a while.

I set the plate of food on the table along with silverware and a piece of paper towel as a napkin and began to quietly gather up plates, listening to the men talk.

"This her?" the blond man asked.

"Yeah, Ember, sorry I didn't mean to be a rude asshole, this is Tic-Tac, we all call him Tic."

I tilted my head and stopped myself from asking just in time but his green eyes sparkled with mischief as he reached out and took my hand to shake it.

"It's because I'm hung like a half-eaten Tic-Tac," he said and the guys laughed. I admit, I did too at the visual.

"Okay," I said. "Ember, it's nice to meet you."

"Glad you and BJ are okay," he said.

"Me too."

"Ember," Blackjack said, raising his chin and looking down at me from across the kitchen.

"Right." I blushed slightly and said, "Bath time for me, and then bed."

Tic-Tac winked at me and relinquished my hand and said, "Daddy has spoken, huh?"

"Goodnight, everybody," I stammered as I turned red as a beet. I shut my mouth and made my exit to more laughter. I paused at the mouth of the hallway and looked back to Blackjack who winked at me.

"Oh, shit. Thank you, Ember. I'm starved!" I heard Tic-Tac say as one of the kitchen chairs scraped and I presumed he took a seat at the table.

I went down the hall and into our room and shut the door behind me, sighing.

I remembered the rest of the girls at Cipher's saying that Tic had been temporarily banished for bad behavior. That he was helping the new chapter in Eastern Washington build some and that it had all been very messy and had involved a woman named Dahlia who even after a month, I had yet to meet.

I felt a tension I hadn't realized I'd been holding in my shoulders and back ease some once the door to the bedroom was shut behind me, shutting out the dim buzz of their conversation with it.

I went into the bathroom and started up the shower with a sigh, stripping and hanging what I was wearing on the hook behind the door intending to wear it again tomorrow since it'd really only been gently worn around the house today.

I stepped in under the spray and lived under the hot water for a while. When I was done, I got out and toweled off, wrapping myself in it to stand before the mirror to blow dry my hair.

Blackjack must have come in, because the bathroom door had been shut.

When I shut off the hairdryer and set it aside, the bathroom door opened and Blackjack poked his head in.

He opened his mouth to speak as I ran my brush through my hair and I stared at his reflection in the mirror, but he didn't say anything. Instead, he closed his mouth and a strange look came over his face. He let his eyes wander over my back and then his dark eyes flickered to mine, meeting them in the big mirror against the wall.

He stepped into the bathroom and my mouth went slightly dry as the air was sucked out of my lungs, which is just the affect it had on me every time that I saw him naked.

He came up to me, and ripped my towel away, spinning me by my shoulders to turn around and face him; stepping into me and thrusting a knee between mine so my sex was pressed against the top of his thigh. He grabbed twin handfuls of my hair at the back, fisting my hair, pulling my head back in that way that made me moan and my muscles turn to liquid letting go *all* of their tension as he covered my mouth with his.

His tongue plunged into my mouth, past my lips and teeth to stroke against my own with this strong sensuality and I melted into him as a result.

He pulled his mouth from mine, fists still in my hair, controlling my head as he growled into my ear, "My dirty girl's all clean just in time for me to make her absolutely *filthy*, isn't she?"

A "Yes, sir," slipped from my lips, breathy as I felt my body loosen up elsewhere, and I fought not to dry hump his leg like a horny teenage girl.

"You trust me, darlin'?" he asked me, drawing back to look down into my eyes.

"Yes, sir," I answered him and he searched my face.

"You know your safe word, yeah?" he asked and I nodded, his hands tightened in my hair and I sucked in a breath and said it out loud for him.

"Good girl," he murmured. "Now go lay down in the center of the bed."

He let me go, loosening my hair and lowering his leg stepping back from me.

I felt a little strange. This was the most intense exchange we had thus far to date and my heart beat faster than a hummingbird's wings in my breast. I felt tingly all over, half of me 'here' the other half feeling like I should bolt, I should run, far, far, away but I knew that was just lizard brain fight or flight from the intensity of what I was feeling.

I trusted Blackjack. I knew he didn't mean me any harm, still, I froze up a little at the edge of the bed when I saw the restraints at the head of it.

"Ember..." his voice was right behind me and I spooked, jumping slightly in my own skin.

"It's okay, baby. I'm sorry, I'll put them away," he said soothingly, and I swallowed hard.

"No," I said, turning and sitting down, scooting myself back into the center of the bed and laying down as he'd instructed.

"You're not ready for this, I can see it—" he argued and I cut him off.

"I know my safe word," I reminded him.

He cocked his head, looking down at me, and I could see the calculations behind his eyes.

"You know I would never hurt you, right?" he asked.

"I know," I said and raised my arms over my head.

He nodded sagely and went for it, undoing the Velcro on the soft restraints and wrapping my wrist, first one, then the other, snugly; affixing the Velcro around the outside to itself to hold it closed.

I closed my eyes as a different sensation settled over me, a light tingle of fear but not fear, the same kind you got when you were on an amusement park ride or going through a haunted house.

He leaned down and kissed me, and I relaxed some more, kissing him back as he trailed rough fingertips down my body in light streaks that left me writhing just a bit and giggling into his mouth as he lingered on the ticklish spot that he knew my ribs harbored.

I felt him smile against my mouth and he pulled back and asked me, "You think you're brave enough for a blindfold?"

"A blindfold?" I asked a little breathless from his kiss.

"Mm-hm." He searched my face.

I asked, "What for?"

"Take away one sense it heightens the rest," he murmured, and I scraped my bottom lip between my teeth.

"Okay," I whispered and he nodded and brought one out of the drawer of the nightstand next to his bed. A satin one, black and like a sleep mask. That wasn't so bad.

"Lift your head," he ordered gently and I did. He slipped it over my eyes.

Everything was plunged into darkness and I felt... better. Sort of strangely safer, but at the same time it was like all of my nerves came alive with that low, anticipatory, electric hum.

"Spread those legs for me, darlin'," he said in that low and seductive tone of his as I felt the bed dip somewhere down low around my right foot.

I parted my legs and felt him settle between them. I jumped slightly at the light, probative touch of his fingers at the mouth of my pussy as he teased me, his groan of gratification at finding me wet doing something to me that guaranteed he would be finding more of what he was looking for momentarily.

"Look at how beautiful you are," he murmured. "This pretty little pussy laid bare for me..." I jumped again as he kissed the inside of my thigh and slid a finger up inside of me. I cried out a little and writhed to take him in a little further. I couldn't ever seem to get enough of this man touching me.

"You like that?" he asked, voice low and intense, like the finely vibrating steel of a sword blade after impact.

"Yes," I said breathy.

"Yes, what?" he demanded, flexing his fingers inside me and teasing that spot that he just seemed to know exactly where it was.

"Yes, sir!" I cried.

"Hmm, good girl," he murmured and then his warm, wet mouth was on my clit and I was crying out and arching, his shoulders blocking my reflexive action of trying to close my knees.

He worked at me, me struggling at my bonds to bring my arms down, to what purpose I didn't know... I couldn't tell if my reflexes wished to grip his hair and pull him closer or the intensity of what he was doing to me made me want to try and stop him, to push him away.

He pressed down low on my belly between the ridges of my pelvic bone ever so slightly and whatever he touched inside me went from sparks to full raging inferno. I cried out, and he tongued my clit in the sweetest torture I'd ever endured and before I knew it, I was crashing back down to the bed, body jerking over and over with wave after wave of orgasm that tore through me with the force of a tsunami.

I cried out and collapsed panting as he let up from where he pressed on my lower belly and stroked his hand up to palm my breast. He stopped with his mouth on my clit and pumped his fingers in and out of me slowly, keeping the waves going, but the intensity less – he wouldn't stop though and I tried to close my knees and turn to my side, panting.

"Ember, stop…" he ordered, and his voice was still that steel, although it had become molten somehow. "Keep your legs open, darlin', or I'll tie them too. I promised you orgasms until you couldn't think and I aim to deliver."

"I'm sorry!" I panted and forced my knees open.

"I need to tie them too?" he asked, and I knew the answer and told the truth.

"Yes."

"Good girl," he said, his hand leaving from inside of me, his weight coming off the bed. "Thank you for telling me the truth."

The sound of Velcro tearing and he said, "Bring your knees up to your chest."

I did as I was told and felt the soft material of the new restraint, not around my ankle like I expected, but around my *thigh*.

He strapped me up and open, my thighs up, my pussy and asshole exposed, first one side and then the other before he returned to his position between my legs.

"Okay, we'll try this again," he said and his voice held a deep lingering lust I don't think I'd ever heard before. "God, I love looking at you like this. You're so fucking sexy; so fucking beautiful…"

My breath caught but not for long and then his fingers were back inside of me, his mouth back on me, and he was taking me back up into the stars all over again, slower this time, steadier, playing off the still lingering afterglow of the first orgasm. I figured one or two more and he would slake his own lust, and I wanted it. I wanted it so badly, to lay here trussed like a damn turkey while he availed himself of my pussy, stroking his cock in and out of me long and deep.

I couldn't have been more wrong about his intentions, though.

He made me come two or three more times alright, letting me have less and less time to recover panting between them. Eventually, there *was no recovery time at all*, and he kept me rolling somehow, wave after wave after wave until his tongue grew tired and he retired it, only to replace it with some kind of vibration, his fingers stuck firmly in place, seemingly melded to my G-spot as he tortured the fuck out of me with sweet sensation and a pleasure that was impossible to describe.

Eventually, in the pleasure induced madness that ensued, I scraped my temple against my arm, dislodging and unmasking myself to look down my body into the intense burning gaze he had fixed on me.

"One more time, darlin'," he said and I wailed and tipped my head back as he flexed his fingers against that place inside me, my pussy throbbing, my clit almost raw as the bulbous head of the vibrator worked at it.

"I can't!" I wailed piteously, and I thought I was on the verge of tears, the panic rising in my gorge, not about whether I would come yet one more time – I had had more than my fill!

No, my panic was purely about *not* being able to come, my body betraying me and letting him down. I didn't want to disappoint him! And I know how incredibly fucked that sounded but that was where I was at.

"Yes, you can, baby. Just one more!" he encouraged and the wicked grin he gave me was enough to melt the fear away and make my pussy contract around his fingers.

"That's it," he encouraged. "Come on. Just one more."

I screamed, half in frustration and half begging the gods or the powers that be to let me give him what he wanted. To let me please him with this one thing and it was as though my strange little prayer had been heard. As though some great and benevolent goddess had stroked my forehead and fire lanced through me, or lightning. Flickering up through my body from my ravaged pussy, along every vein, sparking out along nerves as synapses fried and I screamed and yelled my pleasure to the high ceiling of our bedroom and collapsed to the bed. Panting, boneless, *exhausted.*

"That's my good girl!" he praised and he let his fingers slip out of me after taking the vibrator away and switching it off.

I lay wrecked and panting, my body trembling as he reared up between my legs and undid his pants, shoving them down just enough for his cock to spring free. He was turned on, like *way the fuck on*, a dark wet spot on the front of his jeans from where he'd been leaking precum the entire time he'd been teasing me to within an inch of my life.

He walked on his knees up the bed and leaned over me, keeping himself from touching my overwrought pussy for now, sliding his hands against my head, sweeping the blindfold off of me, and putting his lips to mine.

I could smell the perfume of my arousal on him, and it was strangely cloying, but not unpleasant. Not when I could smell just *him* beneath it. I quite liked the combination.

"You good?" he asked with a smile that bordered on impish.

All I could manage back was a whimper.

"Ohh." He laughed a little, breaking up the 'oh' with his giggles as he reached up with one hand, bracing himself up off the top of me with his other elbow against the bed and released the straps holding my wrists.

I brought my arms down, my shoulders protesting just a little bit, and wrapped them around him.

"There you go," he whispered carefully. "That's it." I calmed down, my breathing going from rapid panting to deeper and more even. He kissed me some more as the frenetic energy dissipated and I relaxed into something sublime and far more docile. Floating on that post-orgasm high and the afterglow, which should read after*math* of what he'd done to me.

He cradled me in his arms and lowered the lower half of his body against me carefully, sliding inside of me with a groan that sounded like he had finally come *home*. I held him, burying my face into the crook of his shoulder and his neck, the straps holding my legs open still for him and letting me relax as he slipped in and out of my pussy in these long, slow, languorous strokes that turned my blood to quicksilver coursing through my body.

There was no way I could orgasm again, and so sated was I, I didn't care to. I just wanted to live in this time and space of having him inside me properly forever, his warm hard body over mine, moving against mine, in this erotic and sensual dance that probably made angels weep if they were to witness it.

"God, I love you," he whispered in my ear, and I felt my eyes mist with emotion.

I love you.

Not, "I love the way you feel" or "I love *this*," but "*I love you*"

What's more? Even though I had heard it often enough from a multitude of people... their actions had so often proved otherwise that I couldn't and wouldn't believe them. I had been *told* I'd been loved but I had never felt it. Had never been shown it... until now.

"I love you, too," I breathed and moved just so, so I could take him in a little farther, hold him a little tighter, as he moved over and inside me with this special cadence and careful whispered touch that didn't send my overwrought body into fits but rather soothed it into a decadent space to where I felt I lay atop softest clouds and that I remained lighter than air with them.

He looked at me, and our gazes meeting was something altogether unworldly. A different touch, a meeting of souls, and everything just felt so right. So wonderful. So complete.

He loved me. I loved him.

Everything else was just noise.

20

*B*lackjack...

"You sure about this, man?" I asked as Jon clasped my hand and pulled me in for a bear hug.

"Oh, man, I've never been surer of anything in my life," he said. We both turned to Ember trailing up to the door from the truck, a tote bag over one shoulder and another dangling from her hand.

As far as she knew, we were here to help Jon around the meadery for a while. She wanted to come along, which was fine. She could be someplace her fuckwit ex couldn't find her with someone I trusted to keep an eye on her in case the dipshit managed to give me and Fenris the slip.

"Hi, Jon," Ember said shyly and Jon smiled.

"Bring something to do?" he asked.

"Yeah, some stones and wire to make some pendants, Blackjack said I could maybe work at one of the tasting room's tables."

"Heck yeah! That's rad. Let's get you set up."

"Fen here yet?" I asked then quickly followed it up with a, "never mind," as I heard the roar of his piped coming up Andover East.

"You go on in with Jon, darlin', I'll be right there." I gave her a

174

quick kiss, and she smiled at me, her eyes luminous, as she turned to go inside past Jon who held the door for her.

I wandered out to the parking spot that held my bike and made sure she'd secured the saddle bags on it from where she'd retrieved her stuff. One of them could be tricky to get closed.

I fixed that while Fen pulled up and heeled down the kickstand, leaning his bike over onto it and shutting it off.

"Hey," he grunted.

"Hey to you, too," I said straightening up.

"How's the little shield maiden doing?" he asked with a quirk of his lips.

"She's inside and good to go, man," I said.

He gave a decisive nod and stood up, swinging his leg over the saddle of his bike and giving a stretch once he had both feet planted on the cracked asphalt of the meadery's parking lot.

Oppegaard Meadery was located in an industrial office park in the heart of Tukwila. It was an unlikely spot, not gonna lie. The low, modern office park buildings done in gray looked ultra-sleek and modern but didn't exactly boast that a place brewing and serving up a drink something like a thousand years old or some shit lay inside.

We walked up to the door and tugged on the axe it had for a handle. Jon's logo for the meadery an etched out ouroboros, or the serpent eating its own tail in a ring, on the glass.

He was at one of his fancy live edge and resin tables that practically glowed while Ember sorted through some polished stones from her bag. She was seated on the bench and Jon had a foot propped on it next to her, his fist on the table as he looked over her shoulder.

A few months ago, my girl would have quailed under such a looming presence, but she knew Jon sort of after the stay at Cipher's, and a few odd meetups since then. Besides that, Jon was a genuinely good dude who put off genuinely good dude vibes. Still, I was proud of her. She'd really seemed to find her center and with every single day that went by I loved her more for the person she was becoming every day.

Still, there was one more obstacle to overcome. One more shackle holding her back; and the club had decided as a whole that dude had fucked around enough and it was time to find out.

"That's totally cool!" Jon was saying enthusiastically about Ember's art as she bent some wire with a pair of pliers. Her online store wasn't doing much, yet... but she had some avenues and ideas. Aspen was going to have her set up with her and some of her pottery stuff at some of the local farmers' markets and see if she could gain some traction there over the summer.

Fenris cleared his throat and Jon looked up, eyes twinkling and said, "Right! Come on back and let's get this party started."

Ember smiled up at me a little wanly and mouthed 'be careful' at me and Fenris. Fen winked at her and gave her a nod.

She knew.

She knew and had insisted on being here at the meadery, to bolster our alibi. We followed Jon out into the warehouse portion of his operation, in among the tanks of his meads in their current state of fermentation, among the casks and whiskey barrels it was aging in and among the bottling equipment.

You would expect it to be loud back here, but it was silent as the grave.

He tossed Fen a set of keys and I asked Fen, "You got it?" He unzipped his jacket some and pulled the stolen license plate out of his coat.

"Nice," Jon said.

We took out our phones and Jon took them and tossed them on top of one of the closed lids of the mead tanks in a side room, shutting the door behind him as he came out with us.

When we put some distance between us and the electronics he said, "Van's out back. There aren't any operational cameras back here. I took care of 'em last night."

I glance up along the building and laughed a little. "What'd you do? Shoot 'em out?" I asked.

Jon shrugged. "Basically. Building owner was pissed but guess he should have thought about that before he let my plumbing stay fucked for so long." He grinned, his blue eyes twinkling and Fen laughed.

"Right, keep an eye on my lady for me."

"Oh, for sure. I'll have her taste test some shit I got coming up with me and I'll order us some food."

"Thanks," I said, reaching into my jacket to pull out a wad of bills he waved me off.

"Your money's no good here, man. I've got it."

I nodded. Not like he wouldn't get it back out of me anyway. He had some more Ingólfur coming out soon and I needed some of that shit in my supply at home. The man made some seriously good shit. Ingólfur being no exception, I didn't know what the fuck a quince was but it did a mighty fine job of flavoring some mead.

Fenris and I swapped plates on the delivery van we were using and gave Jon's plates back to him. We lucked out that he hadn't gotten around to putting the meadery's logo on anything and that there wasn't anything remarkable about the damn thing that could trace back.

We'd asked him the "what-if" on shit going sideways and he'd shrugged his shoulders and said, "Shit ain't going to go sideways and if it does, I report it stolen and that's what insurance is for."

"Who's driving?" I asked and Fen tossed me the keys.

"You are. No offense, you been out of it for a while and I wrestle goats all day for a living."

"Fair," I said with a nod.

We went up to Capitol Hill and found a parking spot close enough to the bars Ember said he liked to haunt.

We saw some of the guys as we wandered giving a chin lift and little more in acknowledgment.

Finally, Fish drifted up to us as we approached one of the bars on the list.

"He's inside," he said, and I gave a nod.

"Three sheets?" I asked.

"Not yet," he said. "Marisol is working on slipping him a Mickey. She's in there with Maverick."

"Shit," I said surprised.

"She feels bad about that whole thing back at Cipher's," he said.

Fenris grunted. I didn't like it either, but Maverick knew what the fuck he was doing. If Marisol was involved, then it was damn sure by her choice. She was smart, too. If she'd talked Mav into being along on this, then it was because he'd seen more merit to her being here than detractions and she was damn sure a hell of a lot prettier and able to get in close to Devin and the ego the son of a bitch was sporting.

"Shit," Fen grunted as Devin came staggering out, pushing Marisol off of him.

"What'd you do to me?" he slurred. I slipped my namesake out of the inside of my cut, the heavy leather blackjack felt good in my hand. Handing Fish the keys to the van, I slipped up next to Devin, Fen shadowing me and coming up on his other side as I clubbed him with the lead weighted weapon in the head.

Smoothly, we caught him between us, and got his arms over our necks and shoulders. We'd gotten lucky, the street clear when it should have been packed with people. Fenris let out some braying laughter and Marisol melted back up the steps. Fish put on a genial grin and walked with us toward the van.

By all appearances, we were just a group of guys out with our drunk ass best buddy.

Smooth operation.

Fish opened up the van ahead of us, and with a look this way and that to make sure we had the all clear, we dumped ol' Devin into the back. Fen leaped in after him and Fish slid the door shut and handed me back the keys.

Wordlessly, I got into the driver's seat while Fish walked down the sidewalk like nothing had ever happened. I started up the engine drowning out the whisper zip of the tied Fen was using to secure our prisoner in the back.

"Coast or mountains?" I asked.

"Mountains," Fen grunted, and I pulled smoothly into traffic.

He climbed up front to the passenger seat a few moments later as I piloted the van through city streets and down the hill to the nearest I-5 on-ramp.

Around an hour and a half into the drive, dude started coming too, groaning and shifting in the back of the van. I held out my blackjack to Fen, and he stared at me for a long moment. Devin groaned again and scowling Fen turned in his seat and brought a meaty fist crashing down into what I had to guess was Devin's head. I didn't know, I couldn't exactly take my eyes off the road to look.

We pulled up into the tree line off of one of the old logging roads up near Tiger Mountain and the hiking trails and I shut off the van's engine.

"Wake 'im up," I ordered and Fen got out of his seat.

"Not yet," he said as I got out and opened up the van's side door.

"What do you mean not yet?" I asked and Fen Jumped out, grabbing onto Devin whose head was covered by a hood of crudely stitched together purple whiskey bags.

"The fuck?" I asked.

"Brother," Fen grunted as he hauled Devin's dead weight up over his shoulder. "I know you've killed people before, but who outta the two of us is the accomplished murderer?"

I shook my head and said, "Fuck, you got a point. Lead the way," I said and I followed Fenris off into the woods.

We hiked what had to be a good couple miles, Fen snapping branches along the way to lead us back.

Finally, we reached a clearing, the moon high but not providing much light down here in the thick of the underbrush and under the thick canopy of evergreens.

Devin got set down and leaned up against the sap covered trunk of a tree and I turned to Fen who was digging with his hands in the soft loam and earth.

"What're you doing now?" I asked.

"Making a fire," he answered.

"The fuck?" I asked.

"Look, we're gonna be here a while. If getting him dead was the only objective then have at, bro – but I thought you wanted justice. I thought you wanted this motherfucker to *suffer.*"

I looked back at the helpless unconscious form against the tree and sighed. I looked around and started picking up a stick.

"The fuck you doing?" Fen demanded as he worked to find stones to ring his pit.

"The fuck does it look like I'm doing?" I demanded back. "I'm building your fuckin' fire."

Fen snorted, and I felt the hair raise on the back of my neck slightly. I mean, I knew the big bastard was crazy – he'd been spoken about in hushed tones like he was the fuckin' boogeyman not just by some of the dudes in our chapter, but other chapters as well. Some of the shit he'd got up to had even made it to chapters across the country that we'd never even encountered except at the fuckin' Nationals Lake Run.

Now here I was about to be the very fabric of one of Fen's horror shows in the middle of the fuckin' woods where bigfoot could possibly pop up and ass rape us and *Jesus fuck!*

Was I pussing out? I wondered as I dropped a bundle of sticks next to Fen and his firepit.

He looked up at me and said, "What's the matter? Getting cold feet?"

I sighed and said, "I've killed plenty of people. Some deserving, some not – but that was in the service."

Fen grunted, "Way I see it, this is in service too. Or you forget why we're even out here?"

I looked over at the prone figure and turned back as Fen blew and a flicker of light emanated from the ground.

"Good point," I said, the image of the bruising on Ember's fair skin drifting out of the depths just behind my eyes. The fucking tears, the nightmares, the *constant* living in fear which in theory should end the minute I ended him.

"You good?" Fen asked me, squatting across from me the fire casting his face in shadowed relief making him look almost demonic.

I crouched the other side of the flames from him and held my hands out to the flames.

"I'm good," I declared and he nodded solemnly.

"Good," he said, and we sat in silence warming up and waiting –

not really sure what for. We had the ability to wake the dude up. The smelling salts in my fuckin' pocket.

Still, I guess waiting a little longer for him to come around on his own wasn't going to hurt anything.

"Where you going?" I asked as Fen stood.

"I'll be back," he said and he pulled a hatchet out from one of his belt loops.

"Alright," I said with a nod, vaguely unnerved but knowing I could find my way back if I needed to. I was a trained fuckin' Marine and I had the keys to the van in my fuckin' pocket.

A few moments later, I heard chopping from out in the dark.

I looked over to Devin who was still motionless and held my hands out to the fire again.

We had nothing but time.

21

*E*mber...

Jon dropped onto the bench across from me as I tweaked some wire around the piece of rose quartz I was working with. I smiled even as I gritted my teeth to force the wire to do what I wanted to do while simultaneously praying my pliers wouldn't slip.

"Try this," he said when I finally looked up and he set a plastic cup with some kind of mead in it across from me.

"What's this?" I asked.

He said, "A little experiment I've been working on."

I tasted it and blinked, eyes going a little wide.

"Okay, I'm going to need to know what that is, because wow that's good!"

"Took some of the blueberry and cherry mead I made last summer and threw it in an oak barrel for shits and giggles," he said.

"I like it," I said. "I don't know how to describe it, but it's got like this woodsy brandy like finish to it."

"That would probably be the brandy barrel I put it in."

I nodded knowingly and sighed and he said, "I ordered up some food, it'll be here soon."

"Oh, my God. I didn't even think about eating!"

He laughed and nodded and said, "Yeah, I figured. You worried about him?" he asked.

I nodded.

"You know, when I was in the hospital and didn't have anyone to call and I hadn't spoken to or seen him for a couple months and had no idea if he would answer the phone… I pictured myself alone and homeless in a shelter and it was the loneliest feeling."

I breathed out a cleansing breath and Jon smiled and gave a nod.

"Yeah, but you're a badass," he said, and I gave him a dubious look. "It's really hard being badass because most humans are garbage and struggle to meet the basic requirements for badassery needed to hang with other badasses."

I laughed at him and gave him a smiling frown of confusion but he went on. "Once upon a time, I was pretty sure that huge compromises were necessary in order to keep from being lonely. Then I found someone who proved me wrong and made me realize that the concessions I made for previous relationships were unnecessary for companionship. I was hoping the same would happen for Blackjack at some point. He's a good dude and I told him once, 'I dunno dude. Maybe someone will come along and do the same. Or maybe not and you'll be stuck a lonely badass.' Now I'm going to tell you the same thing I told him next: 'No matter what happens, being lonely is better than being in a shit relationship with a douche bag who holds you back from your true potential.'"

"That goes for you, too," he said. "Even if BJ hadn't shown up like he did which," he snorted like the entire notion was absurd, and I had to smile because now that I knew Blackjack like I did the notion of him not showing up *was* completely nuts… "Let's face it, isn't his style. What I'm trying to say is: you're a badass, Ember and you would have figured it out and found a way."

I let that sink in and I nodded.

"Good point," I said, because he wasn't wrong about any of it.

"I'm really glad shit worked out for the both of you," he said getting up and pointing to my glass. "You gonna need more of that?"

I downed the rest in it and gave him an impish look. "Yes please!"

183

He laughed and said, "Okay, I'll be right back. Unlock the door and grab the food if it comes."

"Okay," I said.

I sighed and looked out the front windows into the gloom of the dark front parking lot and to the pair of motorcycles parked side by side that looked… well… lonely and a little forsaken waiting for their riders to return.

I turned back to my art and set my pliers down, running the sweating palms of my hands up and down the tops of my thighs to dry them off. Truth was, I *was* worried. I mean, I knew Blackjack and Fen were more than capable – but it didn't matter how capable you were. Things could always happen.

Jon came back with a bottle and another glass and refreshed mine and poured some in his own.

"To being badasses," he said and held his glass up.

"To doing better," I said, and we clicked cups and drank.

"What's that mean?" he asked after drinking. I savored my sip just a little bit more and sighed.

"I don't know," I said. "To recognizing the signs and not being quiet. To knowing when to make concessions and when not to… that sort of thing."

He smiled at me and nodded. "To not letting the garbage humans get a foot in the door?" he asked.

"Exactly."

"I'll drink to that again," he said and held up his cup and sipped some more. I smiled and took another drink, rolling the rich liquid around on my tongue. "I wouldn't worry," Jon said when he caught me looking out the front windows again. I laughed a little and shook my head.

"It's not that," I said.

"Oh, then what?"

"I think our food is here," I declared and he looked up and over too.

"Oh, shit!" He hopped up, nearly tripped on the bench, and ended up doing this weird thing where he hopped in a circle on one foot his hands in the air like he meant to do it.

I laughed and laughed and he went to the door and got our food.

He'd made me feel better about a few things and my patience for however long Blackjack and Fen would be gone renewed. He'd warned me it could be all night, but I was hoping it wouldn't.

It didn't matter, though. I could wait for as long as it took to feel truly *free* again. Devin had taken enough of my life away from me. Had almost taken Blackjack if one of his shots at us had landed on the mark. The police wouldn't do anything...

I understood now why the club was the way it was in that regard.

The threats, the harassment, only to be told by the police to 'call them when he actually did something...' when he already *had* done something by putting me in the hospital!

The wheels of justice didn't turn slowly. They didn't turn at all, and for someone like me there had never been something even remotely resembling love or justice my entire life...

Until Blackjack.

I smiled across the table at Jon who was the type of person who made it hard to do anything *but* smile and we ate. Talking about this and that, sharing stories, and just generally enjoying each other's company while the stars spun overhead and the time trickled by.

22

*B*lackjack...

I looked up as dude groaned. It didn't take him as long to wake up this time as I'd expected. Fen looked to me and I gave him a nod. He returned it and went over to the dude while I stayed crouched where I was.

When Fen had returned from his chopping, he'd come back with some wood to build up the fire and a big round from a fallen log or branch that he'd worked a flat on one side.

I knew what was coming, but fuck if I didn't think I was prepared to do it – even if the motherfucker deserved it.

Fen swept the hood off dude's face and I looked across the fire at him as he looked around and finally settled on me.

I must have looked like I was straight outta the depths of hell, and the way his eyes turned hard and he nutted up right in front of me? It's like it flipped a damn switch in me just *knowing* what the look he was giving me would have done to Ember after all the systematic abuse and bullshit she'd been through before him and the rest of the way he'd torn her ass down, and *for what?* For what?

She was so fucking *eager* to please and all she fucking asked for? All she fucking wanted? To be loved, and to have a rock to lean on, and to be told she'd done a good job at *anything* and all of those things, *none of those things*, would have cost him fucking anything.

Instead, he'd demanded more. *More, more, more!* Eroded her trust, damaged her ability to believe in anything and gaslit her into oblivion and beyond and had driven her absolutely fucking *mad* with the grief of having to live with a broken heart, feeling forced to make him the center of her world, isolated from everyone else and feeling so fucking lonely in her relationship that she literally felt like she'd had only one way out... he'd nearly killed her, and when she'd finally opened up about it and told me what his reaction had been after I'd returned her home that morning?

No, he didn't deserve a second chance. Not to do it to someone else.

She'd said he'd just smirked at her and said, *"God, you can't even do that right. What the fuck, Ember?"*

"Glad to see you're awake," I intoned.

"The fuck is this?" he demanded.

"Your funeral," Fenris said.

I cocked my head and lifted one shoulder in a shrug. "More like execution," I clarified.

Something moved behind Devin's eyes. Not quite fear, but the first stirrings of uncertainty were there.

"You see," I drawled. "We do it old school around here. No cushy cell, no three hots and a cot. We're a strictly do not pass go, do not collect anything but a real punishment befitting your fuckin' crimes," I told him.

I thrust a chin at Fenris who hoisted the man to his feet, going behind him with a knife and snapping the ties around his wrists.

Devin tried to jerk, tried to make a run for it, but Fen socked him right in the solar plexus.

Ol' Devin fell to his knees, clutching his gut, coughing, retching, and wheezing trying to pull in air.

Fen worked at his belt and Devin tried to crawl. I stood up, and the motherfucker *flinched*. Good. Now he was afraid...

Fen pulled his belt out from the loops and fashioned it into a loop, pulling the tongue through the buckle and cinching it down. Devin reached out like he was beseeching for something and that just made Fen's job easier. He looped his belt around dude's wrist and dragged him across the dirt and litter of pine needles, dragging his arm up over the flat of the halved log piece.

I sniffed and let Fen's hatchet handle slide through my fingers, giving me some length to heft it.

"No!" Devin choked out.

"Should have thought of that," I told him. "Before you put your fuckin' hands on her."

"*No!*" he screamed and Fen put tension on the belt. The guy tried to pull back, which just made my job easier as I hacked, one, two, and a third time down on the middle of his fuckin' forearm. Blood squirted, bone cracked and the arm made a sickening squelch as it fuckin' parted, the last of the tendon and muscle giving way.

Devin lay on his back, like a turtle capsized onto its shell holding up the stump of his arm, gushing, bleeding, screaming as Fen pulled his belt off from the freshly detached limb and let it fall to the dirt.

Wordlessly, the big man, my *brother*, got the loop around the other wrist while Devin screamed himself horse. He was crying, begging, and I had no fuckin' mercy in my heart as I took the other arm off too.

"Please don't let me die, please don't let me die," he begged, whining, and I looked to Fen who hauled him to his feet and pointed him out into the woods giving him a shove.

"Survive if you can," he intoned. Bawling, his arms bleeding, his tee soaked in blood and sweat, he took a staggering step out into the dark.

I watched him go, and finally pulled my piece out from the small of my back, sighing. Fen gave me some side-eye, standing there with his arms crossed over his chest and a strange sort of demonic light in his eyes.

He stopped me from taking aim for a second and said, "I like Ember."

I nodded and lowered my gun and let him get a little way in, sobbing and tripping over his own fuckin' feet and the underbrush.

"Man, this is just fuckin' pathetic," I muttered and raised my gun and took aim. One shot, and it took him in the back of the head, blowing his face out. He fell forward, and I cocked my head, waiting for my gun to cool before I holstered it.

Fen nodded.

"Bury him?" I asked.

He sniffed.

"Nah, ain't nobody coming up here. Critters'll tear him apart and drag him off in pieces. If he ever is found? It'll just be bones."

"Teeth?" I asked.

"Like I said, ain't nobody coming up here," he said.

"Why you so sure?" I asked.

"I own this chunk of property," he said. "Anyone comes up here, it'll be trespassing."

He turned and started kicking dirt over the fire to put it out.

I turned slowly and asked, "Did you seriously buy your own fuckin' dumping ground?" I asked.

"Nah," he said with a shrug. "My dad did."

I blinked and shook my head. "Talk about keepin' it all in the family," I muttered.

He barked a laugh.

"Let's get back to our women."

I nodded and followed Fen's lead outta here. We had a long ride back to the city and we needed to stop and get cleaned up before we made it all the way back.

We stopped at a cheap motel, the kind with a number in the name right off the highway, and Fen who was the cleaner of the two of us went in and booked us a room. I slid up to it along with him and we each showered and bagged up our bloody shit. We spent some time spraying down our leathers with hydrogen peroxide and wiping it clean of any blood that foamed up for us. We redressed in the clean packaged shit we had on hand in a duffel and drove out to one of the homeless camps under the freeway.

We found their burn barrel and ditched our bloody clothed, saturating them in lighter fluid and lighting them up. We stayed, handing out some sandwiches from a fast-food joint we'd swung through and waited for things to burn down enough to our satisfaction before leaving.

The people down here knew that when our kind showed up doing shady shit like this? That you damn sure bet 'cha a chicken sandwich had better buy their silence.

It was past midnight by the time we rolled up behind Jon's shop. Fen pounded on the big metal roll-up garage door and what felt like a few minutes later it started moving thanks to the press of a button from the inside.

Jon stood by looking a little worried but once he saw us, he gave a solid nod and asked, "Need a drink?"

Fen said, "Nah."

I said, "Fuck yes."

He didn't even bother with his mead; he stopped by a shelf and took down a bottle of the hard shit. A good bourbon from a local distillery run by one of the local tribes.

Ember came forward, a bundle of nervous energy and buried herself against my chest the moment I walked through the door into the tasting room and I put my arms around her, holding her tight.

I kissed the top of her hair as she shifted, like she was burrowing deep into me and didn't want to come back out again. Like I was her comfort object. A civilian version of a woobie or some shit and all I could do was hold her tighter.

"You're okay, darlin'," I murmured. "Ain't no one ever gonna hurt you like that again. You ain't gotta be lookin' over your shoulder anymore."

She held tight to me and rested her chin on my chest and looked up into my face, concern swimming in the brilliant pools of her eyes as she asked, "Are you okay?"

I cocked my head and nodded. "I'm okay," I said finally. I honestly felt dead inside, and I didn't know what that meant really. I mean, I'd been here before, just not quite like this.

I did a shot with Jon and Fen – who wasn't about to pass one up even though he didn't feel like he needed a drink and I sat with Ember on my lap as she showed me what she made while I'd been gone.

You know, normal stuff.

I was struck by how much more *peaceful* the world's spin felt now... how much weight had just been lifted off of me as much as her and a sense of, rightness about the world still turning without that dude on it settled over me and there was no guilt.

I think I honestly was more fucked up over *that* than I was over killing the guy in the first place.

We sat and talked about mundane shit, like Fen and I hadn't just hauled my girl's ex out into the woods and chopped his arms off before blowing his brains out and it was something. Pretty soon, it was like two in the fuckin' morning with a long-ass ride back up north and to home ahead of me and my girl who looked sleepy.

"You wanna go home or you wanna stay in one of the club apartments which is closer?" I asked her, jostling her in my arms a bit.

"Home," she answered, and I was glad for it. I sorta wanted to be back at the ol' fortress of solitude, myself.

"Okay, come on. Let's go."

We packed her shit up and stowed it on the bike and Jon locked up and saw us out.

Fen and I gave him a good-natured ribbing about getting a bike as he got into his fuckin' sport car roller-skate thing and he laughed at us, flipped us off and said he'd see us later.

I knew he had a person to get home to, and she was lovely. Quiet, organic, and as sweet as the honey he used to make his fuckin' mead. We didn't see her too often but that was alright. She had kids and a life and the club wasn't really any kind of place for kids – at least not our chapter.

Fen headed for 167 South and his farm, Ember held on tight to me and I made for I-5 North and home.

When we got there, I pulled us into the garage and she dismounted carefully after I shut off the bike.

"Are you really okay?" she asked when we were alone and I nodded.

"I'm the villain, baby. I'd watch the whole fuckin' world burn for you," I told her and she shook her head and combed her fingers through my hair after I took off my helmet.

"Bullshit," she said. "You're a hero, always have been and always will be," she said. "You don't get to feel guilty over that asshole."

I felt a surge of pride in her that she would call him a name, she'd refrained from it for a good long while, her programming having run sorta deep... He had her fear trained like a motherfucker and I wasn't entirely sure how long it would take for her to heal, but it didn't matter. I was here for it.

"Come to bed with me," she murmured and stroking her fingers through my hair leaned down and kissed my forehead.

I smiled and said, "Yes, ma'am," and she giggled a little.

"Somehow I think you need a break from being in charge," she said softly and I nodded slowly.

"Not often," I said. "But yeah, I think you might be right on that for tonight."

"Then come here," she said tugging on my hands. "Let me take care of you for once."

I liked the sound of that, and I was wondering exactly what she had in mind. I got off my bike and followed her in through the garage door, pausing at the hooks inside the door to hang up my shit. She hung hers up too and said, "Come find me in the bedroom," and just those words alone in her soft voice was enough to get me going, my cock giving a twitch in my jeans.

She came to me almost as soon as I stepped through the bedroom door and her hands went to undressing me. I stood patiently as she stripped a piece off of me then one or two off of her, then me, then her deconstructing our clothing until we were both nude, candles flickering on just the bedside table. I took her into my arms and leaned down to kiss her and she melted into me, kissing me back like I was her very air to breathe and I liked that. Maybe a little too much.

I pulled back from her and looked at her, and she smiled up at me and asked, "What?" her lips losing that easy smile, the sparkle in her eyes dimming the longer she took in my expression.

I cradled her cheek and smoothed a thumb along her jaw and

gritted my teeth and was honest with her. "I sometimes worry that I'm no better than him," I said.

"What?" she asked, her voice shocked and her tone horrified as she asked me, "How could you think that?"

"I worry that I'm selfishly holding you here, holding you back from going out and making friends in the name of keeping you safe and—"

She put both of her hands over my mouth, and I smirked behind them, partially at her audacity but mostly in amusement.

"You haven't let me make new friends?" she demanded. "And what about Jon, and Raven, and Little Bird, and Aspen, and yes even Kinzleigh and Marisol?" she demanded. "What about the rest of the club who have been so nice and welcoming?" she demanded, and I shut my mouth and nodded.

"You know if anything were to happen to me, they would continue to take good care of you, right?" I asked.

"I know that," she said and looked a little heartbroken at the thought. "All because of you... which is the complete opposite of... of where I come from," she said.

"Yeah," I agreed.

"I don't know what the voices in your head are saying right now but they're stupid and they need to shut up," she said.

I laughed. Sometimes she slipped into this childlike way of saying things and it was so fucking adorable and I loved it.

Her expression changed and she asked so softly I almost didn't hear it, "He *is* dead, right?"

I smoothed her hair back from her face and nodded. "Yeah, darlin', he is."

"Then why would you say that?" she asked. "About something happening to you?"

"I mean, you never know, right?" I asked.

Her face crumpled some and I could see the gears turning, and I instantly felt guilty for putting the thought in her head. I should have known she would overthink it to death, dammit.

"I don't want to think about it," she said.

"I know, I'm sorry," I murmured.

"It's okay, just... come here." She pulled away, and I hated it, but she went and propped pillows against the headboard and popped herself up onto the mattress making grabby hands at me. I smiled and went to her, flopping on the bed and laying face first into her chest, turning my head and listening to her heartbeat.

I loved it, lying between her legs like this, ear pressed over her heart, listening to its steady Cadence. She pushed her fingers into my hair, scratching nails along my scalp and I felt all the tension leave my body.

This was my peace, and the way she gave it to me, the way she nurtured me and just let me have this... God, she really was just the perfect woman.

I loved that it didn't have to be all or just about sex with her. No, the connection we forged, that we were sharing, it was about so much more than that.

I sighed and relaxed into her and closed my eyes and soaked up the attention. That was honestly the whole point of any power exchange, that at the heart of it, it went both ways whether the polarities got reversed sometimes or not.

It was all I'd ever wanted, and it wasn't until her that I felt like I truly had it and understood why it'd just never worked out or even come close with anyone else.

23

*E*mber...
    He fell asleep in my arms and that was alright, it seemed like he never really slept. Almost always coming to bed after me and up before me, always taking care of me in small and big ways and I tried very hard to take care of him back. Keeping things neat and clean, cooking too, all the domestic things… but this… this was something I didn't get to do often and I felt like maybe I should.

I closed my eyes and leaned up against the headboard, and even though it wasn't the most comfortable position to sleep in, I somehow did manage to drift off.

When I woke the next morning, it was late, I could hear Blackjack out in the kitchen and I was tucked comfortably into bed. I rubbed my eyes and yawned, stretching, and found one of his shirts laid out for me at the foot of the bed. I smiled and shrugged it over my head and slipped my arms through the sleeves.

The bedroom door opened just as my head popped free and he stepped in with a plate with silverware balanced on it and a cup of coffee in his other hand.

I sighed and smiled and he smiled back and came over to me, handing me the coffee first like the very god among men that he was.

"Good morning," he murmured and traced some of my hair behind my ear with a light touch. I swallowed a big mouthful of the blessed caffeine in my cup and smiled at him over the rim murmuring, "Good morning," back to him.

"How'd you sleep?" he asked. I gave a little shrug and laughed and said, "I did okay for how it started out. I'm not so used to sleeping sitting up like that, but it was fine."

He leaned forward and kissed my forehead and said, "Thank you for that, I think I needed it."

I smiled and nodded happily, happy to have done it and he held up my plate. I set my coffee aside and took it.

"Come join me?" I asked.

"Be just a second," he promised and he got up and slipped out of the room. He returned a moment later with his coffee and a plate and posted up on the other side of the bed with me, our legs outstretched as we ate and just enjoyed each other's silent company.

"What do you feel like doing today?" I asked eventually.

"Hmm, I figured we could just take it easy," he said with a hand atop my thigh. I raised eyebrows and gave him a salacious little grin.

"Why, are you propositioning me, sir?"

He laughed a little and leaned way over to put his mouth against mine in a quick kiss.

"You're goddamn right I am," he said, and I giggled.

We finished our breakfast and I gathered the plates and such to take to the kitchen. He followed me in there and put his arms around my waist, nuzzling the side of my neck and kissing me behind my ear. I put my hands over his and leaned back into him, tipping my face up to his and begging for a kiss with a small sound from my throat when he didn't give it to me right away.

He chuckled lightly and put his lips to mine and I opened my mouth to his deepening the kiss into something decadent and sultry sweet.

"Hmm," he hummed in satisfaction and I flashed on what I knew he'd done the night before for me... for us... and I couldn't find it in me to feel the slightest bit guilty or bad for Devin.

He was dead, and yet he'd been given every opportunity to just *leave me alone,* and he hadn't. He'd come here and had tried to hurt us, and for what?

No, I didn't feel bad, all I could muster emotionally at the thought of him was *relief.* Relief that he was gone and just this *high,* this soaring sense of freedom that I was able to start my life now.

Like, I didn't realize how much I'd felt that he held me back and Blackjack? Blackjack had been the one to free me, and to tell me he loved me and not just *tell me,* but *showed me,* every day, without fail.

From insisting that I take care of myself, to taking care of me, this man was such a positive driving force in my life now, and I didn't know what or how, but I swore I would spend every day trying to be a positive and driving force in his. I swore to dream big with him, and that I wouldn't rest until all of our dreams were achieved.

I turned in his embrace and returned it, wrapping my arms around him and kissing him with a fervent delight and felt him smile against my mouth. Both of us breaking out in a fit of giggles and I marveled at how quickly he bounced back from the awful thing he'd been forced to do the night before, all in the name of keeping me *safe.*

I looked up at him, and he looked down at me and murmured, "Bedroom," and I nodded, agreeing. I wanted to feel him. I actually *loved* the feel of him on top of me, between my thighs, *inside of me...*

He picked me up, grunting as I wrapped my legs around him and put my arms around him, kissing him the whole way down the hall to our room.

He threw me down on the bed and worked open the front of his jeans. I wasn't wearing any panties beneath the shirt of his I'd thrown over my head and so there was no resistance when he worked the head of his cock inside me, just that I wasn't entirely ready but that didn't take long at all.

He drove into me, working his way in and out to spread my wetness and ease his way, and it only took a few thrusts.

"God, *fuck!*" he moaned and shoved the tee on my body up over my breasts so he could bow over me and take one into his mouth.

I cried out and arched into him, my pussy fluttering around his dick with my arousal and he hummed in appreciation against my breast, the sound sending pleasing vibrations through the sensitive nipple.

I gasped, and panted as the sensations he wrought stole my breath completely from my lungs and he worked his hips back and forth, his strokes short, but the angle with which he delivered them so much more powerful and impactful than anything I'd ever felt before.

He wrapped his arms around me, delving them far beneath me and forcing my back into an arch that was borderline obscene and sucked at my tit, his cock moving inside of me, the head of his dick running over my G-spot torturing me exquisitely. The cage of his warm, hard body pinned me like a butterfly, my pussy fluttering around him with every stroke as I tried desperately to reach that shining fall, but it was as though he had me tethered to this reality by one shining golden thread and while I was high, so very high, to the point I could reach out and almost touch that burning light within me that would send me tumbling, free falling into the devastating orgasm that would rock me to my core... I was damnably just short, just barely out of reach and the beautiful bastard *knew it.*

24

*B*lackjack...

I made her come until she did that wonderful slide into languidness that told me she was floating in that afterglow river. The point where her body was relaxed and all boneless, her muscles fluid and her movements slower and like liquid stardust.

I wanted her nice and relaxed. I had a craving, and I figured the time was right to indulge in it.

I withdrew from her snug little pussy and went down on her, working her through yet another orgasm, only this time, I teased her tight little asshole with a fingertip as I pumped the rest in and out of her.

She was soaking wet, primed and ready, but I'd already indulged in her sweet pussy and I was here for some forbidden fruit as it were. She watched me down the length of her body, her hands fisting the covers at her hips as her body tightened and she almost convulsed against the bed with the power of her orgasm. It was while she was coming so hard that I slipped a finger into her ass, going slow, working my way in and out in a steady rhythm, working my way deeper every time.

She cried out and her hips writhed and I asked her, "You doing okay?"

"Mm-hm." She put an arm over her eyes and I homed in. "Am I hurting you?" I asked.

"No," she answered, voice breathy.

"Are you just uncomfortable because I'm playing with your ass?" I asked.

"Yes," she answered tightly.

"Feels good though, doesn't it, baby girl?" I asked, and she shivered. I laughed slightly and said, "Answer me."

"Yes!" she admitted but I could tell her embarrassment was there.

"Nothing to be embarrassed about, darlin', it's just you and me and I plan to fuck this tight little asshole of yours and make you come like never before."

She sucked in a deep breath as I probed with another finger and she tightened up on me.

"Relax," I ordered and she did, marginally.

"Going to add another finger, now. Okay?"

"Mm." it was neither an endorsement nor a detraction and I smiled. She still wouldn't look at me, and her face and chest were flushed with her exertion from the orgasms I'd pummeled her with. I added my middle finger to the first slowly and told her to push out, she did and I managed to get past her tight little sphincter with only a slight note out of her that could have meant surprise as much as pain. I stopped and checked on her, feeling her body sort of pulse around me as her anus got used to the current invasion.

"You good?" I asked her.

"Mm," she moaned out, and it was definitely not a bad sound.

I smiled and spoke low and insistent, keeping it hot, telling her how sexy she looked, how proud I was of her and how I was going to fuck her tight little asshole and how much I was looking forward to making her come again.

She fell into the sound of my voice and when I deemed her relaxed enough and ready to take me, I removed my fingers, went for the lube in the bedside drawer and lubed up my cock with one hand and plunging my lubed fingers in her ass with the other keeping her nice and open for me, ready to take me.

"You ready for me to try this?" I asked and she nodded.

I positioned myself, folding her legs back, the tops of her thighs touching her chest and I pressed the head of my cock to her asshole. I went in easy thanks to my prep work and her eyes very nearly rolled into the back of her head. I smiled and bit my bottom lip, sliding in slow and easy. It was a different sort of sensation. Whereas her pussy was tight all along the length of me, her ass was only tight at the entrance. It was also less slick, even with the benefit of the lubricant.

I couldn't go as hard or as fast here, I wasn't out to hurt her – just claim her, and the hotness and appeal of this act was more about the trust, domination, and taboo than it was about the sensation for my cock.

I eased in and out of her and watched her expression as she went limp beneath me, her eyes practically rolling into the back of her head. My gaze flicked from her face to where I disappeared inside her and I smiled. She was coming, her pussy pulsing rhythmically as I fucked her ass slow and sweet and I had her there, right where I wanted her, in that state of perpetual never ending orgasm and I couldn't tell you how high that got me.

Even lubed, fucking my girl's ass felt drier than if I'd fucked her pussy. Less slick, the tightness centered around the base of my cock at her entrance rather than along the whole length of me.

I loved this. Especially with her.

It took an inordinate amount of trust for her to let me do this so I was determined to do it right. To go slow and steady, to make it as good for her as possible. It had the added bonus of feeling good, but not so good as her pussy that it allowed me to last longer. To be inside of her for longer, and I had to like that.

No, I *loved* that.

I let us both revel in the absolute euphoria, paying attention to her moans, her breathing, her facial expressions. If she showed any signs of discomfort we were done, regardless of if I finished or not.

I wasn't about to go from her ass to her pussy to finish up myself.

That was just setting her up for failure by way of an infection. I wasn't fucking stupid, nor was I cruel.

What she was doing by submitting to this was a rare and precious gift of trust. One that I would hold sacrosanct.

I moved above her, inside her, and watched her go free, her body going lax, her eyes closing, as she gave herself over to the sensations completely and it made me so proud. She felt so good, my body doing that slow climb up the stairway to the heavens as my balls tightened and that tingling sort of warmth started in them and wrapped around to my lower back.

My breathing became deeper, harder, my blood oxygenating further as the chemical chain reaction in my body started and went rapid fire down the line. My cock jerked, my body along with it as though it were led by a string and I lost my slow and steady rhythm, grunting, moaning as it felt like my fucking soul was ripped through my body and out my dick.

I spilled deep in my woman's ass, and the sheer dirty taboo nature of it made me fire off at least two extra pulses.

I pulled out of her so carefully, making sure she was alright and that things were still good, but *fuck* it did something to me to watch her sweet little asshole gape for me as I pulled out of it; some of the pearl droplets of my cum spilling to the waterproof blanket I kept on the bed.

"Gimme just a moment, baby," I murmured between panting breaths. She gasped beneath me, but she was so far gone on the river of pleasure and afterglow I didn't think she could think let alone speak.

I let my eyes wander every curve of her, every lean angle and plane of her body and I felt a surge of such love, honor, and possession. I smiled and got it together enough to go run a bath.

A washcloth wasn't even going to begin to fix this mess.

25

Four months later...

*E*mber...

I took in a deep breath of the salty Puget Sound air and looked out over the sound. We were at the Des Moines Marina and park. The sight of the fisherman fishing off the pier under the bright sunshine and the endless rolling blue sky made my heart happy.

"Thanks, Vyking," Aspen said to what I just called her father-in-law in my head, even though she and Fenris weren't married.

"You bet," the older man said. He hoisted another apple crate loaded with cardboard shreds and Aspen's pottery into the back of his waiting pickup, out from under the big ten foot by ten foot easy-up.

We were packing up after another successful Saturday market.

"You okay, Em?" she called to me and I smiled and nodded.

"Yeah," I said. "Sorry if I'm slacking off."

I laughed and worked at unthreading more of my necklaces off of the easy-up's frame.

"Looking for Blackjack?" she asked.

"Oh, no! We would have heard them by now if there was anything to hear."

She giggled and said, "Well, yeah, there's that."

"No, I was just taking a moment to appreciate how idyllic it is out here."

"We couldn't have asked for a better day, that's for sure," she agreed.

"Not too hot, not too cold," I said and Vyking chuckled at the both of us.

"Good day for fishin', for sure."

"You catch anything?" Aspen asked curiously, and he shook his head.

"Nah, but it was worth comin' out here," he said with a smile and I couldn't help but smile to myself. He'd come out and been here all day, coming around from time to time to check on us and relieve one or the other for a bathroom break. Bugging me for Blackjack about drinking my water.

"Ah, there are the boys," Vyking declared and I cocked my head and listened as I pulled down another pendant on its black cord.

Sure enough, from somewhere up on the hill there was a roar of pipes. I smiled as the sound rolled out over us and the bay and taking my eyes off of the cords that I was untangling I looked back over my shoulder to the glint of chrome coming down the hill to stop at the little parking kiosk to take a ticket and to be let into the parking lot.

The fee was nominal to park here, one to two dollars an hour, and would have been free had they come while the market was going.

Oh, well... I thought to myself. *You snooze you lose.*

I worked a little more swiftly to get the necklaces down off the easy-up frame as Aspen hurried a bit to finish up taking down her display of pottery and hand thrown earthenware, tucking them away in crates for the ride home.

"Hey, baby," Fen called and went to Aspen, kissing her soundly. I smiled at the shadow coming up on me and turned.

"Hey, darlin'." Blackjack's smile was something serene and I couldn't help but smile back and drop my hands from unlooping my wares from around the easy-up frame.

He bent and kissed me and I kissed him back, my arms threading around his trim waist as he pulled me in tight to him, his hands on the globes of my ass.

"Need help?" he asked.

"It'll get me out of here faster," I said with a wink and he set himself to unlooping the pendants on their cords with me. He and Fenris took down the tent stall and packed it away in the back of Vyking's truck with the rest of our things.

"There you go, old man," Fenris declared, lifting and latching the tailgate on the old pickup.

"Watch who you callin' *old*, yah fuckin' child," Vyking said and winked at me. I giggled.

"Alright, you two ladies watch yourselves around these heathens," Vyking told us and Aspen hugged him.

"See you later, at home," she said.

"Thank you for everything today," I said.

"Aw, it was my pleasure," he said with a nod.

He went around, moving a little slower, and got into his truck firing it up. The old beast lurched and lumbered toward the exit with Aspen and I waving joyfully.

"You girls do good?" Fenris asked.

"We made our money back and then some," Aspen declared.

I beamed and nodded.

"Aspen sold three pieces," I said.

"You sold *twelve*!"

"Yeah?" Blackjack asked, leaning back from me just enough to look me over, the shine of pride in his dark brown eyes.

"Yeah." I nodded and beamed.

"Good job, babe!" He gave me a squeeze.

"You ready for some barbecue and some cold beer?" Fen asked.

"Thought you'd never ask," Aspen declared. "Lead the way, I'm starved!"

"To the club!" Blackjack crouched down and laughing I leaped on his back and he gave me a bouncing piggyback ride across the parking lot to the bikes that were waiting all while I shrieked half in joy half in thrill ride as he made like he would fall backward or drop me.

Aspen giggled as she and Fen walked a little more sedately behind us.

We took the scenic route to the club; and by the scenic route, I meant we rolled all the way along First Ave through Burien and skated over to Ambaum at the last minute rather than jaunting over to 509 which would have been faster.

The day was too pretty, the light summer breeze too nice to sacrifice cruising the surface streets, stereo on the bike blasting good music, in favor of screaming up the freeway dodging the idiots in their cages.

We pulled into the lot in front of the club and rolled up to the line of bikes on the side. The small lot in front of the bone yard was already full, and I did a count and realized there were far more bikes than there were club members here in the Western Washington chapter which meant we had visitors.

"Babe?" I asked when I got off the bike and pulled off my helmet.

"I gotcha," Blackjack said. He stood and went for his saddlebag on his side. He pulled out my *property of Blackjack* leather cut and he handed it over. I smiled and gave a nod, pulling it on over my jacket for now.

Raven came around the side of the building squealing and excited, all but jumping up and down, hugging Aspen then hurrying over to me. I pulled the pendant I'd been saving for her out of my pocket and handed it over. She looked at the chunk of mossy agate wrapped in bronze wire and giggled giddily and jumped up and down.

She'd found the stone, and I'd tumbled it for her and it'd turned out an exceptional piece.

"Thank you so much!" she cried and threw her arms around me. I hugged her tightly and said, "Oh, you're welcome!"

Little Bird poked her head around the corner and called to Raven, "Did you get it?"

"Oh my, God, yes! Look at it! It's so pretty!" she went dashing over and Blackjack came around the bike and threw an arm over my shoulders, so we could walk around the front of the club together.

Aspen had put on her 'Property of Fenris' cut, too and I hugged in a little tighter to Blackjack's side.

The other chapters, sometimes the guys could be intimidating and a little... different.

"Who's here?" I asked Blackjack quietly, leaning into him.

"Don't know," he said. "Didn't think we were expecting visitors." He sniffed and we waded into the crowd inside the front door.

They were club members from down in California intermingled with Western Oregon chapter members by their bottom rockers and I didn't like the look of confusion marred by suspicion on Blackjack's face when we'd first entered the building to the strange faces from California, but when recognition dawned on him with some of the others from Oregon that he knew were picked out of the crowd, his tense posture eased and I started to feel better.

"Hey, Druid, what's up man?" Blackjack asked one of the men he recognized from Oregon. I'd met Druid around two months after Blackjack and I had sort of officially started being together and I liked him. He was broad shouldered, with long light brown hair, long on top with a shaved undercut. He was a sweet soul, loved plants and flowers and to garden and had a gentle, soothing voice and he was absolutely in love with love. A gentle giant, if you will, and obsessed with finding his one.

"Some of the boys from the redwoods and Humboldt County wanted to come up and see your boys who run the dispensary now," he said affably.

"Ahhh." Blackjack nodded knowingly.

Major, Tic-Tac, Nine, and Squatch had combined forces and money to build a pot shop and had launched it around the New Year, before I'd officially, well, landed with Blackjack.

It was still a new venture for them but so far had been wildly successful for them given the culture surrounding weed in Seattle. They had plenty of competition with just how many marijuana dispensaries were in the area, but they'd really carved themselves out with their location between a tattoo shop and a popular bar.

"Tryin' to cut some middlemen?" Blackjack asked conspiratorially.

Druid nodded his look serious and said, "Now Ms. Darlin', you know that us Western Oregon boys are respectful, but when the liquor flows, we haven't had much experience with these California men. Best keep your wits and stay close to your man." He winked at me and gave me a serene smile and I smiled back and nodded.

"Thanks, man," Blackjack patted Druid's large shoulder and Druid gave a nod.

"What can I get you, honey?" Ms. Momma Kat asked him and Druid turned back to the bar to ask for a Hefeweizen.

I tucked a little closer to Blackjack, and he gave me a squeeze.

It turned out; the California boys weren't so bad. There were three of them here, Mooney, Cognac, and Omen. They were affable, if a little rough looking from all their time spent outdoors up in the hills with their grow operations.

Their business was conducted, even without the benefit of Tic being here because he was held up in Eastern Washington helping the chapter there for the time being while they worked on rebuilding still.

He was supposed to come home in the next month or so, though.

I spent most of my time near Blackjack and with the knot of girls. Marisol and I were okay now, but I felt badly for her. She didn't quite fit in with the rest of us girls that well. She just didn't have many of the same interests as we did and while the rest of us found common ground all over the place, she just seemed frustrated that she couldn't as much.

She seemed to be fire to the rest of us being Earth, Water, or in Little Bird's case – Air and her element while a powerful one was distinctly 'other' a topic that Raven was discussing as we took up one of the large picnic tables under the jutting roof out over the front of the club. We were set far back from the door at the furthest one under the bare, old school arcade lightbulbs the guys had strung up around the perimeter of the covering out here.

The sun was setting and Raven had her tarot cards out and was giving Marisol a reading when Glass Jaw came up, leaning down and giving Cadence a kiss on her temple.

"Hey, any of you ladies hear from Dahlia?" he asked. Mostly looking at Marisol and Little Bird who shook their heads. Kinz looked away out over the parking lot and the guys in the easy-up manning the grill, beers in hand. Which that was mostly just Fenris and Dump Truck.

"No, why?" Marisol asked and Glass frowned.

"Mav wanted to know. He invited her to see if she could behave herself and he hasn't even been left on 'read' he was wondering if she was just mad at him and talking to one of you guys."

Looks were traded and various 'No's and 'uh-uhs' rippled through our little gathering.

Glass grunted, "I'll let him know."

I had only encountered Dahlia once a few months back, she had been acerbic, rude, cold, and it was like she was angry. She had this affectation of being a bitch but she pushed it too hard right into *being* a bitch for real and she'd ended up arguing with Mav and had been sent away from the party early for trying to cause drama which is why she'd been kind of sort of exiled to begin with according to the rest of the girls.

No one knew what was going on, but she had been pushing everyone away for a while and had just been so negative no one wanted to deal with her anymore.

When Glass left the table, Marisol said, "Raven, can we take a picture of this or something and can we finish later? I want to go check on Mav."

"Sure," Raven brought out her phone and snapped a photo of the cards in their spread on their silk cloth.

"Thank you," Marisol said, getting up and untangling herself from the picnic bench.

I frowned slightly and looked after her.

"Is she okay?" I asked.

"Yeah," Little Bird frowned after her as well.

"That's a complicated situation," Raven said with a sigh.

"Right," Cadence said nodding.

"I really hate asking," I said, "But I just don't understand the dynamic there."

Aspen sighed, "Neither do we, honestly."

"Dahlia is Mav's best friend," Little Bird said. "They've been friends since they were kids and they grew up in... in similarly unhealthy households," she said finally. "They've been close for ages, but it's not a romantic kind of close. It's more like siblings if anything."

"Okay," I said.

"Marisol is absolutely the love of Maverick's life, but sometimes she feels neglected because Mav is so focused on Dahlia and her bull-shit," Kinz said bitterly.

Everyone went silent and Kinzleigh demanded, "What? It's true," her southern twang coming out a bit.

Everyone reluctantly started to nod.

"A lot of us used to be more forgiving about it," Raven said.

"But it's been steadily getting worse and she was dragging Tic into it so bad and finally enough was enough," Aspen said.

Kinz snorted and nodded. I'd heard about her getting shoved and hit and that honestly scared me but none of the guys seemed like that was a thing with them and it really sounded like Tic did it to defend Dahlia which still wasn't an excuse, especially since Dahlia had clearly deserved what she'd had coming or whatever. I mean, if *I* had been so bold and was being an asshole like that, I wouldn't expect Blackjack to come to my rescue.

Kinz made a slightly disgusted noise and said, "I mean look at her now, she's not even here and she's still somehow managing to disrupt the party. I think she's given way too much power."

Everyone looked uncomfortable, and no one was willing to break the brittle tension that was forming between everyone like ice.

Raven was finally the one to sweep it away with a gusty sigh and a "Well, who's next?" as she swept up her cards and stacked them back into her deck.

"I'll go," Cadence said cheerfully.

"Okay, what's your question?" Raven asked.

We sat and talked and interpreted the cards and discussed and just generally indulged in some girly sort of mysticism time that was leaving me questioning what exactly I did believe. I mean, I wasn't really religious, I wasn't exactly spiritual – I mean, was I?

It was an interesting and eye-opening set of questions.

Eventually Druid wandered over to us and we all rearranged ourselves so that he could sit across from Raven and, of course, his question was *'will I ever find love?'* Was surprised to find out in the course of his reading that he was only a couple of years younger than *I* was. Twenty-seven to my twenty-nine.

"Druid here is an old soul," Raven said with a wink, and I laughed and had to agree.

We were all laughing at something or other that was said when it happened. Our laughter nearly drowning out the cry of anguish from the back of the club. A deathly silence fell over everyone outside, and we all just sort of froze, looking at each other for a handful of heartbeats.

"Stay here," Fen ordered sternly, abandoning the grill and I got up immediately. Not to be a defiant little shit, but because Fen didn't own me, Blackjack did. I didn't know where he was or who had made that sound.

"Ember!" Aspen tried to stop me, but I was already through the front door to the club, darting through bodies and black leather until I fetched up hard into Blackjack's side as he stood in the mouth of the hall leading back to the chapel and Maverick's office.

Inconsolable male weeping emanated from Mav's office and Blackjack moved with me up the hall.

"What happened?" I asked.

"I don't know," he said. "Just stay with me. I've never heard anything like it."

I stuck with him as he shoved through some brothers crowding the door and we went into the office. Mav was on the floor, both he and Marisol crying. Marisol had a hold on Mav, his phone screen lit and lying on the floor as he howled in the most pain that I had ever heard anyone in.

Glass scooped up the phone and said into the receiver, "Hello?"

Blackjack went to Mav while I knelt next to Marisol. I hugged her and asked, "Oh, honey, what's happened?"

There was a mass amount of confusion but eventually the story came out.

Mav had gotten a call from someone from Dahlia's phone. He was her programmed emergency contact... Dahlia was dead.

26

---

*B*lackjack...

Ember stubbornly clung to me, her arms wrapped around my waist, tucked into my side.

Mav sat on the couch in his office, Marisol holding a glass of water at the ready, smoothing back some of his hair while Glass stood by, butt leaning against Mav's desk, arms crossed. We'd shut the rest of the club out for now while we just sort of tried to process the news.

All we knew was that she was gone, and drugs were involved. We didn't know anything else.

"Somebody needs to call Tic," Mav said distraught, and I piped up.

"No. Nobody needs to call him. I'll go. This isn't something he should get over the phone."

Ember's arms tightened around me, and I gave her a squeeze, letting my hands smooth over her back as I went to hold her at arm's length.

"I'm sure one of our boys can give you a ride home," I said and immediately she started shaking her head.

"No," she said, and her voice was steel wrapped in silk.

"Baby, please. I have to do this. Tic came all that way when our house got shot up, I can't let him find this shit out over the phone."

"Take Deacon with you," Glass Jaw said, and I looked over. He gave me a hard look and I knew he wasn't going to budge on this.

"I'll see if he can…" I said, low-key upset that he didn't think I could break the bad news without backup. "I got this, though. Really."

"Clint…" Glass Jaw said, using my given name. I nodded and took a deep breath.

"I'm going with you," Ember repeated when I turned back to her. Something in those blue-green eyes of hers… she was standing her ground, standing firm and strong in the face of this and I simply nodded. Truthfully, I wanted her. I may need her. I could shove my heartache aside for now but… but not forever and I wanted my woman, needed my woman to be there when I got my chance to break.

"Okay," I said. "Let's go."

I found Deacon and spoke to him low while Ember grabbed her gear and mine to ride out of the closet upstairs. Deacon didn't say shit just thrust his beer into someone else's hands and went for his gear.

He met up with us out by the bikes and said, "I'm glad you came and got me."

I nodded, and didn't say anything about it being on Glass's orders.

It was a long hard ride up over the pass. We had to be careful. Night was falling fast and hitting a deer on a bike was pretty much instant fucking death and we didn't need more of that.

Glass had come out and told us to check our phones before we talked to Tic, that there would be updates as he got them. He'd already sent guys to Dahlia's and Mav was preparing to go to the medical examiners for an ID. Glass was going with him.

We divided and conquered, which was our chapter's MO.

We rode in somber silence, Ember holding onto me fast and like a trouper. She'd been up hella fuckin' early to do her sales thing all day at the Marina and now it would probably be the wee hours of the fuckin' morning before we reached the fuckin' clubhouse over in Moses Lake.

We rode hard, breaking speed limits where we knew it was alright to do so, and slowing when we came to populated areas, or areas we knew the State Patrol liked to camp to earn the state the most in revenue. We didn't run into any Staties, thank fuck, and when we pulled up outside the clubhouse out here, the party was in full fuckin' swing.

Lone Wolf, the chapter president for Eastern Washington pushed off the wall out front and dropped his cigarette, grinding it out under his boot.

"Glass called me. I haven't said shit. This is best coming from you guys," he said once the silence flooded in after we'd shut off the bikes. The music was so loud inside ain't nobody hear us.

Ember stood close and looked worried but stayed out of mine and Deacon's way. Wolf gave her a nod, and she smiled and somberly gave a nod in return. I checked my phone.

There was a string of texts from Glass letting us know everything he knew from all points of information gathering that could be done in the last few hours and it was a lot...

What it boiled down to was she'd OD'ed, but whether that OD was a genuine OD or a suicide was up in the air. There was no note, which if you knew anything about suicides like I did from all the twenty-two-a-day veteran's affairs type shit I'd been into, you'd know that suicide notes actually weren't all that commonplace which made shit all the more depressing, but it was sadly true.

I understood that. The few times I'd thought about offing myself? Leaving a note had been the last fuckin' thing on my mind.

As we went over the information on our phones – Deac having the same texts that I did, Ember and I exchanged a knowing look and she tucked herself back into my side.

"I didn't leave a note," she murmured. "I didn't even think about it. I just wanted the pain to stop." She sounded sorrowful and guilty, and I hugged her a little tighter and kissed the top of her head.

"I know, darlin'," I told her. "Me either."

"I don't know what would be easier," Wolf grunted, tossing his long ponytail that hung damn near to his waist back over his shoulder. "Accidental overdose or suicide."

"Neither," Deacon declared. "Not when it's someone that you love like Tic loved her. He was willing to walk through *fire* for her."

"Just..." I took a deep fortifying breath. "Just let me be the one to do the talking on this, okay?" I looked to Deacon. "I owe it to him."

Deacon nodded and said, "I work best after someone's already falling the fuck apart," he said honestly, and I hadn't considered that when Glass had ordered me to bring him along. I nodded.

"You can use my office," Wolf said, and he turned to push open the door to the front of the club. We were immediately assaulted by the blaring music and Ember flinched from the hard and sudden noise. I tightened my hold on her and went through into the club first.

It took a second to adjust to the dim lighting after the bright flood lights out front illuminating the bikes. I stopped with Deac and Wolf at my back as I blinked letting my eyes adjust as I scanned the room.

There were a shit ton of bodies in here.

The Eastern Washington chapter was growing and growing strong under Lone Wolf's leadership. Most of the guys in here were lateral transfers from other clubs or were nomads looking to settle. One or two were fresh meat coming off of prospecting, like Albatross over there.

I spotted Tic sitting around a coffee table, laughing like a lunatic, a card of some kind stuck to his forehead, a glass of whiskey in one hand and a blunt between his fingers as he leaned way back.

He looked good. Way better than he had in a good long while and Deacon stepped up beside me and we exchanged a look.

It was Ember that moved first. She slipped from my side and ghosted through the bodies. One of the guys standing around took a step back and practically stepped *on* her and I recognized him as one of the boys from Idaho. He started to hit on her, saw my rag on her, and held up his hands and just apologized and let her go.

There was no shortage of free pussy wandering around in various states of dress. There was one girl up on the bar with a brother's face in her pussy as she arched back, hands flat to the glowing wood, thrusting her tits to the overhead bar lighting.

Yep, the party was in *full* swing around here.

Ember slipped up beside Tic's seat on the couch and slipped her hand into his free one that he was gesticulating with. He stopped and looked over and then up at my girl. He frowned slightly. She gave his hand a little jostle and jerked her head to the back of the club where she had to presume the offices were. He looked out over the front of the house and spotted me and Deac by the door and stood up.

Ember never let his hand go.

Deacon and I surged forward as one and I gestured that Ember and Tic should lead the way, pointing out Wolf's office.

Ember shoved her way through into the space that was much more cramped than Mav's back home. Tic followed her and then me and Deac. We shut the door behind us, and the noise was dulled by half- to three-quarters. There was a window in here, that was a mirror out there, but it helped keep the tiny office from feeling claustrophobic. I mean, the desk and the one chair across from it took up the majority of the space.

"What's going on, guys?" Tic asked cheerfully. "You look like somebody's died!"

Our grim silence had the smile sliding off his face. He looked down at Ember and jerked his hand from hers.

Ember took a half step back as I shoved him down into the seat at the desk and leaned my butt on the wood surface. Keeping my hand clamped to his shoulder, I swallowed hard and said, "Man, I'm so sorry to tell you this—"

"What?" he demanded. "Spit it out, man. *What?*"

"Dahlia…" His face went ashen, and he jerked back as if he'd been slapped. "I'm so sorry, dude. She OD'ed. She's gone, man."

The look on his face was sick. Stricken with a dash of disbelief at first and breaking this kind of news to a brother? It was a special kind of hell only made more special by the fact that it seemed like the whole of time slowed so that I had a front-row seat to every nuanced thing he had going through his head, playing out on his face.

It was as though I watched his soul tear in fucking two, the pain playing out behind his eyes which were as green as anything I'd ever seen. He looked to Deacon as if Deac would tell him I was lying, but the passive yet somber expression on Deacon's face just seemed to clinch it. Ember took a half step forward just to Tic's side and I held up a hand.

I couldn't predict what Tic would do and I didn't want her to get hurt if lashing out was his answer. He looked from me to Deac, from Deac to me, and his face crumbled. It was like his voice returned with the air to his lungs that'd been unceremoniously ripped the fuck out from my proclamation and he fucking *screamed.*

That sound was guttural and gutting all at the same time. Filled with so much rage and pain it brought a tear to everyone's eye that was front row and center to hear it. To *see it,* as he slid out of his seat and onto the floor. He ran out of air again and sucked in a ragged war-torn breath only to let it out in a wail of absolute fucking despair.

I tilted my head back to the sky and Ember went to her knees beside Tic and gathered him into her lap.

He was lost. As lost as I'd ever seen a grown man as he sought shelter and comfort like a small child. His arms going around her waist, his face buried in her stomach as he just sobbed over and over in these jagged half screams when he had enough air to do it.

She rubbed his back through his cut, and I dropped heavy in the chair he'd vacated and gripped his shoulder.

Ember looked up at me, tears slipping down her own cheeks in the face of such pain and something crossed between us. A silent under-standing that no matter how bad shit felt. No matter how barren, scalded, and blasted a-fucking-part we ever got or felt, that leaving this type of fucking emotional damage behind wasn't going to be a fucking option.

This was a harsh lesson, but a lesson learned.

There was a permanence to pain. It didn't ever leave. It just compounded and grew, all-consuming and swallowed a person fucking whole if given half a chance and if you let it digest you, if you gave up and gave in, it didn't die with you. No, it just rolled on, gobbling up and swallowing the people closest to you destroying them as well.

Pain, like anger, couldn't be satiated. Couldn't be fed into compla-
cency. It had to be *contained.*

We let Tic go through the devastation because some things were
just too personal to fully intervene. The hellfire that we'd brought
with us with this type of news burned harsh and bright and super-
heated our brother beyond anything.

It was up to us to guide him through the process like a smith with
whatever he happened to be forging, but it was up to Tic on if he'd
come out the other side stronger or if he'd become so brittle that he'd
break. All we could do was make sure to have the right support or
ingredients to ensure the best outcome – flux to bond the pieces, oil
to quench versus just water. Shit like that.

I mean, no matter what, he was going to be forever changed after
this – the broken pieces or different pieces of his mettle melded back
together. The scarring from it causing a sort of Damascus pattern in
his psyche.

I don't know, maybe this was a stupid analogy, maybe not. All I
knew is that we were here, and we would not let him down.

Like my old Drill Instructor used to say, *I won't give up until long
after you give up on yourself.*

Ember took the brunt of the first wave, after I'd made the splash,
then Deacon took over asking me and Em to give him a bit.

We'd left the room and had stepped out into a club filled with
silence. We hadn't even realized that the music had shut off.

Lore wandered over, his phone in his hand and said, "We booked
you guys a couple of rooms over at the motel. They're paid for. You
can't hope to go back tonight."

"Thanks, man," I said.

"We take care of our own, and you guys are club no matter what
division or chapter," Ryder said, arms crossed over his chest as he
stood with the bar at his back. I nodded. He was a Jarhead like me, so
he got it.

"Come here, honey," Dane called and reached out a hand to Ember,
waving her in. She looked up at me and I nodded and let her go. She
went over and Dane sat her up on one of the bar stools, dipping a

bandanna into a glass of water and wiping at her face like she was a child. She jerked back at first and he gave her a firm and kind look, and with another look to me, I gave her a nod that it was okay.

I didn't mind, really. I knew Dane to be a Daddy Dominant type, and she was in good hands.

A glass of something stiff was pushed into my hand and I was led over to a stool beside Ember's. I put my hand on her knee and gave it a squeeze and downed what was in the glass, coughing at the harsh burn as it went down.

"Got a couple boys back at Tic's room packing up his shit and bringing it," Wolf said. "I can more than spare him by now. I think it's time for him to go home."

I nodded. "Yeah. Thanks, we appreciate it."

Wolf nodded. "Sacred Hearts Forever..." he said.

"Forever Sacred Hearts," I replied, and we clasped hands and pulled each other in for a hard back slapping hug.

"What's even going on?" someone asked and there was a smack of a hand against leather.

"This is how you kept your name, Albatross," someone else hissed.

"No, it's fine. Someone close to our chapter OD'ed," I answered. "She, uh... we don't know more than that right now. We just don't know."

I looked over at Ember, her face freshly scrubbed of her muddy mascara, her hand clamped over mine lending me strength when my voice cracked slightly on the last "know."

"Oh, shit, man, I'm sorry to hear that," the fucking new guy they called Albatross said.

"It's okay," I said, running my other hand over the top of my thigh over and over, the palm sweating. "I mean, it's not okay, but it's... I don't know." I cleared my throat. "It is what it is, I guess."

"Yeah, man," Dane nodded and asked, "Another?" I shook my head. "Nah."

We still had to ride to the nearby motel whenever Tic and Deac came out of the office.

"Parties over boys," Wolf grunted. "Tic's not gonna need all of us standing around here gawking when he comes out of there. Let's give the man some space."

I nodded to Wolf, and the guys started to clear out.

I wanted to say sorry for crashing the party, but I wasn't. Fuck their good time in the face of something like this.

To their credit, no one complained. They all just gave their condolences to me and Em and left.

Wasn't long after, when it was just Wolf, Ember, and I remaining that the door to the office opened and Tic, eyes red rimmed and face looking like he'd aged twenty fuckin' years in the matter of minutes, emerged.

"We got a motel," I called to Deac and he nodded.

"I'll show you where it's at," Wolf said. "Just follow me."

We rode in formation, keeping Tic insulated. I honestly didn't know how he was even good to drive. When we pulled up outside the motel, a couple of guys from the chapter were already there, just getting off their bikes with a couple of big duffels.

Tic's stuff.

We got our rooms. One with two queens for Tic and Deacon and a smaller single queen room for me and Ember.

"Thanks, you guys," Tic said dully.

"Don't mention it," Wolf said. "For real."

He made a hand motion and his boys straightened up and they departed.

"Hell of a homecoming," Tic said and stared at me, empty, hollow. I think he was just numb for right now.

I nodded. "I'm so sorry, bro."

He shook his head, his face crumbling, and he just couldn't look any of us in the eye.

"Get some good rest," Ember murmured empathetically, and we parted ways.

I let us into our room, the bedside lamp aglow and as Ember shut the door behind us on the world, I dropped onto the end of the bed.

She turned all the locks and set the weird bar thing over the ball that'd replaced the old sliding chain setup and turned.

We stared at each other for several heartbeats, and I rubbed my lips together, trying like a motherfucker to remain stoic.

"Oh, baby no," she murmured, and she came to me, wrapping her arms around my shoulders and head and crushing me to her.

I broke.

No shame in it.

I'd been with Dahlia, had known her for years, had loved her too as a friend, and I knew Ember understood that. At least I hoped that she did.

27

*E*mber...

I held onto Blackjack while he wept into my middle, clutching him to me, raking my fingers through his hair and holding it back as I pressed lips to his forehead, once, twice, bending my neck at an awkward angle down so close to my body to do it.

I stood firm as he had for me so many times before and let him have his break. Returned all the strength that he'd poured into me that he needed and finally, after a while, he calmed against me.

"I'm sorry, babe," he said, and I shook my head.

"Hush! No... this is serious. This is big. Don't you be sorry... I only met her the once, but I could tell she meant so much to so many of you."

He tilted back his head and looked up at me and I cupped his face, brushing my thumbs along his cheeks above the line of his beard on either side.

"Yeah..." he said dully and I smiled a little sadly.

"I had no idea," I murmured, and the guilt resurfaced, gnawing at me.

"Yeah," he said softly and he let me go, looking off somewhere to the side, into the depths of himself. The introspection clear in his vacant-eyed stare.

I knelt on the floor and put my hands on his knee and looked up at him. The movement brought him back around to look down into my eyes.

"I am so fucking grateful for you," I said, moved in the moment and after all I had witnessed tonight. My eyes welled, and he looked down at me, palming the side of my face and smoothing his thumb over my skin.

Cherished.

It's the only word I could use to describe how I felt, and that feeling warmed me all the way through. Injected life into the parts of me that felt stiff and numb from long neglect and abuse.

"I think I'm just as grateful for you, darlin'," he said.

"Why?" I asked. Just needing to hear it.

He smiled, and it was like I watched the brittleness of it strengthen just by virtue of his gaze drinking in my face.

"I love you," he said. They weren't words that he uttered often, which is one of the reasons that when he did? It made them all the more special. "Before you, I was just going through the motions. Keeping busy for the sake of keeping busy. Moving from one project to the next, to the next just to have... I don't know... *something*. Then there was you, and you gave me real reasons a *damn good reason*, to stop just going through the fucking motions and to fuckin' grab life by the balls."

I laughed and he smiled, and it was good for a moment, and while it faded a bit around the edges, it didn't diminish as much as I expected given the circumstances. I mean, the corners of his mouth dropped slightly, but the smile never left his eyes. Warming them into something that suffused me from the inside out with a feeling that was lighter than air.

"I love you, too," I murmured. "You gave me a reason to keep fighting and you wouldn't let me quit and I promise you, I *never will quit*. Not while we're both breathing."

He leaned down and captured my lips with his and my eyes fluttered shut. Months and months in and his lips on mine *never* failed to make me swoon like the very first time he kissed me. The shiny newness of our relationship never seemed to wane even though I thought surely it must by now.

The kiss intensified and his hand delved into my hair at the back, his fists clenching in the strands, my scalp tightening deliciously as he took control of the kiss completely and held me at his mercy.

I loved this feeling, even though you would think it a thing that would be the exact opposite of what I would or should love given my dark origin story.

I think part of the reason I loved it so when Blackjack exerted his will over mine in a physical sense was because I knew how implicitly I could trust him. I knew that he would never hurt me, and I felt cradled safely by his love emotionally, and the safety I felt? That safe feeling was *magical*, and so even when he pulled my hair or caged me with his body so I couldn't get away, instead of feeling oppressed, I felt *empowered*, because I knew one word from me and it would all stop. It would stop and he would seamlessly shift gears and this primal dominated feeling would go from dangerous to nurtured in an instant.

God, it was such a heady sensation, too.

The kissing deepened, and I felt it too, knew that this was different somehow, that it wasn't sex for the sake of fun, or just to feel good. No. This was something more primal. This was a contact that was borne of a deep-seated *need* for the both of us. A need to stave off the dark emotions and the night. A need to stave off the specter, to lift the pall of death that'd settled over us like a burial shroud.

We struggled against that muslin cloth of despair and fought to regain that sense of life and vitality that we'd shared in all day before the pervading sense of pain had crept in like a shadow, draining the color from our hearts and darkening our souls.

The world was a dark and depressing place anymore. The older we grew. Finding that vitality in such times was becoming increasingly crucial in the battle to remain healthy. To find that sense of happiness.

When brushed so completely and frighteningly by death, the need to do something life affirming became crucial. Especially for people like me and like Blackjack.

His long fingers and strong hands went to the zipper at the front of my vest that was layered above a thick, well-constructed jacket. He unzipped my vest and went for the zipper on my jacket as well.

I pulled the hair tie from his loose ponytail and combed my fingers through his hair as he parted my jacket and vest and pushed up the tee that I had on beneath to lay wet kisses on my stomach.

I tipped my head back and let my breath out in a desperate silent plea for more as he palmed my pussy, between my legs over my jeans and rocked his hand to stimulate me through the thick material.

"Oh!" I cried out and he grunted shoving my jacket and vest back off my shoulders. I let it slip from me and it thudded to the threadbare but clean carpet beneath my booted feet.

"Hmm," he hummed out in satisfaction and went for my chaps to get me out of them, then attacked my jeans all while I only managed to shove *his* jacket and cut off of his shoulders and back onto the bed before I walked his tee shirt up his back with my fingers.

He let me pull it off over his head and drop it to the floor but he was intent on getting his hand down the front of my pants, slipping his rough fingers between the thin cotton of my panties and my flesh.

He teased my pussy lips apart with gently fingertips, and finally plunged his hand into my jeans more fully, kicking my feet apart with his foot, and shoving fingers between my lips to find my wet and waiting center.

"Oh, yeah," he groaned when he made contact with what he wanted and found me wet and waiting.

I cried out, digging nails into his shoulders and throwing my head back once more and he shoved three fingers inside me, pressing the heel of his hand tight against my clit.

"You're gonna come for me like this," he growled. "I'm going to make you come all over my fucking hand and you're going to do it for me, aren't you baby? You're gonna take these orgasms like the pro you are at it, aren't you?"

"Yes!" I gasped as he rocked his hand steady and even and flexed his fingers inside of me.

"You're my good girl, aren't you baby?"

"Yes!"

He savagely shoved his fingers into me harder and demanded, "Yes, what?"

"Yes, Sir!" I cried and my legs trembled.

"That's my girl," he praised. "Fuck you're so pretty when I fuck you with my fingers like this," he said. He demanded, "Get your shirt and bra off while I feel you like this. I want to watch those titties bounce, I want to watch them heave while you breathe for me. Okay? Mm-hm."

I scrambled to comply, lifting my tee lightly by the hem, peeling it up my body and off from over my head while he drove me crazy with his hand, using his other to jerk down my jeans and panties to give himself better access.

I got rid of my bra next, as quickly as I could while he pulled his hand from my pussy and sucked his fingers.

"Mm! God that's fucking good!" he sucked in a breath between his teeth and blew it out and got up, turning me and shoving me down on the bed. He made quick work of getting the rest of my clothes off and knelt at the side of the bed.

He wrapped his arms around my thighs and dragged me bodily and aggressively toward him. I slid along the coverlet half laying on his jacket and cut, but I didn't care. I didn't care about anything but getting him back inside of me, his mouth on me.

He shoved fingers back in and pumped them in and out of my wetness, his mouth descending on my pussy and suckling at my clit like this was the only sustenance he needed to give him life.

I shoved my hands against my mouth to muffle the throaty cry that tried to escape out of it, for consideration that we were in an older motel and that the walls weren't likely well sound proofed.

I lay as still as I could for Blackjack as he absolutely, passionately, ravaged my pussy with fingers and mouth making me come in a beautiful explosion of silvered shattered bits of me until I wriggled and begged breathlessly for him to stop, that it was too much and he finally relented, but only long enough for him to get his cock out of his own jeans and involved.

He brought himself out and dragged me off the bed to straddle him growling, "C'mere." I slid over the length of him, my pussy greedy and taking him in deep as I wrapped my arms around his shoulders and his arms twined around my back, crushing me to him.

Breathlessly, I rocked on his rock-hard shaft, the motion doing *amazing* things for me but I doubted the grind did much for him. He held me down onto him and grunted, saying, "That's it, baby; use that dick. Take your pleasure and fucking come all over me."

Holy shit, the dirty ass mouth on this man. I couldn't get enough of it as I rocked with him, moving him against my walls in that way that drove me fucking crazy but had seemingly bored the shit out of every other partner I'd ever been with.

Fucking losers, I thought savagely then half wondered where that had come from! But I knew the answer to that. It came from the confidence that Blackjack worked diligently to instill in me every day.

"Oh, God!" I cried as I tipped closer to that shining fall, rocking faster, frantically trying to get there as my man grunted and groaned his own pleasure into the room. As he praised me and told me things, things like 'that's it' and 'fuck yes' and 'you're so fucking beautiful when you come for me' and I just couldn't stand it anymore and I felt like I fucking *burst* from the love and praise he poured into me.

I threw back my head, feeling like a wild thing, and cried out my pleasure, unable to contain my voice as my pussy gripped and trembled around him. His arms skid down my back, his big hands gripping my ass, as he tipped me back against the side of the bed for a slightly different angle and he drove himself violently into me, over and fucking over, both of us panting, both of us feeling like we were dying in the only acceptable way there was. In each other's arms, from the sheer force of pleasure we managed to raise between us.

The passion explosion between us was so intense, so incredibly fast and furious and so *devastating*, I swear I blacked out or something. Only coming back to myself pinned between him and the bed, his body leaning forward to hold me up as I went completely limp in his arms and I gasped, "What happened?"

"I don't know," he declared, gasping himself. "But it was so fucking good, I want to know how the fuck we do it again."

I laughed. I couldn't help it. The laughter tittering and stuttering out of me from between my gasping breaths as I clung to him in the midst of the wreckage of our clothes in the shabby little motel room.

Pretty soon, his stuttering laughter joined mine, and we collapsed in a fit of ridiculous giggles, clinging to one another in our joy which felt so right despite how wrong it must look given the circumstances...

Or maybe it was right. Just right. Long overdue for the both of us...

At any rate, I couldn't think of anyone else I would rather share this type of joy with. I hadn't even realized how much I could love someone or feel loved as I felt with this man right here.

I looked into his eyes from inches away, touched his face with reverence and loved the way he held me close, the way he touched me like I was his only tether to this world; because lord knows he was mine.

"I love you," I murmured and he kissed me, our tongues tracing the inside of each other's mouths, slowly, surely, carefully.

I gasped as he powerlifted me off the floor and stood with me beside the bed. He laid me down and climbed over the top of me, showering my body with kisses.

"I love you, too," he murmured his dark eyes somehow darker with that decadence he alone seemed to have and he kissed me *there*, his lips light and gentle against my clit as he started to destroy me with his mouth all over again.

28

*B*lackjack...

We were exhausted the next morning as we showered. I worried about it. About the ride home, not so much for me but for Ember. This was only the second long-ass ride over a couple of days that she'd ever taken and in the midst of so much of an emotional toll, I would be lying if I said I wasn't worried.

She'd been fucking magnificent last night.

So lithe, so beautiful, so incredibly sexy and confident as she'd ridden me. I mean, she had been a sight to behold, and it was like I wanted someone to pinch me as I looked at her back, over by my bike and the rockers that declared *'property of Blackjack.'*

I didn't understand how such an ethereal, celestial creature could be mine.

I went out to her after doing a last check of our motel room that we hadn't left anything behind and smiled as she squirmed adorably and made a pouty face at me. Her panties were in my hip pocket.

"Don't like your choice?" I asked, teasing her some.

She'd had her choice between dirty panties or going without, and she'd fully confessed that she'd liked neither.

"What choice?" she complained. "There really wasn't any choice and it's bullshit."

I laughed and took her hands, pulling myself close to her and swaying gently with her and said, "We'll put some emergency panties in a Ziploc and stash them on the bike," I said.

She looked up at me and stuck out her bottom lip in a cute little pout and demanded, "Why didn't you think of that before?"

I laughed a little and said, "Because I didn't think a trip like this would have to be a thing with you," I said softly.

Her face lost its easy smile and the ghost of sorrow chased her joy away. I felt bad about that, but it had to happen eventually. The pall of the reason we were here settling back in, like rain clouds blocking out the sun.

The door to Deac and Tic's room opened behind us and we turned. Ember let me go, taking a step back as Tic looked up at me. Deac shut the door behind them as Tic walked out to the bikes and me.

He came up to me and opened his arms and I crushed him in a tight hug.

"Thank you, man," he said, full of emotion.

"You showed up for me, bro," I told him.

"Always. I might be a fucking asshole sometimes, but I try not to be a cunt."

I pounded him on the back and we broke apart.

"I wasn't going to let you find out like we did," I said shaking my head. "Like Mav did."

"Fuck," he muttered and shook his head, dropping it to stare at the ground. "I wouldn't deal. Thank you for being here for me," he said.

"Always," I parroted back at him and gripped his shoulder, giving him a shake. "Let's get you home."

Ember smiled, but it held a tinge of tired sadness as she looked on at us and Tic went to her and wrapped her up in a hug too.

"Thank you," he muttered over her head and she gave him a squeeze.

"You're welcome," she said softly.

We hit the road just long enough to find some fucking breakfast somewhere. As we ate, Ember chattered about rocks and how she wished we could come back through the pass, that there were places in the Cascades that had some good stuff in the rivers and streams to hunt up for her tumblers and projects.

Tic sort of seized on the distraction she was providing, asking questions and nodding along and she was happily supplying all the answers.

"How do you even know where these places are?" Deacon asked, and she looked up from her plate.

"There was a manila envelope of papers from the Washington State Geological Department or whatever in on of the filing cabinets in the garage," she answered. "Only like thirty pages or so, but it detailed where some semi-precious stones could be found all throughout the Cascade region. I looked up the places they mentioned and some of them are through Snoqualmie Pass and along the river here."

Deacon nodded like he was impressed.

"I think I'd like to go with you guys when you start looking," Tic said. "Just being out there looking sounds fun," he said. "Always like those 'Where's Waldo' books when I was a kid, this sounds like more of a challenge."

Ember laughed, "You know, there's a lot of gold out there in the same places," she said.

I perked up a bit, "I've got some prospecting shit back at Cipher's place," I said.

"Really?" she asked.

"Yeah, precious metals are more stable than currency," he said. "We just never really managed to find the time."

"We should go," Tic said. "Like all of us. People can pan or hunt for Ember's rocks. We should all just go before the summer is over." He shook his head and wouldn't look at any of us when he added, "Life is too fuckin' short."

Deacon and I traded a look and Ember's chin raised slightly when she caught it as well. We were all worried about Tic, but if he was suggesting this type of shit, then that was good. Real good. It meant he wanted to surround himself with people. He wanted to keep himself occupied, and those were all good things. Deacon nodded at me and I figured he had to have a hand in this. That there may have been a long talk about coping and coping mechanisms last night.

I knew, because Deacon and I had had a talk a time or two over the same subject when I'd been low.

"Sounds good, man. I can dig it," Deacon said and Ember groaned. It took her groaning for me to catch it.

"You motherfucker," I said and Tic looked up from where he'd been pushing the food around on his plate.

"Get it?" Deacon said with a proud grin. "Dig it?"

Tic closed his eyes and shook his head, "What this motherfucker said," he said jabbing a fork at me. "You motherfucker!"

We laughed and the clouds lifted for a precious second.

The long ride back over the pass was a somber one, even more that the night before. One, we had Tic with us and that honestly felt like we carried with us some fragile and precious cargo. I don't think anyone outside of Mav loved Dahlia better than Tic and I didn't even know if that was an entirely fair observation.

Mav and Tic probably loved Dahlia equally, just in different ways.

Even though... well, the more I thought about it, the worse I felt for thinking it... but even though Dahlia was toxic as fuck for all involved.

She had been so fuckin' broken by her childhood. In ways I don't think anyone *but* Maverick could begin to understand. Broken to the point she hid behind that proud, beautiful, strong and bitch façade and let her issues consume her. Not only her, but anyone else the gravitational pull of her personality managed to drag into orbit.

It was tough, what Mav had been forced to do. Putting her and Tic both in time-out in hopes that they'd be willing to work on themselves. In hopes that with some time and separation that Dahlia wouldn't take Tic down with her, but damn had Dahlia fought Mav every step of the fuckin' way.

I'd heard about it. I'd even seen it.

She didn't want to think there was anything wrong with her. With her attitude or with how she was treating people. The way she tried playing people against each other to start some drama so she could feed off of the chaos.

Deacon had talked about it once. About how her home life growing up must have been pure chaos in order for her to seek it out like she did.

Mav had pretty much confirmed his suspicion without giving anything away on that. Which was rough, because who among us *didn't* have some kind of shit time growing up?

I mean, some of us had it easier than others, sure but I couldn't understand D and why, why when she had so much shit going for her, she just couldn't leave some of that shit behind...

I don't think it was weakness, I mean, *just fuckin' why, Dahlia?*

Except she wasn't here to answer and she never would be able to and so we just had to wait and see if any clues came up to give us any insight into just what the hell she'd been thinking.

Ember started shifting and fidgeting as we came down the other side of the pass. When we got to Issaquah, I gave her knee a squeeze, and she hugged me tighter back, the indication that she was hanging in there, but I knew she had to be getting sore.

When we reached Bellevue, I signaled the boys that we were splitting off. They gave the hand signal that we were all good, and I parted with them, skating across the lanes of traffic to get up onto I-405 North while they continued I-90 West to go to the club.

I took the Bothell/Kenmore exit and pointed Ember and I toward home.

I tell you what, my house never looked so fuckin' good when we got to it.

I pulled up into the garage and shut off the bike, Ember hopping off almost immediately and groaning, putting her hands to her lower back and the top of her butt and bending backward, getting a stretch into her lower back.

I took off my helmet and she reached up to undo and take off her own.

"I have never wanted a hot bath so bad in my life," she said and huffed out a sigh.

"I'm right fuckin' there with you, darlin'."

She smiled at me and we set our helmets on top of the deep freezer on our way into the house, stopping at the hall closet just inside the door to put up the rest of our riding gear.

"I'm hungry," she said, and I looked at the time.

"Yeah, breakfast was a minute ago," I agreed and she flopped onto the couch and made grabby hands in my direction.

I laughed and sat down with her, turning and laying back against her chest as she put her arms around me. I held up my phone so we could both see it and opened up one of those food delivery apps.

"What looks good?" I asked.

"Fuck, I don't know, anything we don't have to cook sounds amazing. Um…" she thought for a second. "Teriyaki!"

"A woman after my own heart," I said absently and ordered our usuals.

"I love that you know what to get me," she said, and I smiled, after putting the order through and closing my eyes and setting my phone aside, laid my head back. She buried her hands in my hair and massaged my scalp.

"Oh, fuck," I groaned. "Keep doing that, you're going to put me to sleep," I said, finishing on a yawn.

"Food first, then bath, then sleep," she said and yawned too.

We both laughed a little and she picked up the remote to put something on the television. We were still startled awake by the knock on the door when the food arrived. We ate while we watched some campy paranormal show of hers where it was just a bunch of talking heads breaking down viral internet clips where more than half of them looked like shitty early 2000s quality computer-generated shit.

We went back and forth, Mystery Science Theater 3000 style on them, talking back and forth on if they were fake or not, and laughing. Cracking jokes… and my girl had some good jokes.

Finally, food in our bellies I switched off the television and held down a hand to Ember.

"Bath and then bed," I declared.

"Sir, yes, sir," she said coolly, and I smiled.

She lit the candles while I measured out some Epsom salts into the running water, and then, because she liked it, I added bubbles.

I loved the feel of her in the circle of my arms and legs as she settled into the hot water with me.

"Mm," I murmured lazily, fighting not to fall asleep. "You know if you go, I go, at this point, right?"

She snorted and said, "I thought it was a given there was no other option then the both of us going together."

"Reminds me of this shit that happened out east," I said.

"Oh?"

"Yeah, mother chapter. Brother laid his bike, freak fuckin' accident. His ol' lady went flying with him and she... she didn't make it. Died on the scene before help arrived and rather than let her go alone, he took his own head off. Couldn't live without her."

"Oh, God..." she said soberly.

"Yeah," I said quietly, my mind flashing right back to Tic's anguish. I didn't know how he was doing it. If it'd been my girl...

I held her tighter and kissed her shoulder.

"I don't want to think about it," she said after a while.

"About what?" I asked.

"A life without you in it," she said craning her neck way back to look up at me. I looked into her eyes and somberly said how I felt.

"I love you too much," I said. "I don't think it's an option for me, either."

She sighed and said, "We both have so much going for us and so much to live for now."

I smiled and nodded.

"Yeah, we do, darlin', yeah we do," I agreed, and I kissed the top of her head.

We sat in our bath in the magical twilight of golden candlelight and just soaked each other in.

"I love you," she murmured and I could tell that she needed to hear it.

"I love you, too."

Like the time what felt like an age ago, when she first came to me and fell asleep in the bathtub on me? This time, we both fell asleep together.

EPILOGUE

A little over a year later...

*T*ic-Tac...

A bunch of us were rolling up through Pike's Place Market for shits and giggles. The sky was high and blue without a fuckin' cloud in it and I had my camera up and running. I'd started recording a bunch of shit, my rides and times with the rest of the guys after... well, after last year.

We were stopped trying to work our way through the brick side street between the two halves of the market but the fuckin' tourists and pedestrians seemed to be fuckin' oblivious to the fact that this was a fuckin' *street*, for *traffic*, and not just *for* pedestrians and so typical me, I decided to be a bit of a passive aggressive asshole about it.

I revved my bike, makin' shit *loud* while Major, Cipher, and Nine laughed around me.

"You like that?" I yelled over to them as they cracked up and I twisted the throttle again, *vroom! Vroom! Vrooooooooooom!*

We all fell out laughing, giggling like a bunch of fuckin' schoolboy ninnies while the citizens turned and looked and whispered behind their hands and pointed from the sides.

Major was just fuckin' howling with laughter, I mean laughing until he cried and I didn't think it was *that* funny, but then again, we were all baked and high as shit with no fucks to give, just coming up through and enjoying the summer weather while we could after we got done visiting our shop, *Sacred Leaf.*

I revved again, and again, and I knew I was being an obnoxious fucker – but I didn't care. It was all in good fun. I revved and my bike fuckin' died and I looked down, a lovely set of manicured nails slipping off my fuckin' kill switch.

The guys fuckin' *howled* while I looked up the shapely slender arm to the girl that flipped it. She turned, auburn hair foaming around her face, stirring in the breeze through the market and I damn near swallowed my tongue. She had a round face, was padded and curvy in *all* the right places, and she winked one silvery blue eye over her shoulder and yeah, I popped a fuckin' boner right then and there.

Her back was almost completely exposed except for the thin strings at the back of her neck and across her lower back. Alluring, gorgeous, fuckin' *feisty* with the way she grinned at me and melted into the crowd.

I rocked back in my seat and fired up my bike again, revving it like never before in ornery defiance.

Holy shit... I thought to myself. *Who the fuck was that?*

I hoped that my go pro had caught her, and I couldn't wait to see...

SEVERAL HOURS LATER, I was back at my computer and downloading the footage from my camera. My place was quiet.

It was lonely out here, but worth it for the fucking view. I looked up out the floor to ceiling windows out over the valley floor. I lived in SnoCo, or Snohomish County, and while my house wasn't really all that big, it had a million-dollar fuckin' view.

I stared out over that view and the far distant twinkling lights in a line that was the highway leading up to the small city of Lake Stevens and sighed.

It was late nights like these that I could almost see her reflected in the glass, her nude body a work of art, better than the ink under her skin as she crooked a finger at me to come crawl to her.

Fuck I loved her, and I missed her, and I never knew and never would know why I just wasn't enough for her.

I sighed and hung my head when my computer chimed that the upload was complete.

I sighed and went triple time through the footage of the day and stopped on the clip from the market.

Fuck, she was only on the screen a few seconds, but I froze it, and I felt a smile curve my lips. She was so sassy, the smirk on her lips sending me right back into instant lust as she cast it back over her shoulder at me and I couldn't resist.

"Okay, internet," I muttered, cutting the clip and sending it to my phone. "Let's do your thing."

I tapped out on the screen, *yeah, I was being an asshole, but does anyone know who she is? Does she ride?*

I took a deep breath and let it out slow and shot my shot, putting it out into the ether. I set my phone aside and leaned back in my chair and sighed.

Am I ready for this?

I asked myself, staring out of the windows into the dark.

Shit, I was getting ahead of myself. There wasn't anything to be ready *for.*

I didn't know this girl, and I somehow doubted that she was going to be found. Even if she was, how did I know if she would want a twisted kinky fuck like me?

I pushed to my feet and swept up my phone, walking across the living room with its spectacular views to the stairs up to my second floor and my bedroom. I stopped at the railing, the vaulted ceiling reaching a point, the moon riding high in the sky and I stared at it.

I felt a pang of grief, and I bowed my head.

I wanted so desperately to move on, but... I couldn't necessarily say this was the best way of going about doing it.

I went to bed, laying there playing and replaying the clip with the music I'd paired with it, watching her lush lips twist into that little confident smirk. I mean *she had to ride*. Either that, or she had a boyfriend who rode. The latter was probably the likeliest scenario.

I closed my eyes and for the first time in a long time, it wasn't Dahlia I saw when I slept. I worried vaguely about that... I mean, *was I obsessed?*

The next morning when I woke proved that I wasn't the only one obsessed, the fucking internet was on *fire*. The clock app where I'd posted my video clip had already racked up something like thirty-eight-thousand likes and over two-thousand comments but as I scrolled my notifications, not a soul knew who she was.

Damn.

I got up and got my ass into the shower. I had to hit a supplier meeting and go be an adult for a while today.

It was midway through the day my phone started exploding with text messages from the club group chat. I glanced at the screen to Major's *Yo, yo, yo! She answered! She tagged you in a video! Tic. Man quit playin' and go look!*

My heart leaped into my throat, and I swallowed hard.

I opened up the app, went to my notifications, and found the reply.

The video opened on a person sitting on a Harley, facing away from the camera. Their booted feet planted to the ground to either side, a full facemask helmet on their head which was profile and their jacket one of those weatherproof Kevlar deals.

Do I ride? The caption asked as the person unzipped their coat. *What do you think?* Flashed on the screen and they dropped their jacket. Her back was revealed, the same distinctive tied on shirt covered her front, nothing but the strings at the back.

Fuck, it's her!

I went to her profile which had followed mine and I followed her back at the speed of light.

I opened up the direct messaging function and paused over the screen. *What did I say?*

I hesitated.

Should I even say anything?

"Fortune favors the brave," I muttered and I took in a slow deep breath in through my nose and out through my mouth before I put my thumbs to the keys on my screen.

What is your name?

I hit 'send' then immediately was like *fuck!*

"Smooth asshole, real smooth," I muttered to myself.

What is your name?

Jesus.

My phone alerted with a notification and I stared at the emblem for the app at the top of everything and swiped down.

You have received a direct message!

"Shit. Shit, shit, *shit!*"

My heart hammered in my chest as I dropped my ass onto the saddle of my bike. I rubbed my sweating palm up and down the top of my chaps and swallowed. My mouth was so dry I swore my throat fucking clicked.

I opened the message.

Shona... you?

It was her. Don't ask me why or how I knew. I just knew it was her... *holy shit.*

"Uh, fuck."

What did I say?

Brothers call me Tic-Tac.

God, that was going to be so dumb finally explaining that one.

As in hung like one? She asked.

I laughed, closing my eyes and bouncing my chin off my chest with how hard I hung my head.

Uh, yeah. I see you've heard the joke, except I've always said hung like a half-eaten Tic-Tac.

God! Why did I say that!?

LMAO! That's even better. I like it. So, Tic-Tac… where do we go from here?

I felt a fine tremble in my hands and they shook slightly as I tapped out:

How about for a ride?

I waited, and waited with bated breath for the reply to come through and finally, it did…

Sounds good. Where should we meet up? Seems the internet is determined to ship us, let's give 'em a little taste of what they want.

Holy shit, she was serious. She was fearless!

Uh, I don't know. Where abouts you located?

She responded promptly, and it was disappointing.

Lacy, just north of Olympia. You?

Damn, that ways *a way…*

Snohomish County, just outside Lake Stevens.

She hit me back with exactly what I'd been thinking.

Damn, that's a ways… let me think about it. Uh, meet me halfway somewhere?

I put some thought into it and said:

Seattle is pretty much halfway.

Her last message came through:

LOL that's true. I hate texting in this damn thing, here's my phone number… don't call me, though. I hate talking on the phone.

Holy fuck, the connection just got a whole lot less tenuous. I switched over to text messaging and plugged in her number.

Me: It's Tic

Her: Hi, Tic! This is much better.

Me: Yeah.

Her: So, what are your days off?

Me: I'm the boss, so I work when I want and when I need to.

Her: Cool. I'm not the boss, I work Monday through Friday.

Me: Okay, so do you want to set something up for next weekend?

Her: Yeah, sounds good! Saturday work for you?

I checked the club's calendar and was grateful that I was clear.

Me: Yeah, that works for me.

Her: Cool. Tell you what. I've wanted to take the Hurricane Ridge ride how about we meet for the Ferry over and take the ride together?

Me: That sounds fucking awesome.

Her: Alright, hang on...

She sent me the sailing schedule for the Edmunds to Kingston Ferry run and then texted back.

Her: 10 o'clock sailing?

Me: Fuck yeah.

Her: Dope, I'll see you on the boat. Bring your camera and maybe a friend to film it.

Me: LOL, you got it. You bringing a friend?

Her: You're my friend now! See you then, Tic.

Me: See you then, Shona.

Well, damn.

ALSO BY A.J. DOWNEY

Christmas with the Brotherhood

Indigo Knights

1. Her Thin Blue Lifeline

2. His Cold Blue Command

3. A Low Blue Flame

4. His Wild Blue Rose

5. Her Pained Blue Silence

6. A Cold Blue Call

7. Her Reluctant Blue Cavalier

8. Forged Under Fire

9. Under A Blue Moon

Sacred Hearts MC Pacific Northwest

1. Over the High Side

2. Wind Therapy

3. Apex of the Curve

4. Low Sided

5. Eating Asphalt

6. Hammer Down

Paranormal Romance (with Ryan Kells)

1. I Am The Alpha

2. Omega's Run

3. Hunter's End

Indigo City Darker (with Jared KingPacal Lain)

1. Triple Threat

2. Double Shot

Standalones

Synchronicity

ABOUT A.J. DOWNEY

A.J. Downey is a Pacific Northwest girl living in an East Tennessee world who finds inspiration from her surroundings, through the people she meets, and likely as a byproduct of way too much caffeine. She specializes in real and relatable romance stories featuring that real-life kind of love that everyone craves.

Stalker Information:

Website
www.ajdowney.com

Sign up for her newsletter at
http://eepurl.com/dkQiIH

Facebook Group - AJ's Sacred Circle
https://www.facebook.com/groups/authorajdowney/

facebook.com/authorajdowney
twitter.com/authorajdowney
instagram.com/ajdowney
bookbub.com/authors/a-j-downey